ESCAPE!

A Writing Bloc Anthology

First printing, 2019

ISBN: 9781795252300

Cover designed by Christopher Lee

Formatted by Christopher Lee and Michael Haase

Head of Editing: Cari Dubiel

Edited cooperatively by all the authors

The Writing Bloc
Visit my website at www.writingbloc.com
Follow on Twitter @ChristLeeEich

Printed in the United States of America

CONTENTS

"How did I escape? With difficulty. How did I plan this moment? With pleasure."

— ALEXANDRE DUMAS, THE COUNT OF MONTE CRISTO

FOREWORD

Escape!

What a perfect theme for what is to be the first in a series of anthologies by Writing Bloc.

Escape is why so many of us read and write, after all.

As readers, we open books ready to be swept out of our seats and deposited in a world entirely new and exciting. Reading is an escape from our normal lives and thoughts.

As writers, the goal is much the same when constructing a story, except that we want the world to escape with us. We want to guide our readers around a world of our own construction, far away from daily life.

Even building this anthology was in and of itself a means of escape. Allow me to explain...

The process of writing often embodies a dichotomy between wanting to include the whole world and needing to be entirely alone. When authors compose a story, when that light bulb pops on and that inspiration hits hard, we think of our audience. We become excited for our potential readers to see directly into our minds and hearts. We hope the entire world loves the brilliant lucid dreams we have composed. But on the flip side, writing itself is typically a rather secluded and lonely journey.

There are first drafts, second drafts, seventeenth drafts... all with an odd anxiety fueling them. Awful, unhelpful thoughts cloud the mind. *Do I have the writing talent this story deserves? Am I ready for someone else to read this? Am I any good at all?* These are the types of questions that can infect the writer's mind and story. And all too frequently, writers don't seek the answers from other people, because we fear the vulnerability of having our hearts and souls exposed, even though we long to have our work read.

I have felt this vulnerability firsthand. I remember the first person who absolutely shut down a story of mine and made me question pursuing the craft of writing altogether. His criticisms were harsh and cruel, with no regard toward my feelings. His incessant need to spot every single plot hole, typo, and grammatical error was relentless. His first critique of my work crushed me almost to the point of quitting writing altogether.

Who was this critic?

It was me, of course.

In response, I clutched my writing close to my chest, so convinced that no one would like any of it that I hunched my shoulders high as I wrote as though I were covering my answers to a test. Despite this wretched anxiety, I still felt compelled to tell stories, to keep going... and I dreamed of my tales being enjoyed by readers all over the world.

Unable to chase away the dream, I accepted the fact that I had to let at least one person read my work. In order to do this, I had to break away from my fears. I had to escape from myself.

In the fall of 2015, I joined some of the random writing communities online. I gobbled up what advice I could. I even started offering little bits of my work to people, cringing as I sent it off and flinching as soon as they told me they finished, expecting a great blow to come crashing down upon my ego like a tsunami. Much to my surprise, no one could trample over my work as well as my inner critic.

Naturally, I received plenty of criticism, but it was mostly constructive and encouraging. The more I showed my work, the more the support came. Soon enough, I became bold enough to enter my writing into a few contests. I even won one.

During the process of my escape, what has proven to be far more valuable than any contest has been the community of writers in which I have surrounded myself. These are people I have come to know as great friends, wonderful people, and damned talented authors. Within this core group, we realized that writers need support, we need a community, and we need each other.

From these needs, Writing Bloc was formed. We escaped the solitude of authorhood by banding together.

This first anthology is overflowing with people I am honored to call friends. These authors work constantly to hone their craft. I invited everyone to Writing Bloc at first with the simple intention of supporting one another as a group. Within two weeks, the ideas were flowing freely as all of our collective inspiration united into great goals we could accomplish together. The concept of forming an anthology of short stories quickly transitioned from idea to reality. We were confident in our ability to assemble a wonderful collection of short stories, and the results far exceeded my high expectations. I am proud of this collection.

I'm also proud of the diversity of backgrounds represented in this anthology. We have writers spanning the globe from the United Kingdom to New Zealand, from South Korea to Ohio, and from one end of the United States to the other. Every writer in this anthology is from a different part of the world, from a different walk of life, and we all came together for this project.

Twenty of us formed a team to write, edit, produce, design, and release this book in your hands. It was a ton of work, but we did it all together as a cooperative, and I have yet to find another compilation constructed quite like this one. We all had a say in the process, and we had a great time doing it.

We worked as a team to bring you something we think is pretty special. This is our escape, and we welcome you to come along with us.

I hope you enjoy this anthology as much as we enjoyed putting it all together.

Happy reading. Happy escaping.

-MICHAEL HAASE, FOUNDER OF WRITING BLOC

MRS. RAVENSTEIN

By Jason Pomerance

This all started when I landed in Director Jail. And, if I can speak frankly, it sucked. Do you know what I mean by Director Jail? Well, in case you don't, I'll tell you all about it. But first, I must confess that I don't know how I ended up in that place. I mean, come the fuck on, the movie wasn't that bad. I mean, okay, it was no masterpiece—no *Citizen Kane* or *Star Wars Episode Ten Thousand*, or *Spartacus*, or whatever you might consider a masterpiece. And everybody's got a freaking opinion, right?—but it wasn't meant to be a masterpiece. It was meant to be small, an illumination on the human condition, about the existential and philosophical...

Okay, it was a piece of shit.

It set a record on Rotten Tomatoes for negative reviews. I took the job because I had mortgage payments to make. But other directors have thrown crap up on the screen and not landed in Director Jail. I can name several, actually. But I'm a classy inmate, so I won't do that.

Director Jail consists of sitting around waiting for the phone to ring, or a text to come in, or any communication from the outside world, really. Or a hello from a colleague you might run into while picking up a grain bowl and a matcha at Cafe Gratitude. (Do you want to hear another secret? I hate that place. Fuck you and your fucking gratitude. What a huge stinking crock of shit).

But I digress. I, Sean Van Der Slocum, am admitting the movie sucked. I'm not blaming the cast. Or the edit, or the costumes or production design. Or the writer (okay, well, I kind of wrote it too, so...don't you believe what the other dude who claims the original idea was his is running around town saying). But nobody in Hollywood wanted anything to do with me. It was like I was this big stinking piece of turd. That right there is your definition of Director Jail. I just couldn't get arrested in this town after the whole debacle.

And then, actually, I did get arrested.

And put in real jail!

And I'm going to be honest with you: real jail is no freaking joke.

It was after a super bad day. I'd gotten my agent on the phone after only texting her about ten thousand times, and all she says to me is, "Dude. Right at this moment, I can't even get you a corporate training video. Which, I know, is sort of pathetic. But I believe in you, Sean. I'll keep trying and we'll get something done, so just sit tight!"

"Great. But I'm kind of running low on cash," I said, hoping desperation wasn't creeping into my voice. "Like seriously low."

"Well, why not Kickstart something? Or a Gofundme. Like that idea you had about the...Jesus, Sean, what was that idea again?"

How many times had I pitched her this idea? Ten? One hundred? When I was in the room with her, I'd know Jamie was tuning me out because she'd swear she was taking notes, but one day I caught a reflection of her screen off that new glass tower that sprung up next door and she was playing fucking Minecraft. Or she'd return a text (or, for all I know, sexting, because there were stories, believe me—with clients even, not that I'd gossip about stuff like that). Anyway, I launched into the pitch one more time: "We open close, on the face of a woman..."

"Dude, hold that thought," she interrupted. "You're not gonna believe this. I just got pinged asking about your availability!"

"You what?"

So Jamie, for the first time in what seemed like forever, came through. She got me a gig.

Well, it was an episode of a reality show, but that qualifies as a job. Maybe I justified taking it by thinking I could elevate things a little. You know, hopefully make the audience care about the bigger picture, the human condition, the status of...

Okay, it was that show with the ladies with the tits who are always drinking and calling each other names and stabbing each other in the back, and then crying and slobbering all over each other and making up. And after a really, really, really long day on set, when all I was basically doing was directing freaking traffic, I got into the Model X to head home. Now how many fucking times have I told goddamn Siri that I like to go home via Coldwater Canyon and not Laurel? But I was tired. And, frankly, annoyed. I wasn't really paying attention, just making turns where I was told to make turns, and before I knew it I was stuck in this endless line of barely moving traffic on Laurel Canyon, and so, yeah, I pulled this totally illegal u-turn and sped off back down the hill and before I knew it this douchebag cop was right up my ass. I pulled over all nice and everything. The shit started because suddenly I was all nervous (okay, I'm not black, but you hear what these cops are doing these days) and instead of putting the fucking Tesla in park, I hit reverse and backed into the black and white, and in a split second the cops are all like out with their guns and shit and making me get down on the ground and I'm suddenly yelling at them to go fuck themselves I'm a fucking citizen and I have rights.

And that's how I wound up in real jail.

Also, real jail is not a good time to get the shits, which happens to me when I get nervous. Don't even ask me about this, because it's just too gross. I mean, a bunch of big goon dudes and one freaking toilet? And no doors? Or air freshener? Anyway, part of this whole deal is actually just like you'd see in a movie, or on some TV show. It came time for me to make my one phone call, and I was led down this caged hallway with a bunch of other guys and waited my turn. Of course I called my lawyer, but remember I wasn't just in jail, but also Director Jail, which means nobody—not even your reps—wants to take your call, so I had to beg my lawyer's assistant Craig as if I was on hands and knees. But then there was this: my guy does entertainment law—he redlines contracts all day long. He knows squat about petty criminal stuff, so he foisted me onto this "colleague," but I'm pretty certain he just googled *criminal attorney Los Angeles* because the kid who showed up looked barely out of high school. He was like "We're going to go before the judge and just let me do the talking and it's all going to be copacetic, dig?"

And I said, "Dude, so awesome! After we grab some burritos let's go hang-ten down at El Porto!"

He went, "Um, what?"

"Never mind. Jesus."

Anyway, it's not like I had much of a choice. Next thing I knew I was in this courtroom, again behind a cage like some kind of animal. Everything was going good—it looked like the kid was actually going to get me off with a warning and then the judge, this not-very-nice-looking short, squat lady with, like, the butchiest buzz cut, says, "I see you're a director, Mr. Van Der Slocum. I love the movies. Would I have seen any of your work?"

"Yeah," I said, rattling off the name of the last movie, and she made this face like I just sharted and she was standing right behind me. So before I could get a grasp on impulse control, I said, "Fuck you, Lady, why don't you try doing what I do!"

Well...

So I earned myself three months of community service, and if I didn't show up, deputies were going to come back and haul my ass into jail. Again, real jail, not Director Jail. For a year or something awful. Oh, yeah, not to mention a gigantic fine, as if I could afford that right then.

And I was like, *Okay, I got this. I can handle this community service shit. No worries, right, it'll be a breeze.*

And then I met Mrs. Ravenstein.

Hers was a plain little house on a street of similar-looking homes way out in Van Nuys. It needed a fresh coat of paint, and the yard had gone to seed. This was the address I was told to go to and pick up Mrs. Ravenstein and take her on a couple of errands. She was 85 years old, you understand, half deaf and blind, and no longer drove. She was taking part in some county program where the able-bodied step in and help the elderly and infirm, and run their errands or ferry them to doctors' appointments or whatever. Anyway, I pulled up to the house after Siri's fucked-up directions from the canyon, again, so I was kind of in a shitty mood, but I was a little shocked at the response when I rang the doorbell.

"Go the fuck away!"

And this wasn't said in any nice sort of way. It was a reedy, old lady voice for sure, but it was the voice of a woman who meant business. Well, I couldn't just go away or I'd be, like, violating a court order. And honestly, I was a little curious.

"Hello?" I called out. "Mrs. Ravenstein? My name is Sean Van Der Slocum. I was sent by the county to take you on some errands."

The door creaked open.

She was tiny, just a skinny little slip of a thing in an oddly perky flowered dress, a close-cropped pageboy dyed jet black, and lips painted the color of ripe strawberries. Also, she was lighting a cigarette off the one she was finishing. She flung the still-lit butt at me as she leaned on her walker and headed for the curb. "Well, get the lead out, kid. We got shit to do."

Getting her into the Model X, by the way, was no easy task, with its gull-wing doors and all its other gadgets. She sputtered something about me being too stupid to buy a proper car, like a Lincoln, or an Oldsmobile. I didn't have the heart to tell her they didn't make Oldsmobiles anymore. But anyway, I got her strapped in, and we headed on our merry way. And by merry way, I mean this little lady cussed up a storm pretty much everywhere. Stop one, for example, was CVS to pick up her, like, ten prescriptions. "Now, Mrs. Ravenstein," the pharmacist began, "you understand this drug has powerful side effects, don't you?"

"Do I look like a fucking moron?" was the response.

At Whole Foods, she began helping herself to food from the salad bar. Not just a tomato or a slice of cucumber, or a little hunk of cheese like we all do. I'm talking like entire meal-size samplings. When an employee came over to reprimand her, she threatened to stick a plastic fork through his retina. This brought the manager, which brought on what appeared to be stroke symptoms, but a wink in my direction indicated the old bird was faking, and only my rushing her toward the exit prevented a call to 911.

Our last stop was the post office. Let's not even discuss how that went down.

I got Mrs. Ravenstein home and settled into a big cushy chair in her den. "I'll be back in a couple of days," I said.

"Right," said Mrs. Ravenstein. "And not because you give a shit. Because they'll haul your skinny ass into jail if you don't."

"Yes. Well. Anyway, I think you have a doctor's appointment in Beverly Hills."

"That doctor's an ass."

"Ok. Still, I..."

"Don't bother coming."

"Again, Mrs. Ravenstein, I don't have a choice. I have to. It's a court order."

"In two days, I plan to be dead," she said. And then, to my utter surprise, she burst into tears.

Okay, yeah, okay—I'm a director. I work in Hollywood. So I'm guessing you just assume I'm a heartless douche. And, don't get me wrong—I can be a major dick. However, something about this poor, sad, old woman, all shrunk up in that big puffy chair, tugged at my heart—a curious feeling, admittedly. I didn't want to leave her sitting there sobbing. "Why would you say you plan to be dead, Mrs. Ravenstein?" I asked.

"Because I'm going to kill myself."

"And why would you want to do that?"

"Pick a reason. I'm a burden. I can't do anything for myself. I need a putz like you to come and drive me to the damn drugstore. Soon enough I'll need somebody to wipe my ass."

"Everybody's a burden to somebody."

She lifted the lid of a small box on the coffee table, pulled out a cigarette, and lit it up. "I'm old, and I'm falling apart. It will only get worse."

She was drying her eyes. I felt like I needed to keep her talking. But also, because I couldn't help it, I put my phone on camera. I pointed it at Mrs. Ravenstein. And I began to record the conversation. "We're all falling apart," I said. "Sometimes it takes me five minutes to get a good pee to start. Especially after a night of Jager shots."

She let out a small laugh at that. "Yeah? I haven't had a regular bowel movement in three years!"

Now it was my turn to laugh a little. Still, I was curious. "Why are you so sad, Mrs. Ravenstein?"

There was a pause before she answered.

"It's all a big nothing."

"What is?" I asked.

"Life.

She talked for hours that day. She was born Isabelle Evans, she began. Her childhood was hardscrabble and unforgiving, but as a young girl—like any young child—she had hopes and dreams about her future. She fled the Dust Bowl state of her formative years, arriving in a still-blossoming California that seemed like the promised land, with its palm trees, the sweet smell of eucalyptus, and of course the mighty Pacific—the very edge of the world as she knew it.

"I was going to do something important," Mrs. Ravenstein said. "Something big."

"So what happened?"

She gave me a small shrug. "What didn't? Life throws shit at you. Every day you duck some sort of bullet, it seems Doesn't it?"

I had to nod in agreement.

"Why do you keep pointing that goddamn phone at me?"

"I'm recording you, Mrs. Ravenstein."

"Why?"

"I'm not really sure."

She gave a short snort. But she kept talking, as if something was compelling her to get the words out.

She met a man. Mr. Ravenstein was his name. He promised her things. A home. Children. Vacations every summer to a little cottage his family had on the beach up north. They married, and then one day he up and left her for one of her best friends. She was alone. She was broke, and so she began working, one odd job after another, until she landed at the corner of Sherman Way and Woodman, at the then-spanking-new Ralphs. She was hired as a checkout clerk. This was the 1950s, when ladies dressed to go to the supermarket and smoked in the aisles. Her story continued through the shagadelic sixties, when the smell of cigarette smoke was replaced by the pungent aroma of weed. The seventies saw women Mrs. Ravenstein knew were married suddenly looking unmoored—forlorn and shellshocked. The divorce craze was in full swing. And somehow she stayed in this place for the next fifty or so years. She was friendly, but not too forthcoming. She knew many of her customers by name, ringing up their orders and chatting amiably, not noticing years passing until babies grew up into teenagers, and then became mothers and fathers themselves. "I would often wonder," Mrs. Ravenstein said, "how I let this happen. How did I let life just pass me by?"

She peered at me closely, searching my face as if I had some kind of clue, but I had no answer.

I went home, and I looked around my empty house. Yeah, you know, I had all these things—every new gadget and giant flat screens everywhere—but what else did I have? What did I have that mattered? I didn't even have a freaking plant. I looked in the mirror that night as I was brushing my teeth, and suddenly it hit me—I wasn't so young anymore either. Where once my face was smooth and unlined there were wrinkles.

On my forehead. Around my eyes. At the corners of my mouth. When did this start? What was happening to my hair? The thought that flew through my mind was '*who will love me now that I'm old, and that my career is in the crapper?*' I'd dated tons of women. Not one for more than a couple of months. And then all the hookups. Why did they all leave me? Okay, admittedly some were just as awful as I was, but still...

I crawled into bed, but I couldn't sleep. Not even a couple of Ambiens worked. I felt trapped, and totally, totally alone.

My court-appointed time with Mrs. Ravenstein came to an end. I was free to do whatever—mostly to try and land another gig. But something kept drawing me back to that little house in Van Nuys. I wanted to know more. Also, I sensed that if I didn't show up, she'd follow through with her plan, to make herself no longer exist, and I didn't want that. I suddenly felt responsible for her, as if she were my own mom (don't ask), or my grandmother. So I'd appear every couple of days. I continued recording the conversations, and even little outings we took. Once I offered to treat her to lunch. I drove us to Cafe Gratitude, but she took one look at the menu and said, "Fuck this, I want a cheeseburger."

We sat outside at the In-N-Out on Sunset. Mrs. Ravenstein gleefully attacked a Double-Double, fries, and a vanilla shake. We were finishing lunch when suddenly I heard, "Hey, you."

I looked up. There was Ava, sunlight filtering through the long black hair she parted on the side so it fell across her face on a slant. With a Latino father and Asian mom, Ava always struck me as a curious mix, darkly beautiful, enigmatic as hell. She set-decorated one of my pictures, and we dated briefly, but when the production wrapped, so did we. "I heard you got thrown in the pokey," she said, grinning, while her friend grabbed a nearby table.

"Yeah," I answered. "But this lady here is my ticket out."

Ava smiled at Mrs. Ravenstein. "I hope," she said, "that you got a thank you out of him. Because Sean was never so good with his pleases and thank yous."

Mrs. Ravenstein smiled cryptically and finished off her shake.

"Ciao, Sean." Ava threw her hair over her shoulder as she joined her friend.

I was watching her go and didn't notice, but Mrs. Ravenstein had grabbed my phone and was recording me. "Put that thing down," I said, trying to grab it back, but she kept moving it out of my reach. "Do you even know what you're doing?"

"I'm old, Sean. I'm not a fucking idiot."

"Give me that phone!"

"What? You can dish it out but you can't take it?"

"Fine. You want to interview me too, Mrs. R?"

"Who's the girl?"

"Somebody I used to know is all."

"You let *that* one slip away?"

"I guess. I can be an asshole."

"I bet you can be, kid. Fix that," said Mrs. Ravenstein.

She turned off the camera. She handed me back the phone and then polished off the last of her fries.

Mrs. Ravenstein had told me her feet hadn't touched the ocean in years, so we took another outing, this time to the beach. I headed to Point Dume and parked on Westward Beach Road, just south of Zuma. She couldn't wait to get out of the Model X, but her walker kept sinking in the sand. I ended up carrying her to the water's edge. At one moment, her face was very close to mine. "Don't get any funny ideas. This isn't *Harold and Maude*," she said.

"You an Ashby fan?"

"I saw every movie he made. But *Harold and Maud*e was my favorite."

"Mine too."

"Now put me the fuck down."

She kicked off the big clunky shoes she had to wear. I had to pull off the compression-style socks that were good for her circulation. Her feet were not a pretty sight, and I had to avert my eyes, because I sensed she was embarrassed. Then Mrs. Ravenstein dipped her toes in the water. The smile she gave the camera was both sad and gleeful at the same time.

A few days later, I took Mrs. Ravenstein to the dentist (dragged kicking and screaming was more like it) and then she needed groceries. She hadn't been back since she retired, but we were close to Sherman Way and Woodman and the old Ralphs, where she worked all those years ago. It looked totally different—they had torn down the sleek mid-century version and rebuilt something bigger and fancier. She seemed to resist the idea, but I helped her inside, and we wandered the aisles picking up the few things she needed (she seemed to live on nothing but Chock Full O' Nuts coffee, Campbell's Cream of Mushroom Soup, and Oreos). I was recording Mrs. Ravenstein, noting her reactions to how utterly different it all was.

At the checkout, there was a woman. An ID badge pegged her as Nan. She was maybe fifty, with a shock of blond curls, a sharp nose, and a pert mouth outlined in vivid red. She peered closely at Mrs. Ravenstein as she scanned her items. At first she began the typical chatter. "Find everything okay?"

"Yeah, yeah," muttered Mrs. Ravenstein.

"How's your day going?"

"Pretty much like every day," Mrs. Ravenstein said. "It sucks!"

Nan nodded her head in agreement and smiled. "Bring a bag, or you purchasing one?"

I held up Mrs. Ravenstein's little canvas sack and started bagging the items. Mrs. Ravenstein paid with a few bills she dug from her pocketbook. We were about to make our escape when the woman said, "You don't remember me, do you, Mrs. Ravenstein?"

This gave Mrs. Ravenstein pause. Now she inspected the woman, searching for something familiar and seeming to come up empty.

"Well…"

"I got my first job here. At this very store. I was seventeen, and I was trying to save money for college. You trained me. I'm Nan. I was Nancy Bremer then. Now it's Nan Rodriquez."

She handed Mrs. Ravenstein her receipt.

"Well, nice to see you, I guess," Mrs. Ravenstein grumbled.

But Nan wasn't done. "Do you remember the manager here, back in the 1980s?"

Mrs. Ravenstein went silent a moment. Then she perked up, her eyes taking on life like I hadn't seen before. She said, "Craig Yaeger. What a douchebag."

"Yup," said Nancy. She turned to me. "He came on to every woman in the store. He grabbed our asses, or he'd brush against our breasts. He pushed himself on us, and God forbid if he'd been drinking, which he did, on the job.

"Sounds like an asshole," I said.

"One night," Nan continued, "I worked the late shift. Yaeger cornered me in the locker room out back. He pawed at my clothes and he forced his mouth on mine. He would have raped me, I'm sure, if it wasn't for Mrs. Ravenstein.

"I…well, that was…" Mrs. R. began, but her voice trailed off.

"She pulled him off me. She kicked him in the balls. She said if she ever caught him doing this again, she'd do even worse."

Right in the middle of the bad lighting, and the canned Muzak and the impatient lady behind us, Nancy burst into tears. "She saved my life, really. I left this place, and I didn't dare come back for years. I'm covering for somebody today on the register. But I'm the manager now. I manage three stores in the valley, actually. And I owe this lady so much."

She dashed around from her perch behind the scanner, and she wrapped Mrs. Ravenstein in a hug.

I might have expected Mrs. Ravenstein to say something nasty. But my phone recorded the old lady as she too teared up and hugged the younger woman back.

Later, as I was dropping off Mrs. Ravenstein, she tried to brush off what had happened. It was no big deal, she insisted.

Said she was just doing her job, which wasn't true. Dealing with predators was never in her job description, I was sure. When I tried to point that out, she shoved me out the door.

At home, I had begun cutting together footage of Mrs. Ravenstein. I opened with a close shot of the old woman one day when she met me at the door, and I, on the spur of the moment, had brought some flowers some dude was selling at the corner of Coldwater and Ventura. For a brief second, her face lit up. I let that shot linger. Now I looked over footage from the supermarket. Mrs. Ravenstein had insisted that her helping Nancy all those years ago was no big deal, but the footage told a different story—I could see something in her eyes that belied what she said. I could see it did matter to her. It mattered a lot.

The more I dug, the more I learned that, back in the day, there were more women she had helped and defended. A host of women worked at that store, and almost every one had a story to tell. I tracked down as many as I could. I talked to them. Some I brought to Mrs. Ravenstein so they could also thank her, and I cut them into the movie, so they became a kind of Greek Chorus.

"Mrs. Ravenstein" wound up being the hit of the festival circuit. Not just the documentary: the woman herself. Although people now knew her not just as Mrs. Ravenstein, but by the name she was born with, Isabelle Evans. She had become something of a folk hero. She was cheered everywhere she went, even at the Granddaddy of all festivals with the snow and the mountains, and the freebies and the swag and the exclusive parties I would have been dying to get into and didn't really give a shit about anymore. It was that moment in the spotlight she always craved, you could tell, because she drank it all in, hoping it would never stop. After one screening, she took my hand and said something I'll never forget. "Thank you, Sean," she began.

"For what?"

"For reminding me that I did matter, even if it was in a

small way."

"But they weren't small, the things you did."

Her face reconfigured; the edges of her mouth curled up just slightly. I realized she was giving me an uncharacteristic smile.

"Promise me something, Sean?"

"Yes...?"

"Promise me you won't wait to figure out you made a difference. Promise me you'll make yourself happy."

"I will," I said.

She smiled once more and said goodbye.

A short time later I arrived at Mrs. Ravenstein's. I rang the doorbell. I was met with an unearthly stillness. And I knew that she was gone. The Medical Examiner said it was a massive coronary, in her sleep. She probably never knew what hit her, his report said. So, a bad heart. But I had figured out that just wasn't true. And I wondered if she woke up in those last moments, in the dark of night, and what may have gone through her head. I wished I could have been there, to hold her hand and tell her it was all going to be okay.

You know what gets you out of Director Jail fast? An Academy Award nomination. The documentary first made the shortlist of films to be considered, and then it got an official nod. It didn't matter that awards weren't being handed out for months. The film landed a distributor, and with the campaign in full swing, it seemed like everybody wanted to be in the Sean Van Der Slocum business.

Women who had been part of my life in the past wanted back in. Some I knew I had not treated nicely. To those, I apologized. But, to be honest, I wasn't sure what I wanted, or needed, anymore. My calendar was slammed. In fact, I should have left for my next meeting already, but when I climbed into the Model X and powered it up, something compelled me to head in the opposite direction. On the spur of the moment, I shot a text to Ava, asking her if she wanted to take a trip. She answered back quickly. She wasn't sure the time was right, or if it ever would be, but she'd consider the offer. I took that as victory enough.

Soon I found myself cruising the open road with the Mojave shimmering on the horizon. I slipped the car into Ludicrous Mode, and in a flash I was just a speck of dust speeding through the arid landscape.

ABOUT JASON POMERANCE

Website: www.jasonpomerance.com
Instagram and Twitter @whowantsdinner

Jason Pomerance has written film and television projects for numerous studios and production companies, including Warner Brothers, Columbia Pictures, FremantleMedia, and Gold Circle Films. His first novel, Women Like Us, published by the Quill imprint of Inkshares, debuted in 2016, and his novella Falconer was published in four parts on Nikki Finke's site for showbiz fiction, Hollywood Dementia. He's currently working on a new novel.

CHRYSALIS

By Susan K. Hamilton

I met Death today.

I knew who she was, felt it deep down in the marrow of my bones, the moment she pushed her sunglasses up on top of her burnished chestnut hair, revealing eyes that were all midnight sky and dazzling stars.

I stared in disbelief.

"Not what you were expecting?" she asked.

"Not even close," I answered, gazing at her silver butterfly earrings and gunmetal nose ring. She looked satisfied by my answer.

"Good. Predictable is *so* boring."

She closed her eyes and leaned back on the park bench. I looked around, still trying to wrap my brain around what was happening and where we were. We sat in a lovely small park with huge copper beech trees surrounding a little pond dotted with yellow and pink water lilies. The trees were ancient, with massive trunks and dark purplish leaves that reached toward the sun. I ran my fingers down the bark of the tree next to me. I was a reporter—facts mattered to me. The bark on the tree? Well, the fact was, it sure as hell felt real.

"I must be dead if you're here."

Dead. That fact hung heavy in my chest—if I was dead, then I'd failed. I had failed and everything—every sacrifice—had been for nothing.

Death raised an eyebrow and asked, "Are you? You do know what they say about making assumptions, right?"

I couldn't help but laugh, but it was hollow. I had to be dead—didn't I? A few moments before, I'd been in a small gray room, my arms pinned painfully above me while some government thug pounded my face. The ghostly tang of blood filled my mouth. I brushed my fingers against my lip, but when I looked at them, they were dry.

"If I'm not dead, this is one hell of a hallucination."

"Do I look like a hallucination to you?"

As she spoke, the sleeve tattoo covering Death's left arm melted, all the colors running together as it turned from vibrant spring flowers to more muted—but richly colored—fall leaves and bittersweet vines. I watched, utterly mesmerized.

Finally, I said, "Considering I'm talking to Death and your tattoos just turned inside out into a completely different image, I'm kinda leaning toward hallucination. Some of my friends in college would have paid big bucks for peyote that would do this shit to them."

This time Death laughed out loud. "I suppose you're right on that count, but I assure you—I'm no hallucination."

"So where—exactly—is here?"

She paused, clearly contemplating what to tell me.

"We're in the Gray. That place that hangs between life and death, where all souls pass when I come to collect them. The Gray can be whatever I want–from a lustrous expanse to a literal void of grayness. This park is my favorite version. I made this special for me."

She closed her eyes again and took a deep breath. Taking the glasses from her head, she ran a hand through her glossy russet mane and then readjusted the shades while I sat next to her, brow furrowed as anxious thoughts flashed through my mind.

"Then I'm in the process of dying?" That was my reporter brain again. Asking questions. Seeking facts. Needing to understand.

Part of me was horrified at the thought. I couldn't die, not yet, not before I finished my job. But another part was relieved. When I signed up for my mission, I'd been all fire and dedication, but after nearly a week of "interrogation" at the hands of the Electorate's secret police, death was an escape hatch that looked far more appealing than I ever thought it could.

"Everyone dies, there's no getting around that," Death replied.

My fear and anxiety got the better of me, and I snapped, "Stop avoiding my question and tell me the truth. Am I dying?"

I glared at Death while my brain screamed, *What are you doing? That's DEATH you're talking to.* I didn't really care that I sounded like a bitch. I mean, really, what was Death going to do? Kill me?

"I'm being serious, Misha. Can I call you that? Or do you prefer Michelle?"

"Misha's fine." I fidgeted, uncertain about how to respond to the kindness I heard in her voice.

"Misha it is then," Death said, continuing on. She cupped her hands and breathed into them gently, blowing a sparkling sand into the air. When it settled, several dozen scrolls had appeared in her hands. "As I was saying, everyone dies. From the moment of your birth, you are in the process of dying, but how and when you actually die isn't exactly set in stone. These scrolls are maps of your life—each one charted out by Fate at the very instant you draw your first breath. Every living person has a vault full of these. Thousands, even millions, of possible lives and possible deaths, all depending on the choices you make. In the end, only one map will remain."

As she spoke, one of the scrolls in her hand quivered, trembled like a desiccated leaf, and then disintegrated into sand. The grains fell to the ground as she put the rest of the life-maps on the bench in between us.

"Well, you're not going to die from a torture-induced heart attack today," Death observed.

I frowned. "How reassuring."

Death was silent after that, closing her eyes while some unseen birds chirped and tweeted in the mulberry-toned leaves above us.

"You said you made this special for you. Why?" I asked her.

She countered with her own question. "Don't you like it here?

"I do. It beats the interrogation room, but why do you like it?"

Death looked me up and down with those ancient, bottomless eyes. Cocking her head to the side, she said, "I understand why they chose you for this. Not a lot scares you—not even me."

"Well, while the rocker chick look with the tats is pretty timeless, it isn't quite the same as the Grim Reaper." I'd always assumed that if I ever saw Death, it would be a figment of my dying brain's synapses—appearing as a great cloaked figure with a deep cowl and a scythe that I would have no doubt created from all the horror movies I'd ever seen.

"Ugh." Death rolled her eyes. "The Grim Reaper look is so passé. Been there done that for way too long. I can take on any aspect I want, depending on my mood. Last week, I was stern and humorless. Today, I'm going for confident, yet rebellious."

Death paused, and I wondered if she was ever going to answer my question. Her silence gave me a chance to study her. With her tattoos and her nose ring, the jeans and the boots, she looked like she could be fronting a rock band. She'd be right at home wailing into a microphone like Steven Tyler, one of the old-school rock greats my grandmother adored.

One of Death's earrings sparkled, the silver butterfly suddenly vibrating its wings and flying away. It fluttered for a moment before alighting on Death's outstretched hand. Gently beating its now iridescent blue wings, the insect floated up and continued on its way.

Finally, Death said, "To answer your question, I like this place because it's quiet. Peaceful. I come here mostly to get away. Collecting souls is harder work than you realize. Sure, some people die peacefully and are ready to go when their time comes, but most don't. A few fight it tooth and nail—sometimes I have to rip a soul out of its body. Can you even comprehend what that's like?" A scowl darkened Death's face, and she gave a humorless chuckle. "It sucks."

Death shook her head ruefully before she went on. "All they

want to do is escape my reach, but they can't. No one is beyond my grasp. They scream and cry, beg and bargain. A few even threaten me. Sometimes I just want some damn peace and quiet—you know?"

"So you stop here with the occasional lucky soul to have some girl talk in your own personal Fortress of Solitude?"

Death shifted on the bench, turning to rest her arm on the back and face me, her glittery eyes suddenly much more intent. "I like you, Misha. You're funny. You do know that you'll have to crush that part of you if things work out the way you planned, right?"

The question cut deep, and I tried ignoring it.

"What's the point of all of this?" I barked.

Death's expression turned sly. She'd touched a nerve, and she knew it. It pissed me off a little.

"Does there have to be a point? I like to talk to the would-be martyrs sometimes—you tend to be interesting souls. At least the ones who have sincere reasons for throwing themselves into my arms as opposed to the brainwashed fools who just act out of blind allegiance."

"A would-be martyr?" I heard the defensiveness in my voice.

"Oh, please. Spare me the fake indignation, Misha. You stepped on the path to martyrdom the instant you let Doctor Fadden inject you with those edited genes and turn you into a walking time bomb. Your willingness to sacrifice everything you love—and everything you are—to *perhaps* change the future. Sounds like martyr material to me."

My cheeks flushed, and I absently touched my arm where Doc Fadden had done his work.

"I'm not judging you, sweetie. Not my job. I just don't feel compelled to listen to bullshit when it's served up like that. You knew if you got that injection you were Dead Woman Walking, one way or the other."

"But if you're here for me now, then I've failed." I looked away and ground my teeth, too ashamed to let Death see the doubt, fear, and tears in my eyes. I knew what I was doing was right, but it was so much harder than I thought it would be.

"Tell me something, Misha. Do you want to die today? Or do you want to fulfill this mission of yours, even knowing what it means for you?" Death's voice was soft and kind.

My fists clenched as the anger flooded back. Five years ago, just after the 2028 election, the president and multiple members of his cabinet were assassinated, and the Electorate took control during the pandemonium. Like other reporters, I did my best to find out what was really going on, but it gutted me to see the country I loved fade into a pale shadow of itself. When our newly minted "prime minister" unleashed his media machine, my faith was shattered as he released lie after blatant lie.

And the masses ate it up.

Fucking lemmings.

Did I want to die? Fleeing the insanity created by the Electorate was an unexpected temptation, one so visceral I could nearly taste it. It would be so simple to slip out of my chains and run free. To just give up... and condemn everyone I cared about to a living hell.

"No!" I shouted. "I don't want to die!"

My heart shattered, because I knew exactly what those words meant for me. As the sound of my voice faded away, the pile of scrolls on the bench shuddered violently, browning and cracking until they too turned to dust, leaving one single map behind.

The map of the rest of my life.

The map of my death.

Death picked up the scroll. "Well, then. A martyr you shall be." Reaching out, she touched a single finger to my forehead.

"Wait. What are you—"?

Everything around me melted, running together like Death's tattoos had earlier, becoming a whirling vortex that probably should have made me sick to my stomach.

Blackness swallowed me.

Then... the bright stab of pain.

All the pain came rushing back.

I knew in an instant I had returned to that drab gray interrogation room, the metallic taste of blood no longer a memory as I felt it seep out of my mouth. A gloved hand grabbed a fistful of my hair and yanked my head upright.

"Good. You're back. Your death would have been very inconvenient for me."

General Maldonado's thin pockmarked face was inches from mine, and the smell of feta cheese on his breath made my stomach revolt. He had small eyes set close together, and a permanent sneer slashed across his face.

I threw a pleading tone into my voice. "General, I told you, I'll do what you want. But only if... Prime Minister... Darrow tells me in person."

It took all of my focus to call Richard Darrow, our illustrious prime minister, by his real name. After the Electorate took control, we started calling him "El Jefe," knowing that any comparison to the old dictator-led juntas of Central America went right up his ass sideways. And by "we" I mean those of us who saw this shitshow for what it was: the collapse of our country. But we refused to sit back and watch it happen quietly. We had relentlessly questioned his authority, and he had hunted us down in kind.

"The Prime Minister is not going to come visit vermin like you. You're beneath him. You and all your *journalist* friends," sneered Maldonado.

I bit the inside of my cheek to keep from responding the way I wanted to. Instead, I just whispered, "I only want to tell the truth."

"Whose truth?"

Maldonado leaned in close, salivating at the prospect of my resistance. And I wanted to, I ached to, but I had to give in. That was the plan. Let them take me—El Jefe's most vocal critic—and let them think they'd broken me. All for the chance to get close to El Jefe and change everything. Letting them take me was all part of the plan. As soon as Doc Fadden had injected me, the clock started ticking. We made sure someone informed the Electorate's secret police as to where I was hiding, and they swept in like vultures.

On the first day in this gray holding room, I flipped them the double-bird and yelled, "Come at me, bitches," to the interrogation room mirror.

Oh, they came for me.

I think I lasted four days, maybe five, but I lost track. They never turned the lights off, and they cycled the temperature from center-of-Hell hot to Siberia cold. They tried what they thought to be obnoxious music turned beyond eleven, but my grandmother raised me on the old classics: AC/DC, Black Sabbath, Dio, Metallica. My jailers gave up on the music when I started singing along with Ozzy. Then Maldonado decided to go more old-school with his torture. That was when the beatings started, followed by waterboarding. He'd even used electric shock—always taking far too much pleasure in my pain.

"Whose truth? *Your* truth," I said to Maldonado. "I told you! I'll do whatever you want, say whatever you want, but I want to hear the deal from the man in charge."

I let my head hang down. Saying those words nearly killed me inside.

"I'm the man in charge," Maldonado growled.

"No, you're not. You're just the puppet—the Prime Minister's the master."

I knew it was a mistake the moment I said it. Maldonado's whole expression changed, rage flooding his eyes, his sallow skin flushing a dull red. I cringed away, and this time it wasn't pretend. The last time I saw that expression on his face, he'd brought in the car battery, and I'd suffered. I started to cry. Real, terrified tears.

"You little bitch! You won't get anywhere near—"

"Please don't hurt—"

"General!"

The sharp voice behind him was deep and authoritative,

and it made Maldonado blanch. Hastily, he spun and saluted sharply. “Vice-Minister! We were not expecting you. No one informed me of your visit! We...”

Vice-Minister Williams, El Jefe’s right-hand man, was tall and handsome, with just a smattering of gray throughout his dark hair. His teeth were ridiculously straight and white—his parents had probably mortgaged their house to pay for that orthodontic work.

“What is the meaning of this, Maldonado? We received word two days ago that Miss Blackstone was amenable to our offer. Why haven’t you brought her to Prime Minister Darrow? We need to get her into the news cycle as soon as possible.”

“She needs to be broken, sir. Those were our orders. She’s still too willful. I don’t believe—” Maldonado stood stiff and rigid.

“Why does she look like this? Your orders were to break her, not disfigure her,” Williams interrupted. “We can’t put her in front of cameras looking like this, you idiot!”

I watched the disgust wash over the Vice-Minister as he looked me up and down.

“She wasn’t breaking, sir.” Maldonado flushed a darker, somehow uglier red.

My throat closed as fear swamped me. It wasn’t supposed to be Williams here, it was supposed to be El Jefe who came to gloat over me. We’d all banked on that. We’d counted on his ego being so big, he wouldn’t be able to resist seeing me in prison. Wouldn’t be able to pass up the chance to see me beg for my life. Now I was going to have to improvise. I tried to go even limper in my shackles and offered a pained whimper.

“She looks broken to me,” Williams snapped. “Jesus Christ. This is an unmitigated disaster! If she can’t go on the air, I’m holding you personally responsible.”

The general kept his mouth shut after that. Williams walked up to me. He raised my chin with his fingers—the gentlest touch I’d felt in nearly a week. I was grateful for it and despised myself for feeling that way.

"Miss Blackstone, I apologize that you've gone through this. Our orders for how to treat you were clearly misunderstood."

I nodded, even though I knew it was a bald-faced lie. The only truth he'd spoken so far was the fact that they couldn't put me on TV. Not in my tortured, broken state.

"Water?" I croaked. "Please?"

"Of course." Williams looked at his bodyguard. "Jones, escort the general and his entourage in the observation room out of this wing. Turn off the recording equipment and then return. And bring Miss Blackstone a glass of water when you come back."

"Yes, sir."

The name and the unexpected voice startled me. Jones was our inside man—and he normally was part of El Jefe's entourage of guards. If he was here, then the Big Kahuna wasn't coming, and somehow Jones had managed to get his assignment changed. Williams really was as good as it was going to get, and I was only going to have one opportunity.

Jones gave me the subtlest nod as he gestured for Maldonado to leave the room. Maldonado huffed and objected, but he couldn't refuse a direct order from the Vice Minister—not without risking his job and his own life. I guessed that Maldonado really didn't have the balls for that.

The next ten minutes were an eternity as I listened to Williams drone on about how I was doing the right thing, and that convincing my brethren to go along with the program was going to be better for everyone. It made me sick to listen to him, but I needed him to see nothing more than a broken little lamb when he looked at me.

"Of course," I mumbled during a pause. "I was so confused before."

Jones finally returned with a plastic cup of water. Williams sat at the table in the room and looked from the water to me and back again. Chained up the way I was, there was no way for me to drink. I didn't really care about the water—but I had to be out of these restraints. As the seconds ticked by, fear started to wash up inside me. Did he suspect? Was he cruel? Clueless? Or was he also playing a game?

"Shall I unchain her, sir?" asked Jones.

"Yes, of course. How thoughtless of me." Williams put on a smiling, false face again. "You poor thing. I am so sorry for how General Maldonado treated you."

I so badly wanted to scream *LIAR!* at him.

"And I do hope that our agreement stands? I would hate to have that Neanderthal's grotesque behavior give you the wrong impression about what we're trying to accomplish. The good we're trying to do." Williams watched me carefully, and I didn't miss the malicious light that flashed in his eyes when I mumbled something about not changing my mind.

Jones released my arms, and I nearly fell, but he caught me and helped me to the other chair. I made sure Williams saw my hand shake as I reached for the cup. After a drink, I took one of the pieces of ice and rubbed it over the raw chafes on my wrists. It stung terribly, but a moment later, the skin started to numb.

"This really will be for the best," Williams said.

"Of course you're right, Vice Minister," I said meekly. I shifted, the legs of the chair scraping on the floor as I moved it, while Williams continued his oration. I had to be a little closer to him. Maldonado's beatings had taken a lot out of me, and there weren't going to be any second chances.

"Having you as the face of our media network will be so helpful. You'll be instrumental in establishing peace. Helping people understand the truth. Our vision for the future..." His voice trailed away as he looked into the distance and closed his eyes, imagining some future only he could see.

All I could see was that last scroll in Death's hand... and my opportunity.

I lunged out of the chair and across the corner of the table, grabbing Williams by the suit jacket and pulling him close. His bellow of surprise turned to one of pain as I sank my teeth into his ear with all my might. The blood was hot on my tongue and made me want to gag, but I swallowed as much as I could before he pushed me away. I collapsed back in the chair.

I'd done it.

"You bitch! You bit me!" Williams shouted, pressing his hand to his ear. He whipped around to turn his ire on Jones, alternating between telling him what an inept bodyguard he was and ordering him to call a doctor.

I grinned, knowing the blood on my lips and teeth gave me a macabre look. His blood was exactly what I needed—his DNA would trigger the edited genes Doc Fadden had injected me with.

My whole body shuddered abruptly as the transformation started. My shoulders hunched and my joints screamed, and the unnatural grunt I uttered silenced Williams. With a cry of pain, I arched back in the chair, digging my fingers into the arms. I didn't want to, but something drove me to look in that damn mirror again. My face looked strange, waxy, like I was seeing myself in a carnival fun house. Then the blood pooled up out of my pores, and another searing pain lanced through me. The last thing I clearly saw was Williams' horrified expression as he backed up, only to be stopped and held in place by Jones.

What happened next, I really don't know. The pain that engulfed me made what I'd endured at Maldonado's hands feel like a day at the spa. Fadden had warned me, but this was beyond anything I had imagined. Bones cracked, joints popped. My muscles shredded as they tore and reconnected. My blood felt so hot, I thought my skin was peeling off. I guessed it looked like the blackened skin of a fire-roasted pepper but didn't know for sure as my eyes shriveled in my sockets as they remade themselves.

I was convinced an eternity passed, but in all, the transformation lasted maybe five minutes. Five minutes to metamorphose, to utterly change. Five minutes to break out of my chrysalis—as the mirror image of a monster.

I straightened and stared at the two men. Williams was slack-jawed and pale, as was Jones. Jones was part of our resistance, but even he didn't know what Fadden's modified genes were going to do. Again, I looked toward the mirror on the far wall. The transformation was astounding. The edited genes in my body had latched onto the DNA in Williams's blood and completely transformed my appearance into an exact replica of the man himself.

"Jesus Christ... what the hell is going on here?" he yelled, his voice nearly cracking.

"What the hell is going on here?" I parroted. My voice started out sounding like my own but then deepened into a masculine baritone.

"This is an abomination!"

"This is an abomination!" I shouted, my voice now indistinguishable from his.

"Guards! Guards!" Williams shouted. There was sweat on his forehead, and I knew panic was setting in because he'd finally realized that Jones wasn't going to protect him.

"You sent all the guards away," I reminded him. The deep, manly voice coming out of my mouth felt alien. I stood up, bumping the table hard, spilling the rest of the water and knocking my chair over. I was going to have to readjust my spatial relations quickly, because the real Williams was a very graceful man. I felt like an ox in this big, muscular body.

"You won't get away with this!" Williams blustered, but I could hear the fear rolling off him.

I locked eyes with Jones. "Do it," I ordered.

Everything in my world slowed down as Jones pulled out a syringe and plunged it toward Williams's exposed neck. The tetrodotoxin would kill him in a matter of minutes. Then I'd simply dress in his clothes and assume his life as El Jefe's closest advisor. A role that would put me in the Electorate's inner circle.

Jones stabbed the needle in.

The Vice Minister slapped his hand against his neck and

glared at Jones. "You traitor! I'll see you publicly executed! Neither of you will get away with this. What are you going to do? You can't get out of this facility, it's too well-guarded."

I watched Williams' eyes dart side to side, looking for a way out, but there was only one door, and Jones stood between him and the illusion of freedom. With the tetrodotoxin coursing through him, the Vice Minister only had a minute, maybe two, left to live. He twitched. Grunted. Loosened his tie in a desperate attempt to breathe. I saw his hand tremble but couldn't tell if it was from terror or pain. Or both. He jerked again.

"I'm going to walk out of here just fine," I told him. "Remember, I'm you now. Your life is mine. Misha Blackstone died at the hands of General Maldonado. No one's going to have the audacity to inspect the body bag I take out of here." This time the cadence of his voice—my new voice—felt right to me.

Williams's eyes rounded. He grimaced and twitched again, his breath labored, and I knew his nerves were blazing. "What did you give me?" he wheezed.

"Tetrodotoxin. In a few seconds, you're going to lose your ability to move, and then your ability to breathe."

He was going to die horribly, in agony and fear, and I didn't care. I wondered what that said about me.

Williams staggered, clutching the edge of the table, and I leaned forward to say... something. Instead, I gasped as the room spun. As the room seemed to recede, I clutched the back of my chair to keep my balance. It suddenly felt like I was watching the world from inside a fishbowl.

I shook my head to clear it, and when I looked up, I saw Death for the second time. She looked just the way I saw her in the park, and our eyes met.

"Today wasn't your day, Misha, but your turn is coming. No one can avoid their time. Not Williams. Or Jones. Or you," Death said.

"Can you tell me when?"

"No."

"Will you tell me how?"

"You already know that answer."

Death was right, I did know. The doctor had told me from the outset that my transformation wasn't permanent. I had a year if I was lucky. It would start like the flu, but the end? It wouldn't be pleasant, and I shuddered, remembering the photos Doc Fadden had shown me of the test subjects.

"Will it be as painful as Fadden said?"

"No," Death said softly. "It will be far worse."

Then a shadow crossed Death's face, the way the earth's shadow covers the moon during an eclipse, and when it passed, she looked totally different. Gone was the flame-haired woman with star-filled eyes and tattoos on her arm. In her stead was an old banshee, with stooped shoulders, milky eyes, and ragged, savagely long nails at the ends of her bony fingers.

Jones, who clearly could see none of this, had propped Williams in the other chair. Death reached out and grabbed the Vice Minister by the shoulder, burrowing her claws in hard. He shuddered once more, and I knew it wasn't from the poison coursing through him, but because he could feel Death's touch. The light drained from his eyes.

As I watched, I rubbed my fingers over the spot where Fadden had put the needle in my arm. I looked in the mirror at a face that was no longer my own, a face I had despised for years. A face and body that would now be my prison until Death came for me.

"You'll never get away..." Williams's last words were slurred from the toxin as it robbed him of his ability to breathe, to move, but not to feel or understand. His last few breaths rattled in his throat.

"Neither of us will," I said with a heavy voice.

Death smiled at me as she grabbed Williams' soul and ripped it from his body.

ABOUT SUSAN K. HAMILTON

Website: https://www.susankhamilton.com/
Twitter @RealSKHamilton

Susan K. Hamilton is the author of *Shadow King, Darkstar Rising,* and the forthcoming *The Devil Inside*. She lives outside of Boston with her husband, Jeff, and their cat, Rio. An avid equestrian, when she's not tapping away at a computer, chances are you'll find her at the barn. She loves fun movies, pizza, and pretty much any furry creature on the planet, and is currently working on a new, follow-up project to *Shadow King.*

CEDRIC

By Michael Haase

Your Majesty, I would like to extend my humble apologies for the corpse at your doorstep. My only hope is that you were able to look past the horrific scene and retrieve this note. I assure you, these words will explain everything.

I love your daughter more than the breath of life itself. This has been true for as long as I care to remember. I was only a boy of thirteen when my mother sent me to find work in your palace. I became a stable boy: a miserable and grueling existence, but the meager earnings were enough to stave off the Great Hunger. I resented it at first, but soon I found myself unable to stay away.

I have the clearest vision of the first time your younger daughter, Princess Mazzy, rode toward me. I had never seen her before. All I had known about Mazzy was that she was the daughter who would never inherit your Crown, the one who could only hope to find a prince from another kingdom to make her his queen. Otherwise, she would languish as a waste of royal blood, forever marked as the daughter who brought shame unto your family. Her fate was determined from the moment of her birth, and even I, a peasant boy, was aware of her cruel plight.

But I was never aware of her bloom and elegance until that moment. Thereafter, she defined beauty for me. I know she was dismissed as the least eye-pleasing of your children, but I never saw her that way. When she locked eyes with me, there was instant understanding. She saw beyond my tattered robes and filth and discerned the core of my being. I recognized her true warmth through the forced pomp and ostentation. I remember her riding up to me on her storm-gray mare, both of us reluctant to shatter the world we had created in a single gaze. I will never forget the moment when she first spoke to me with the soft cadence and sweet charm of her young, musical voice.

"You look like a Cedric to me," she said, wearing a smile that filled my heart to bursting.

The moment stole my breath. There was no chance she could have known my name. The recruiters had plucked me from a sea of boys, all of us desperate to make a coin a day. I was no one.

Yet we knew one another as soon as our first gaze entangled our fates. The great universe is an endless labyrinth, yet the gods had placed us together. Mazzy and I played out a story dictated by the stars.

We told no one, for no one else mattered.

Peasant workers received beatings if caught speaking to the royals. Your guards were ruthless in their discipline. However, Mazzy still made time to meet with me almost every day for the next few years, using her clever mind to conjure up ways for us to rendezvous in secret. On the rare occasions we were caught, the guards waited for Mazzy to retire back to the castle, then came to the stables to whip me. Even so, I was never deterred from seeing her the next day.

For what punishment is greater than depriving oneself of true love?

By age sixteen, I was finally banished from the palace grounds for being caught with Mazzy too often. This infuriated my mother to no end. She beat me for losing our family's income, and it was true that we never ate well again. I tried explaining to her how I felt, but she called me a fool. My brothers and sisters joined in mocking my love for Mazzy, and my home life became an even poorer existence. When I could escape the barrage of abuse from my mother and siblings, I walked to the foothills and found a high peak which looked down over the castle gates, in an attempt to catch a single glimpse of my love.

I knew I saw Mazzy astride her storm-gray mare, even though she looked as small as a single grain of rice from where I was perched. I was certain she could see my filthy visage amongst the rocky terrain surrounding me. I was not forgotten. Though we were separate, our hearts remained near.

It was upon my eighteenth birthday that we finally reunited. She snuck from the castle and found me in the foothills. Despite years of absence, we found no reason to speak.

Instead, we kissed.

It was a dream realized.

And then she returned home. It was not easy watching her walk away, but I had no doubt I would see her again.

And I did.

Every day, we met and embraced, sharing and expressing our love as we looked over the kingdom that would have mocked and abused us for following our hearts. The doubters never mattered; our love was as natural as a heartbeat.

It did not take long for us to discuss fleeing the Kingdom. As always, the difficulty was money. None of the royal wealth would be available should she declare her love for me. And there was no chance a man ostracized from working within the palace grounds would be able to make a decent enough wage within the Kingdom to afford elopement.

It was I who came up with the plan to leave the Kingdom to find work. This is a decision I would forever regret, yet there were no other options. I loathed leaving my love, but I saw it as a temporary evil for the greater good. I could roam and work hard labor for years, and once I had saved up enough, I would return and steal Mazzy away. We would make a life together in another land. It was a dream I carried with me as I worked in neighboring villages for the next several months, and it kept me strong and focused.

Then that dark day descended. The gods no longer seemed to favor our union.

The town crier sang out the words that brought me to my knees. Princess Mazzy, my true love, was dead.

My soul shredded. My heart was wrung out by cold and ruthless hands. I cursed the gods and swore off all allegiance to them.

Mere moments later, I took the wages I had saved to the nearest tavern and began grieving under the foolish cloak of heavy drink. My traumatized and intoxicated mind relived the tale of my love for Mazzy to anyone who would listen, and eventually my story landed upon the ears of an elderly man with a black mustache curling up into sharp, pointed ends. He invited me out to the front of the building, where he had parked a cart of his wares. In my drunkenness, I followed him, as I was curious about his claim that he could help me. Part of me hoped he was a criminal, leading me off to stab me in the heart and end my misery.

His cart was packed to the brim with ointments, potions, and trinkets. He pointed out numerous items designed to help with coping, with forgetting, with moving on—and I must admit that in my despair I was tempted. But amongst all the flash and distraction, a small vial filled with an opaque black liquid drew my attention. He caught me staring at the bottle and complimented my taste, stating that what I had found was an elixir of his own creation.

The old man said his elixir could bring back the dead, but at a cost. It required an exchange, a life for a life. Half of the bottle had to be consumed by someone alive before the other half was poured into the mouth of someone dead. The dead would revive, and both people would remain alive until the following sunset. Once the last sliver of the sun's light slipped off the horizon, the exchange of life would be complete. The dead would live once more, and the living would perish.

I was at first appalled at the claim of the liquid's effects, so I accused him of being either a warlock or a wizard. He chuckled, stating he was merely a struggling entrepreneur, but he guaranteed his product would work. In all honesty, I cared not if his potion was dark magic. All I knew was that I had a chance to bring Mazzy back. I spent the remainder of my wages on the old man's elixir and immediately began my return journey home, never once stopping for rest.

Even so, the journey took three days, and I did not make

it back before her corpse was interred beneath several feet of earth.

I slunk onto the cemetery grounds just before dusk. The dirt in front of her headstone was freshly turned with lilacs and lavender strewn upon it. For a moment, I considered myself to be too late. It felt like a violation to dig up my one love's remains.

But then I read her headstone. My task had changed. I did not wish to rescue my love any longer. The purpose of my mission had become far greater than I imagined.

I clawed the earth away from the grave in what felt like mere minutes, tears streaming from my eyes to the point of blinding me. My fingernails tore and bled with my efforts, yet I felt nothing but love and desperation. At last, I reached the casket and pried it open with a strength I never before knew I had.

The headstone was true. Cradled in Mazzy's lifeless arms was the body of a newborn—our child. This tiny infant boy meant everything to me, to us, to our love. I fell to my knees, sobbing, hoping for everything to be a nightmare. My gaze shifted back and forth between the baby boy and the headstone declaring Mazzy, my love, to be the victim of a difficult childbirth. Next to her name was another with the birth and death date being the same as the day my love died.

The inscription declared his name to be Cedric.

I will admit that I was unsure of the elixir when I first sipped my half. My skepticism did not matter, though. Your Majesty, I had to try and reignite the fire of the love I shared with your daughter. I wanted to give the other half to my child right away, but I realized that I had no means of caring for the boy. I thought of all the nursemaids at the palace and the care little Cedric would receive there. I brought his body to your front door, and we arrived in the early evening.

I gave Cedric his half of the elixir on your doorstep. The old man's concoction worked exactly as promised.

You will see what I saw. He has her soft, powder blue eyes.

His cry is strong. He is healthy. I only had a few glowing moments with my son before I knocked at your door. I don't remember quite what happened, but the guard sent for one of your nursemaids, and they took him from me, to safety.

I do not know what was said of Mazzy's pregnancy, but I am certain the news was not met with great enthusiasm. Perhaps she told you the truth, and you thought the child was only the bastard son of a missing peasant boy. He is much more than that. Cedric, your grandson, is perhaps the most special child to grace your kingdom in history. He is the direct product of true love. He is a perfect creation.

I know I did the most virtuous of deeds. I know I did what your daughter would have wanted. In Cedric, the greatest love carries on. Your Majesty, I plead for you not to reject him.

As I write these words, the sun is settling behind the foothills I used to sit upon while studying my love from afar.

I apologize for my corpse on your doorstep, but I felt you should know the love from which that boy is made. Cedric is the most precious child in your Kingdom. He has already defeated death. Both of his parents sacrificed their lives so he could live on.

I beg you to treat him as your own.

ABOUT MICHAEL HAASE

Website: https://talltalestold.com/
Twitter @authormikehaase

Michael Haase is the author of the forthcoming book, The Man Who Stole the World, to be published by Inkshares. Michael is a happy husband, father, musician, and spontaneous comedian who does nerdy stuff like study computer programming in his spare time. He lives intentionally near Cleveland, believe it or not.

THE TIME BEHIND DYING

By Peter Ryan

It's dark. The breeze is cool, but the day's warmth radiates from the desert floor, making me slippery with sweat. Trucks rumble past on a distant highway, their reverberations softly bouncing off wind-sculpted stone. Twin headlights pierce the gloom, highlighting a stark, red-tinged landscape and striping across my hunched form. The car's tires nestle rim-deep in the sand, its engine block ticking as heat bleeds into the crisp evening air. The rear of the vehicle sags heavy on its springs. And I know why.

There's a body in the trunk.

The shovel's handle is slick with the blood seeping from my blistered hands. The soil is iron-hard, baked barren by an eternity of blazing suns. "What happens in Vegas, stays in Vegas" sounded like bullshit when I first heard it—not so much now I'm digging another grave. I smear the sweat off my brow and shiver, but not because of the breeze.

I wasn't always like this. I used to tally numbers, not body count. I sat in air-conditioned offices, shuffling papers and laundering illegal funds through discreet overseas accounts. I was no saint, but I sure was no killer. Then betrayal and revenge raised their ugly heads, and my life twisted into His control.

I peel off my undershirt and drop it to the dirt. The harsh headlights illuminate the vivid scars stabbed into my flabby gut. The wounds pucker like carp sucking tidbits from the surface of a scummy pond. Ratty jailhouse tattoos dance along my neck and spine. Savage Haitian divinities spiral out over my rib cage and hips, inked on like a crude external skeleton. Sweat streams down my face and chest, running over the coarse-healed lacerations, flowing through the rough-drawn deities, and bringing them to life.

I lean on the shovel and check my watch. Fewer than sixty

minutes left—four feet of grave to go. I need to push it. I raise the shovel high above my head and swing it axe-like at the earth. It clangs, skittering off hidden rock, and wrenches from my hands.

I recall the kill.

The woman bound and screaming, watching wild-eyed as I slit her husband's throat like a sacrificial lamb, arterial blood spurting his life out. It was a righteous execution—he was an abusive prick. And now this blameless woman is being held hostage over me—slated to die unless I reach six feet deep. He likes to play His games. And the price of my losing is her death, but with Him, there's always more.

My wrists ache, and my hands continue to bleed. I retrieve the shovel and place a sharkskin-booted foot against the cross-section of the blade. I drive it hard into the desert earth. This time it's easier. The unyielding surface gives way to loose subsoil. Thin clouds scuttle across a glinting starlit sky as I toss out another shovel load. I might just make it deep enough. I might just save her.

Then the lights flicker.

The rental's brand new, and the battery's fully charged. This is wrong. The breeze stops like the night is holding its breath. The clicking from the cooling engine ceases. The rumbling of the far-off traffic mutes. I hear a gentle *clunk*, and the trunk lid rises. There's a whispered invocation and an easing of suspension springs. I peer into the lights. I can't see much, but I don't need to. The dense starlight of the Milky Way now silhouettes an upright body.

The dead man stands on twisted limbs. I had to break his legs to force him into the trunk. He shouldn't be alive—but then again, I've been dead before. A trickle of sweat crawls down my spine. The jailhouse tattoos gyrate, and fear surges through me.

This is not his grave I'm digging.

The man shuffles over to me—a warped, drunken gait. Gore leaks from his slashed throat like drool from a macabre smile.

His head lolls as he gazes down at me in the grave. Reflected in the lifeless eyes I see all the people He compelled me to kill. I stare, willing Him to show Himself in this man's body. Wanting to negotiate. Wanting to plead.

It doesn't happen. The night breathes.

"Keep going," the man gurgles through torn vocal cords. "We don't want the vermin digging you up."

It *is* my time. Insects of dread burrow into my flesh. I should've killed the wild-eyed woman. I knew the rules, but she had already paid the price through marriage to this thug. But the dead man's presence is the cost of breaking His contract. Everyone pays. No exceptions.

And now the urgency to dig is personal. The grave needs to be deep. I only have one chance. I need to dig beyond my sins.

"Why did you come back from death?" the man asks after a few minutes, squatting beside my grave like a malevolent toad.

I don't stop. The man lays a heavy hand on my shoulder.

"Why?" he repeats.

I empty another shovel load.

"You know why," I tell him. "You've seen what's there."

I heave out more dirt.

"Tell me more," he orders. "I need to know more."

The shiv that shredded my gut finished my first life. I bled out in the prison showers. I deserved it. I wanted to die. But He wasn't finished. He hungered for me. He brought me back. Sharp Haitian bones as needles, and my own blood as ink. He chanted ancient curses to resurrect the fallen and carved tattoos deep into my skin. He came to me and offered me a choice. And I had seen what was next. They were waiting for me—both of them.

I can't return to the time behind dying. When He made His dark bargain of resurrection, I said yes. Anything to delay the reckoning, because the murdered innocent never really die.

"You've been beyond," I tell him. "You've seen what happens to people like us."

In the bottom of the pit, a low haze roils. It sucks the warmth from my calves and thighs. I shudder. The man steps forward and tugs the shovel from my hand. He clasps my forearm to pull me from the hole. We share the twin grips of gladiators. I realize my mistake and try to jerk away. Too late. He yanks me out of the pit and onto the desert floor. His hold tightens.

My tattoos smirk and frolic. I feel them, pinprick-sharp, as they jag themselves from my skin. I sense their malice as they skip down my arm before gliding onto his flesh. They contort around his forearm, disappearing under a sleeve, then moving up and over his torso. The material of his jacket jerks and stains with the blood of my dancing tattoos. His warped body straightens, and he smiles.

Now released from His curse, my scars crease open and seep. Thick, dead blood oozes between my clenched fingers. It has the metallic stench of old coins. I pull my hands tighter, willing it to stop, but it's no use. These wounds are old, and they never really healed.

I now lie at the edge of my grave, listening to the murmurings of the dead. I roll over and stare into the pit. Instead of sand and rock, there are now gray, putrid mouths with decaying, angular teeth—a few of them even belong to children. Between them are grasping fingers with torn nails, wedding rings, and scabrous flesh. Milky white eyes peer blindly from flesh-rotted skulls. They see me. They want me. I need to escape beyond the innocent dead.

He jumps in, landing among the broken bones, oblivious to the death beneath him. All he sees is a job unfinished.

"You need to go deeper," I tell him.

"I'll go deeper, but you need to give me answers."

"Do it for your wife. Or He will take her. Then she'll be waiting. You don't want that."

He grunts. The gash in his throat is already knitting together. The childlike sketches twirl around the gaping flesh. The man strikes with the shovel. The edge pierces a mouth, and a partial skull swings from the end of the blade. Dark hair hangs lank off the bone. A pair of black-rimmed glasses dangle from a shattered eye socket. He was the first of the innocent dead. My wife's lover. The huge man flings it out of the pit. It lands among a pile of splintered bones. The Haitian tattoos no longer insulate me from my part in the dead reality. The pile of earth I'd exhumed now writhes with the limbs, torsos, and entrails of the innocent.

"Deeper," I say again.

He digs. This time the shovel blade bites into the desiccated body of a woman. I recognize the dress. It was summer. The dress was white with a patterning of tiny sunflowers. It's now stained with blood and dirt. Her shrunken skin pulls tight across her ribcage. Her once-full breasts are now flapping flesh exposed through ripped material. The man effortlessly heaves the half torso onto the pile. It wriggles among the battered limbs. My wife's body again entwined with her lover.

My wounds pulse in tune with my dying heart. The sweat I'd worked up is now a crust on my forehead. I watch as the man carves another chunk out of the earth. More limbs. This time the arms of children. One with a baseball mitt. The other clutching a teddy bear.

My heart quickens, and the blood from my gut flows freely. The man notices my distress and flings the pile at me. I flinch as the arms spasm in my lap. The mitt closing and opening, waiting for a summer that never came. The hand holding the toy clenching and unclenching, waiting for a life that never started.

Parts of the limbs have been consumed—gnaw marks pale against dried bone. The brothers were buried shallow in a desert like this one. Their parents failed to pay the ransom. The kids had seen my face. A shot to the back of the head for each. He gave me no choice. I grab both thin arms in one fist. I feel the shriveled muscles and tendons wriggling. I hurl them away. They're waiting for me. Small insistent hands that will never stop grasping at my wounds.

"Deeper," I plead.

The man's blank eyes look at me. His legs have straightened, and he's standing tall. The pit must be at least four feet deep now, yet his chest and shoulders tower above the grave's ragged lip. My legs now dangle into the empty space, my boots kicking at the air. Across from me I see the chunks of bodies moving against each other. The older ones dusty and dry—the newer ones moist with gore.

He thrusts the blade into the loose earth—mouths bite and fingers clutch. Limbs twitch and skulls chatter. He sees none of this. He sees me. Blood leaking from between my fingers. Dried sweat caking my chest and shoulders. My skin devoid of markings.

"How many?" he asks.

The question is obvious. The answer is not. I don't know. I started killing in my thirties. My first two were my first innocents. The lover, then my wife. The heavy-framed glasses. The sunflower dress. She said it was all a mistake. I agreed. What I did next was not. It was deliberate. No remorse. Not for him. Not for her.

My bosses found out and deemed me a risk. I was compromised. I had a choice to make: wait for the inevitable bullet to the brain or turn myself in and let justice take its course. I took the latter. Only it was never that easy. My bosses' contacts were far-reaching. They had me killed in prison. They had Him resurrect me—reborn a killer for hire.

"Too many," I answer.

He rests on the shovel's handle, one hand clasped on top of the other. Leaning like he's peering over a neighbor's fence. He wants to know more. My present is his future.

"It was your job," he says. "To kill."

"Yours, too."

He half nods. This day was always coming. This man was always coming. I'd wanted more time. I can't go back. Not to the grasping hands and the sucking mouths. Not to the time behind dying.

I shiver. I see the bodies. The years of death. The kills. The waste.

"Keep digging," I tell him. "If not for me, then her. For yourself."

He grips the handle and pushes deep, slicing decomposed flesh and bone. His shoes sinking into the rotting dead.

"What do you see?" he asks.

"My past."

"It's a grave, man. There's no past there. Just dirt."

Another shovelful joins the pile. I see the mutilated torso of a fit young man clad in torn running shorts and shoes. Another innocent I couldn't leave alive. The legs convulse and turn. On the back, pressed into the rancid flesh, are tire marks. He went down hard. But he didn't die immediately. That took a knife.

I study the big man's hands. I see the dancing tattoos. Figures made from my blood imbued with the power of life.

"Why you?" I ask.

He shrugs. "It's your time. And I had to take the deal."

"What did He tell you?"

"Tell me? He gave me the same choice he gave you."

"But why me?" I complain, knowing the answer. "What did I do wrong?"

"You didn't finish the job," he says.

He takes another shovel load and heaves it high. He's getting deep now. Around the five- foot mark. The clock is ticking —not long to go. The body parts surrounding me continue to squirm. Tugging at each other. All moving toward me.

I pull my legs up from the pit, wrap my arms around my shins, and rock back and forth. My bloodied fingers interlock around the top of my dirt-caked boots. The man heaves another shovel load of putrefying flesh onto the pile. I clutch my legs tighter. Rivulets of blood flow down my pale torso, over my pants, and drip onto the desert dirt. The dirt that contains my future. I need him to dig beyond my past. To escape to the quiet place where I don't exist. The Man with the needle-sharp bones told me this. It's my one chance for peace.

"What do you see?" he tries again. "I was told you have the answers."

"Answers to what?"

"As to what happens next. To me. To what I become."

I shrug. The grave's deep, but I still see the remains of the crushed and torn humanity. All reaching for me. Handless arms seeking the everlasting embrace. They yearn for me from the pit. I look at my watch.

"You're on the clock," he says.

"Yes."

"How long?"

"Eternity if you don't go deeper."

I look into his eyes. They are blank, black disks of ignorance. The tattoos continue to dance across his flesh—chortling and scornful. My own blood mocking me as my time slips away.

"And if I do?"

"I get Nothing," I mutter. "Nothing at all."

"Nothing?"

I nod. He takes the shovel and digs. I watch while he hauls another load of body parts and dumps them on the waist-high pile. Then he turns and stares—straight at me.

"Do you think you deserve Nothing?" he growls. "You broke the contract."

His eyes are no longer dead; instead, they flare and gleam. His grin widens and the tattoos shriek.

It's *Him*.

I see the skull beneath the skin, the teeth, the sharp cheekbones, the outline of the eye sockets pressing through the drab human flesh. The handle of the shovel now butts against the fleshy part of His underarm. He crosses one leg over the other. The stars begin to fade. I pull my legs tighter to me, folding myself like a frightened child. His face glows. My skin itches with the echo of the prison tattoos.

"So tell me," the Man asks again. "Do you think you deserve

Nothing?"

The alarm on my wrist bleeps. A tiny sound against the background of the cosmos. Time's up. I unwrap my arms and stand. My blood no longer flows. My heart no longer beats. Lumps of humanity squirm at my feet.

"Well, do you?"

I lean in and look into my eternal resting place. And then I see it. Under His feet, half-buried in the human remains—a full body. And at the bottom of the legs are a pair of sharkskin boots.

Not deep enough.

ABOUT PETER RYAN

Website: http://www.synccityjack.com/
Twitter @SyncCityJack

Peter Ryan is a sci-fi lover, motorbike rider, darts player, and T-shirt designer, as well as being an English professor at a university in South Korea. He grew up in Perth, Western Australia, and has traveled much of the world. While on the move, he has done a variety of jobs, including sales support at an insurance company, laborer on the building sites of London and Melbourne, chauffeur/minder for an English lord, and business English consultant in Shanghai.

AMBITION

By Deborah Munro

Bouncing over the curb, Gwen screeched into a narrow parking space, leaving the vehicle askew as she jumped out. The icy wind slapped her loose dark hair against her cheeks as she slammed the car door and hurried to the lab, looping her purse over her shoulder. March in Osaka was always unpredictable, and she had underdressed for the chill. Wrapping her trench around herself more tightly, she splashed through a shallow puddle in her flats, feeling water squelch between her toes and soak into the pant cuffs, which she could already see would be a gray stain. *Damn it!*

The lab was a nondescript concrete structure, cold and bleak in the early morning light. She pulled her card key from under her coat, swiped it through the lock, and waited for the click and green light. But no, it flashed red, and she stamped her foot, splashing dirty water further up her pant leg. She tried again: still red. *It's like the spiteful thing knows I'm running late!* Calming her breathing and her shaking hand, she opened her coat and dried the card on her silk blouse, yet another clothing item ruined by today's fiasco. She swiped the card through, and it grudgingly flashed green.

Stepping through into the anteroom bathed in fluorescent white, Gwen doffed her soggy shoes and coat in a wet heap in the corner. After three years on this project, gowning in had become second nature, as it was essential for not contaminating the experiment: first the indoor slip-ons, then the shoe covers, followed by the first pair of gloves, the hairnet, and the facemask. Then she moved to the inner room and pulled on the head cover, the full "bunny" suit, the outer boots, the eye shields, and the second pair of gloves. With an agitated sigh, she wiped down her phone and tablet computer with isopropyl alcohol and glanced at her phone, cursing at the movement of time. The Japanese didn't tolerate tardiness. There was no excuse good enough here in Japan, especially when she needed to collect the blood samples at the same time every day for the best comparison. The thought of ruining the life-altering results of her research this close to the end because she was late was unbearable. It would not only be a tragic loss, but professional suicide.

Gwen pushed through the vertical plastic flaps into the inner vestibule, which was awash in amber light to protect the light-sensitive samples. The rhesus monkeys, with their naked faces and whiskered cheeks, had grown to be Gwen's closest friends, and she confided in them daily. She couldn't remember the last time she had spent a day away from the lab, but her commitment to her work was paramount. Just a little more time and she'd have the results she needed to prove her genetic alterations reversed Alzheimer's, providing the monkeys with renewal of their deteriorating memories.

Despite this incredible breakthrough, which would no doubt bring Gwen's work to the forefront of science on the search for a cure for Alzheimer's, there was something still confusing her. Some of the monkeys' improvements on the intelligence and memory tests had stagnated. Gwen knew there had to be a difference in one of the gene sequences, which she had narrowed down to the most likely candidates, but she needed more data points. The monkeys seemed to respond to the treatment identically in nearly all ways, save for the fact that as they became smarter, they also became more non-compliant and defiant toward testing. Gwen shook away the unwelcome thought and rubbed her shoulder as she walked from the inner vestibule down the hall toward the supply room.

Lately, some of the most genetically responsive monkeys had begun to show some random signs of aggression. Hugo, one of the large males, had bitten her just beyond the edge of her protective apron last week, forcing her to clean and bandage it in secret. An incident report would compromise her timeline, which was unacceptable. The publication of the initial results of Gwen's study in *Nature*, the premier journal in her field, had been a huge success last year, and she was due to publish her latest results next month. That meant getting the blood tests done this morning before she missed her time window.

Seeing the hallway was empty, she jogged the rest of the way and gave the door a shove.

The supply room door opened easily, catapulting her inside with an undignified clumsiness. Gwen was relieved to see no one was there, and she straightened up, rearranged her garments, and set her tablet down on the workbench to free her hands. Calming herself and re-prioritizing, she slipped back out into the hall, walked across the corridor to the animal lab, and swiped her card through the punch clock. She was barely on time, and she breathed a sigh of relief.

Returning, Gwen grabbed the rack of clean test tubes off the shelf and proceeded to set up syringes for capturing the monkeys' blood. She hated having to poke the little guys every single day. They broke her heart when they had been trained to the point of coming up and voluntarily sticking out their arms, hoping for a simple scratch behind the ears when she finished her work. The monkeys with the more enhanced memories, however, now resisted her. She had to resort to using an animal control pole, which was basically a noose, to pin them down and draw their blood—this was what led to the bite when she leaned forward too far.

Working quickly, Gwen rolled the cart across the hall and entered. This small room required yet another layer of protection. She donned a face shield, rubber apron, and third set of gloves. Leaning her card pocket against the reader with a frustratingly awkward chest thrust, necessary for getting in with the cart before the door lock reset, she bumped the heavy door with her butt and backed carefully into the animal lab, dragging the cart behind her.

The room was completely silent, and Gwen's skin began to crawl. Normally, the monkeys screeched their high-pitched call while climbing around and rattling their latched doors. The lab was a large open space, the walls lined with cages, and had a central workspace with tables and computers. Now, all the cages were empty, doors ajar like Gwen's own shock-laden jaw.

Gwen took a step backward and heard a squish and a crack as she tripped over something on the floor and fell, pulling the contents of the cart down with her. Her face shield flew off as her head jerked back. With a yelp as her tailbone cracked against the concrete floor, Gwen saw what she had tripped over and screamed.

Molly, one of the gentlest monkeys in the group, lay dead in a sludge of congealing blood, her chest cavity crushed where Gwen had stepped on her. Breathing hard, Gwen forced herself to open her eyes and look. Molly's body and even her long, beautiful tail were shredded, bringing Gwen to the point of retching. She tried to push herself up with her bulky hands but slipped back to the floor, her gloves slick with blood. She surveyed her lab and saw that the carcasses of nearly all of Molly's brethren were strewn across the floor, killed in the same gruesome manner. Hearing a raspy screech, Gwen quickly pushed to her feet, rust-red patches staining her garments.

Stifling another scream, Gwen realized that not all the lab animals were dead. Hugo crouched defensively in the corner under a steel counter, now barely recognizable from the cuts, bites, bald patches, missing ear, and eyes overflowing with rage. He gripped a broken glass shard from what remained of a shattered test tube in his tiny bloody hand.

Gwen backed away slowly, desperately judging how she might escape. Edging toward the computer station, she finally noticed Fuji-san, her technician, crumpled on the floor, stab wounds pock-marking his shins and forearms as if he'd fruitlessly grappled with his attacker. Gwen cried out and crossed her gloved arms across her chest, unable to look away from his gouged-out eyes.

Gwen shivered and stared into Hugo's wild eyes. She leapt

for the door and the monkey screamed, lunging for her. She shoved the rolling cart at him. He let out a watery breath as the cart hit him in the throat and knocked him to the ground, sending his makeshift weapon clattering across the floor. Gwen wrenched open her exit door and slammed it shut, hearing a dull scrape and thud, followed by repeated thumping as the monkey battered himself against the door.

Gwen opened the outer door, making sure no one was around, and dashed to the supply room, slipping inside and grasping the table for support. Struggling to breathe, she pulled off the apron and gloves and fished her phone from her pocket with tremoring hands that made it difficult to find the number she was looking for. Focusing on her fiancé's name, she dialed.

Jack's voice answered on the second ring. "What's up babe?"

"Jack! They're dead! My career is over!" She could hear him sit up in bed, clearing the sleepiness from his voice.

"Gwen, calm yourself so I can follow you. What's going on?"

"The monkeys! They're dead! Hugo killed them, and he attacked me. He killed Fuji-san. His eyes....oh god, his eyes were..." Her voice edged toward hysteria as she visualized the gored eye sockets.

Gwen was met with silence for a moment before Jack spoke. "Please slow down and start again, as I'm not following. Who is Hugo?" Although ruthlessly ambitious, Jack was a calm, rational person at all times, but right now his patronizing tone was making Gwen tremble with frustration.

"Hugo is a monkey! The rest of them are dead, and my lab assistant is dead! My entire career is in total ruin, all over the lab floor. What should I do?" Gwen screamed into the phone, then glanced around and lowered her voice, realizing someone might hear her and come investigate. "Listen to me. I'm covered in blood. I don't know what happened—how they got so violent. This is going to destroy my life! There will be an investigation, and I'll never get another chance to do this kind of research again! Do you understand what a fiasco this is?"

"Don't do anything. You're obviously in shock." She heard him stand up, apparently dressing with the phone held to his ear. "I'll come over and we can figure this out together."

"There's no time. Someone is going to discover the bodies in the lab any moment. I need your advice *right now*!"

"Hang on. Let me think, okay?"

Gwen peeked into the hallway. Bloody footprints tracked across the floor. The magnitude of the destruction struck her. Nothing short of complete annihilation of the evidence was going to cover this up. Realizing this, she had a mutinous idea. "I could access the cylinder room from the back of the lab, turn on the oxygen, then throw in one of Fuji-san's cigarettes." Her mind was working rapidly, trying to find a flaw in her plan. "It will look like my assistant was simply careless. That could work, right?"

"It will take me twenty minutes to get there," Jack said, ignoring her question, agitated. Gwen slid down the door onto the floor.

"What else can I do? Throw my future down the drain? I don't know how they escaped. They must have learned how to open the latches, which means this isn't really my fault, but it will ruin me anyhow. I am so close to a breakthrough that will help *millions* of people. How can I just abandon all that over a latch design?"

She heard Jack breathing hard. She knew this meant he could fix this, find a solution.

"Jack?" she whispered, pleading.

"Just do it. Things will die down after a bit, and we can start over, do something revolutionary."

Gwen's throat constricted, and she couldn't breathe. She realized in that instant that her life, her complete image of herself, had been destroyed. She'd wanted him to argue with her, offer an alternative scenario. Tears slipped unheeded down her face. "I...I need time to think."

Ending the call, Gwen realized her phone was sticky with

blood. She found a moist wipe to clean it off. Then, almost mechanically, she pulled out the mop bucket from the corner to clean the floor . She removed her gear, carefully placing it in a laundry sack on the counter. She entered the still-silent hallway and began mopping the floor in her bare feet.

The rhythm of work quieted her mind as she progressed from one bloody smear to the next, the bucket gliding silently behind her. Three long years of research—gone. She scrubbed the animal lab door, and Hugo began to screech and claw, slamming his body against it while she cleaned. Gwen choked back her sobs, trying not to visualize Hugo bludgeoning himself, sitting with her back to the door, feeling the vibrations impale her. As the blows weakened, she waited, willing them to end, and her heart clenched when silence finally reigned. She stood up from where she crouched with her hand against the door and let feeling return to her legs. She shivered from the cold that seeped into her feet from the concrete floor.

Holding the mop in front of her, Gwen unlocked the door and peeked in. Hugo lay against the door, the shard still in his clenched fist. With trembling arms, she poked his lifeless body, just to be sure. She then knelt, pulled the shard from his hand, and threw it across the room. She pushed his body further into the lab with the tip of the mop handle before exiting, wiping off the mop and scanning the outer room, making sure all traces of her presence were gone. She clocked out and returned everything to the supply room, gathering her laundry sack and tablet.

With a sigh, she took a pack of cigarettes from her assistant's bin.

ABOUT DEBORAH MUNRO

Website: https://deborahmunroauthor.com/
Twitter @DebMunro_Author

Deborah Munro is a scientist and biomedical engineer from Oregon who recently expatriated to New Zealand. She is passionate about writing, especially hard science thrillers that engage readers on current issues.

I WISH IT HAPPENED

By Durena Burns

Dana Clemmens hates the rain.

She knows some people who like rain. Some of her college friends say positive things about it. "Rain cleanses you," they sometimes say. Or, "the sound of rain has a calming effect." Maybe the rain reminds you of sitting by the fireplace, having a cup of hot chocolate, and relaxing.

For Dana, rain is awful. She can't stand it. The wetness and chill of it irks her. It's all she can think about as she walks toward her mother's house. Her hair is frizzy from the rain outside, and her cotton sweater is doused in droplets. The streets are slippery and the air is freezing. She can't help but compare the cold weather to the usual hot summer season.

Dana takes a quick glance back at her parked car along the curb. Raindrops continue their descent onto the car's windshield. The houses in the neighborhood are still. The lawns are bare, and there aren't any other people around. Dana stands in contemplative silence longer than necessary. She then looks back at her mother's front door.

Her mom's house is a simple two-story Colonial. Its white exterior, brown trim, and reddish-colored rooftop complete its appearance. The sight of the house normally makes Dana feel comfortable because of its familiarity, but something seems off about it today.

She raises her fist to the door, but it opens before she is able to knock.

"Hey, Daughter." Karen, Dana's mother, greets her with dark, warm eyes. She is wearing a white and black striped blouse, ripped jeans, and brown heels. The fit of her clothes complements her.

Despite Dana's sour mood, she smiles. "Hi, Mom."

"I saw you pull up," her mom says, hugging Dana. Karen then releases her and gestures for the two of them to enter the foyer. "It's great to see you. How's school?"

"School's fine. I'm enjoying my classes." Her low tone trails out into a huff.

"If school's fine, then why all the gruff?"

Dana and her mother stand in the foyer. Dana peers at the window to the right of her—the blinds are shut.

"It's not school. I just wish it would stop raining. Rain is an omen."

Karen frowns momentarily. "I'm not big on rain either," she says. Dana follows her as Karen makes her way to the living room. "Still, not everything has to be gloom and doom."

"Rain's depressing."

"So is your hair," Karen jokes, walking up to her daughter to fix her frizz.

As she runs her fingers through Dana's damp locks, Dana tries to change the subject. "How have you been? Last time we talked, you said you had an audition. How'd that go?"

Karen lets go of Dana's hair as they both take a seat on the couch. "Well, they didn't give me a call back." She appears contemplative, but smiles. "The auditions have slowed down a bit. I'm not too worried about it."

"It was for a commercial, right? I'm sorry they didn't call you back."

Her mother waves away her apology. "Yeah, some dance commercial. It's fine. I'm just glad you're here. I'm glad we're able to see each other."

Something about the way her mother says this causes Dana to tense. She wonders why her mother seems so nonchalant about the commercial. *And, what does she mean she's 'glad' we're able to see each other? She sees me often enough.*

"Let's go to the café," Karen suggests. "It'll be good for us to get out."

"Sure," Dana answers, discomfort long forgotten. "I could go for some coffee."

The drive to the café reignites Dana's nerves. The rain has

eased, but the roads are void of other cars. *Where is everybody?* she muses. *It's normally congested.* Dana watches as the cloudy, Southern Californian landscape passes her through the reflection of the car window. As she looks further outward, she notices several trees have a blue tint to them. She blinks a few times to clear her sight. To her relief, the trees have returned to their common green. Dana chalks up the momentary mistake to her nerves.

Through Dana's peripheral vision, she catches her mom's profile. A ghost of a smile comes to Dana's lips as she realizes that she strongly resembles her mom. They have the same nose, the same dark eyes, the same short, curly hair. The only noticeable difference between them is that Dana is half a foot taller. Karen has more muscle mass to her body. This fact makes Dana proud of her mother.

Dana is an only child, and her extended family isn't in regular contact. Karen rarely mentions Dana's father, and Dana doesn't even know if he's still alive, but she's satisfied with it being her and her mother. Karen is the only family she needs.

"What're you thinking about over there, Dana?"

Still peering at her mother's profile, Dana answers, "I'm thinking about how much we look alike."

"I don't get why," her mother says. Dana sees the teasing grin on her face.

"That's because we're too close to see it."

Dana's mom makes a hum of acknowledgment. "I guess so," she says.

"Just you and me, right?"

Karen pauses. "Yeah," she says. "Just you and me."

They arrive at the parking lot of the café faster than Dana anticipates. The café's L-shaped building is beige, and the pathway to the entrance is gray. The windows in the front are boarded shut with an 'open' sign hanging on the glass door. The parking lot is just as empty as the street.

Dana and her mother saunter side by side before they enter the café. The inside of the building doesn't have any other customers. The lone person is a young, blond man standing behind the counter with an anxious grimace on his face. His name tag says 'Bobby'.

"Hey, Ms. Clemmens," he addresses with a Southern drawl. "What'll it be today?"

"The usual," Karen says. "Coffee. Black."

Bobby tries and fails to smile at Dana. "And for you, Miss?"

His appearance startles Dana somehow. A distant voice in her head whispers that he is familiar. Like she knows him, personally.

"Have we met before?" Dana asks.

His anxious smile eases a bit. "Maybe I have one of those faces," he says. "Are you Ms. Clemmens's daughter?"

She nods. "Yeah. I'm Dana."

Bobby's smile becomes more genuine. "What would you like, Dana?"

"I'd like a caramel frappe, please."

"Good choice," he says before preparing the drinks.

"Thanks," Dana says.

"Sure thing," Bobby says back. He says this with such conviction that it almost floors Dana. She makes her way to the circular table where her mother is sitting.

Dana sits across from her and hears the return of the rain, the droplets hitting against the building's roof. Without warning, a wave of depression and anxiety hits her.

"What's wrong, hon?" Karen looks at her, concerned.

"I'm not sure," Dana confesses. "I just got really sad... and scared."

Karen reaches over the table, her hand on top of Dana's. "It's okay, Dana. There's no reason for you to feel afraid. We're fine here."

"You sure?"

"Of course."

Dana stares at her mother for a full minute. Her mother's words are soothing. Dana moves her hand to interlock with Karen's. Bobby walks over to them to serve their beverages. As he places Dana's cold drink on the table, a loud sound—like a sonic boom—rocks the café.

Dana gasps at the sound. The pleasant grin on Bobby's face slides right off. Karen squeezes her hand—whether out of fear or comfort, Dana doesn't know.

"It's okay," Karen repeats to her daughter in a whisper. Dana turns her head to look at Bobby, but to her surprise and horror, he has vanished.

Dana prepares to scream; her head pounding from the loud sound. The inside of the café is morphing before her eyes, the walls melting, the ceiling disintegrating. The barren tables around the room change as well. Their frames become a different form entirely.

Karen continues to reassure her daughter. She sounds way too calm, considering how crazy this is. Shouldn't she be just as freaked out as Dana? The edges of Dana's vision suddenly close in on her until all she can see is black.

A silent scream is on Dana's lips as she opens her eyes in a panic. Karen is right beside her, holding Dana and shushing her. Dana's eyes adjust to the light on the ceiling as she sits up. She belatedly realizes that she is on a bed. Dana takes in the sight of the simple room with a nightstand, a chair by the wall, and a single bathroom. The small size of the room feels claustrophobic. She is only wearing a hospital gown and slippers.

"It's okay, Dana," her mom says. "We're okay."

It takes Dana a while to calm her shivering body, tears streaming down her face. She becomes lucid enough to realize where she is, where she has stayed for the last month—in a psychiatric hospital. Suddenly, flashes of her life cross her mind, and Dana starts to remember...

It is raining the day she receives the news.

The day the *world* receives the news.

It's finals week. Dana is ready for the semester of college to end, and she's nervous for exams. She is on her tablet, browsing on a search engine. While waiting in the hallway for her next class, an emergency alert appears on her phone. Other students' phones and devices vibrate or ring in unison. Around the campus, drills are heard throughout the hallway.

The large asteroid called W-14A is on a collision course toward Earth and will make an impact in about a year's time. Due to its massive size, scientists warn that the impact will be an extinction-level event.

Dana ignores all the pandemonium as the halls fill with staff and students. The professors are trying to calm the students, yet everyone is scrambling around and shouting. People are running into each other, embracing one another, and crying together. Dana freezes in place, shocked and angry.

W-14A is categorized as a Near-Earth Asteroid, or NEA. Its discovery was more than a century ago, and initially, it wasn't a threat. In fact, W-14A fell out of its orbit thirty years prior and traveled throughout the solar system. Nations around the globe focused on more pressing matters about space at the time.

Somehow, the asteroid's path was disrupted from other planetary interferences. W-14A then flung like a gravitational slingshot and made its way back toward Earth. All plans and attempts to stop the asteroid's impact had failed.

Dana absentmindedly walks through the halls of the school. She reaches the exit of the building after the announcement. She stands, still shocked, in the opened doorway as the rain pours down on her, soaking through her clothes. She hears a recap through her phone mentioning the attempts to stop the asteroid throughout the years:

Nuclear weapons.

Both an unmanned probe and a spacecraft probe.

A mass driver—to hurl objects to stop the asteroid.

Dana tries to have positive thoughts, at least for her own sake. The positive thoughts never come.

"What do you remember?" Karen's voice penetrates through her memories.

Dana knows exactly what her mother means with the question.

It doesn't take Dana long to tell her, "Everything."

Life becomes a routine after the announcement of the asteroid.

Some people decide to stick with their normal lives, going to work and school. Others decide to quit their jobs altogether or pull their children from school for a permanent vacation. Then, there are those who care less about life and become violent toward themselves or others. Crimes, accidents, and a general sense of anarchy goes on the rise.

Dana, all the while, becomes deeply depressed and full of anxiety.

The joys of her life aren't there any longer. She stops attending college, she rarely visits her friends, and she stays alone most of the time. She even stops paying rent for her apartment. The lack of rent doesn't make much difference. Her landlord fled as soon as the news of the impact was announced. The water and electricity later shut off.

Running out of options for a safe place to stay, Dana moves in with her mother. Karen worries for her and tries to keep her company as much as she can. Her mother wants to continue her life as a working actor, but any form of entertainment has ceased. With the dangers of the outside world, Dana's mom settles with saving money for the two of them to survive. They only leave the house when they have no other choice.

A month before W-14A is set for impact, Dana contemplates taking her own life. She locks herself in the upstairs bathroom, away from Karen. She cuts her wrists, but stops at the last minute, terrified of death. Dana doesn't want to die from the asteroid, but she also doesn't want to die by her own hand. She wraps her wrists up with tape. Dana berates herself, feeling guilty that she planned to leave her mom alone. Dana imagines her mother finding her dead body and feels sick.

She decides to tell her mother instead.

"Can you take me to the hospital?" asks Dana.

"Oh my God, what happened? What's wrong? Are you hurt? Sick?"

"I tried to kill myself," Dana says in a monotone. She feels dizzy from the cuts. Her mom's eyes water as Dana reveals her taped wrists.

In the waiting room of the ER, Dana stares at nothing in particular. She's overwhelmed with all the people around her —the crowded space stifles her. The room is chaotic. Family members are crying in despair, the wounded and sick are everywhere, and the hospital's staff are exhausted. The emergency room becomes so packed that doctors and nurses are treating patients in the parking lot. Some people are unlucky as they are turned away from help.

It takes two days for a doctor to see Dana and a whole week before a bed is available to her at the local psychiatric hospital. It's the only mental institute opened in the area.

Dana is diagnosed as clinically depressed. She also hallucinates. Sometimes Dana is coherent enough, but most of the time she's in her own little world. The psychiatrists and psychologists are scarce since most are either gone with their families or committed in the hospital themselves.

As the days pass, Dana indulges deeper into her hallucinations. Doctors, nurses, and patients begin to leave the hospital, either through their own volition or in some extreme cases—through death and suicide. The one person who remains beside Dana is a nurse named Bobby.

Robert, or Bobby for short, is a frequent character in Dana's hallucinations. He's always someone Dana recognizes, but she can never pinpoint why.

In a period of coherence, Dana says to him. "Bobby, why did you decide to stay here?"

Bobby doesn't answer right away. Dana feels bad, thinking her question was insensitive.

After several minutes, Bobby says, "My family... they're gone. My parents died several years ago and my other family disappeared after—after the news about the asteroid. I have nowhere else to go."

Dana doesn't say anything more. She just hugs him.

Dana doesn't want to leave the hospital. She's too afraid.

Her mom decides to stay with her, too. Karen doesn't want to leave this world without her daughter.

Dana's interrupted again from her memories as her mom cries, "I thought I wouldn't be able to talk to you again. I thought you left for good."

Dana returns her embrace, sobs coming from her mouth. "I didn't want to come out of it. I wanted to escape. I wanted to escape it." *But there is no escape*, she thinks. *I know that now. We're going to die.*

"I'm here," her mother kisses her on the forehead. "I'm here, kiddo."

"I know." Dana pauses for a bit. "How long do we have?" Karen doesn't respond; she just holds her tighter. *It's happening soon,* Dana concludes. The hospital has taken away all electronics, and the only TV is in the rest area. She refuses to leave her room.

"Excuse me," a Southern male voice chimes. Karen and Dana look toward the doorway of the room where Bobby is standing, blond hair and all. "Are you two alright? I was going to the rest area for a few minutes and wanted to check on Dana."

Dana wants to yell at Bobby and say to him that they're not alright, that nothing's alright and never will be again. But Karen smiles at him through her tears and says, "Thank you, Robert. We're okay. How are you doing?"

Bobby looks as though he's going to cry himself, but he holds back. "I don't know," he admits. Any anger Dana feels toward Bobby disappears at the look on his face. *He's scared*, she realizes. *Just like me.* For some reason, this thought comforts Dana.

"Stay here with us," Karen insists.

Bobby gives them a sad smile. "I'll be back. I'll just be a few minutes."

He turns to leave, but Dana calls out to him. "Bobby," she says. He turns back to her, a question in his eyes. "Thank you for taking such good care of me and not leaving me alone."

"Sure thing," he says, the tears in his eyes falling. His answer causes a lump in Dana's throat, as she remembers his same words from her false memory. She knows this is his way of saying goodbye. With one last sad look, Bobby walks out of the room.

Time moves by both slowly and quickly all at once.

Dana and Karen are on the bed, lying down and facing each other. Bobby hasn't returned. Dana swallows nervously, petrified for the end and for Bobby's absence. She starts shaking, unable to control herself. A terrible thought occurs to her.

"Mom?" she whispers.

"Yeah, hon?"

Dana says in despair. "I don't think Bobby's coming back."

Her mother is silent for a long time. Finally, she says, "I don't think he's coming back either."

"Why didn't he stay with us?"

"I don't know, sweetheart," her mom says. "Maybe he wanted—to be alone." *To die alone.*

Dana sobs into her mother's chest. Karen hugs her. "I'm sorry, Bobby. So sorry," Dana whispers.

The lights above them abruptly shut off, as does the rest of the electricity in the facility. Dana gasps in alarm as they become shrouded in near-darkness, the afternoon sun hiding below the horizon. She holds on tighter to her mother and Karen does the same. Dana begins to hyperventilate.

"Stay with me, Dana," her mom pleads, a quiver in her voice. "Don't disappear and leave me alone. Take a deep breath. We're okay, right? We're going to be okay."

"No, we're not." Her breath goes faster. Part of Dana hopes that she will pass out.

"Yes, we are," Karen's firm. "It's all going to be alright."

Her mother then hums a song, a song she used to sing to Dana when she was a little girl. Dana's breathing persists for a while until the humming reminds her of childhood memories.

She reminisces about their trips to the beach, family reunions, and the smiling face of her mother as she tells Dana about the jobs she booked. A picture of the two of them appears in her mind, with Dana aging from the time she was a toddler to present day. Dana's breath slows down, and she joins in with her mother, their hums the only sound in the room.

Dana isn't as afraid anymore. As long as her mom stays with her, she'll be fine.

A loud noise from outside causes the room to shake for a moment before it stops. *This is it,* Dana thinks absently. *W-14A is going to hit.*

Dana huddles ever closer to her mother, taking a break in her humming to say: "Just you and me, right?" This is how Dana wants to say her goodbye. Saying 'I love you' seems too sudden, too final.

"Yeah, just you and me."

A massive quake suddenly vibrates the room with violent force. The nightstand falls over, the ceiling cracks with some pieces landing on them, and the bed shifts to the doorway. Even still, mother and daughter continue to hum. A thunderous sound is heard in the distance and then everything goes dark.

ABOUT DURENA BURNS

Durena Burns currently lives in Southern California and has worked for special education in elementary. She mostly writes biographical stories about her family. Her first published book 'Call Me Whitehead' is about her late uncle's experiences as a black man in the Vietnam War.

CAPTIVEEDOM

By Ferd Crôtte

Standing on the roof of our one-story shack, I can see all four walls of the compound where I've lived my entire life. I've been told these walls keep us safe, that they keep the danger out. But it's a lie. The walls are there to keep us in.

The compound is a fifteen-acre patch of reclaimed farmland. It was ten acres when I was born, but we've decontaminated five acres since then, and we're working to clean up five more. It's a hard job, and they've made me work at it since I was a kid.

I like being up here early in the morning, watching the rising sun brighten the hazy, yellow sky. The morning light throws shadows off the eastern wall, illuminating the eight buildings that make up the compound—six shacks like mine, an outhouse, and a barn. Smoke drifts from the chimney of one of the shacks. Kelly's family must be awake and tending the fire. I raise the collar of my jacket and zip it up tight as I suddenly realize I'm cold.

The buildings of our small community are clustered in the center of the compound. The corn and soybeans are planted on the east side; the small apple orchard is on the west, the chicken coop on the north, and the vegetable garden, flowers, and bee boxes on the south.

But my eyes are drawn back to the wall. It's funny how much time I spend looking at that damned ten-foot cinder block wall. I stand up tall to see as much as I can over it, but the angle and the distance make it difficult. I can see part of the wide field to the north, and I think I see a line of bright green by the creek they say is out there. I've never seen the "deadwood," or the "hot land," or that "creek with undrinkable water" the adults are always talking about. We're not allowed up in the watchtowers or to leave the compound until we're eighteen. Only the adults can venture out, dressed up in the yellow beekeeper suits.

I see the guard towers at each corner of the wall. They extend another five feet above the top of the wall, giving the watchman a better look. There's always one watchman on night duty. I spot him on the northwest tower, rifle in hand, looking outside the compound, then looking in.

All my life I've been told the watchmen keep intruders out and keep us safe within the walls. It used to be more often, but I still hear a gunshot every once in a while. Then there is a lot of commotion. "We're safe. No one gets in and no one goes out." I hear a lot of stuff like that after a watchman fires his gun.

I get off the roof, stepping down the same ladder I used to climb up. I head toward the northwest tower to talk to the watchman. I see it was Kelly's father was on the night watch. His shift is almost over.

"Hello there, Thomas. You're up bright and early as usual," he says.

"Hello, Mr. Watchman," I respond. "Any action overnight?"

"Nope. All's quiet on the western front."

Whatever the hell that means. Adults are always saying things like that, stuff from the olden days only they can remember. "So we're safe?" I ask, using a friendly tone to mask my sarcasm.

"You know we are. It's sad in a way; there are fewer and fewer intruders. Most of the people are gone. But the good news is we are here. We are survivors."

That's another thing I hear all the time. *Survivors. Survivors of the final war. Mutual destruction.* Supposedly there is proof outside these walls, and I intend to see it for myself.

"I wanna go outside," I say to the watchman.

"You're safer inside."

"You say that, but I still wanna see what's out there."

"You know, Thomas, the grass is not greener on the other side."

I don't believe it. I saw that line of green.

"I'm sure you feel trapped like a prisoner inside these walls. We all do. But within these walls, you can be happy. Within these walls, you are free to do and to be whatever you can."

"I'm sorry, Mr. Watchman, but I'm going out there. It's my birthday. Today I'm eighteen."

Kelly is my best friend, and now we're the same age again. She turned eighteen last month. I suppose we're meant to be together, especially considering we're among the very few young people in our small community.

I walk over to the deep water well to pump out a bucket of fresh water for Kelly's mother, and then I walk over to their house to see if Kelly is up yet. The front door rattles on its loose hinges as I knock. Her mom opens the door. "There you are," she says, taking the bucket of water with a smile and a nod, "just in time. Breakfast is almost ready. C'mon in!" Her voice is always cheerful, and her welcome is real.

"Thank you," I say, pulling up a chair and sitting at their table. "Is Kelly up?"

"I think so. Kelly, are you awake?" she says, turning her head toward the tiny room where Kelly sleeps. She doesn't have to raise her voice because our shacks are very small. Kelly's room is only a few feet away.

"Coming!" Kelly replies, her sweet voice an echo of her mother's.

Kelly comes out of her room as she finishes buttoning her shirt. The mere sight of her makes me happy. "Good morning," she announces, and joins me at the table.

"I just talked to your dad," I say. "He said no one is talking out west, or something like that." I wink and we all laugh.

Kelly's mom serves us an egg. Kelly and I share it just by ourselves this time, not with the whole family like usual.

"Happy birthday, Thomas!" Kelly's mom says. She adds a scoop of cornmeal and two cherry tomatoes to each of our plates, then pours us each a small glass of water. "You can have some mint tea if you wait for the water to boil." She nods her head toward the fireplace, to the tin pot sitting on a metal grate over the fire. I glance over to the tiny kitchen counter and notice a plate with a few sprigs of fresh mint leaves, chopped up and ready to go.

"Thank you! This is all very nice," I say.

"You're welcome, Thomas. You are very important to us, you know." The forced smile on her face doesn't hide her worry.

My own smile melts off my face. I know what she's getting at. It's no secret I feel confined in our compound. My parents and Kelly's parents are anxious to know what I am going to do now that I've turned eighteen.

"So what have you decided?" Kelly asks, her voice quivering a bit, also in tune with her mother's fears.

I stay quiet, finish my breakfast, and help clean up. Then I say, "Kelly, wanna join me for a walk?"

We say our goodbyes to Kelly's mom and head out. As soon as we are out of earshot of her house, Kelly asks, "Are you really going to do it?" Now she definitely sounds worried.

"Yes, I'm going outside the wall." This should come as no surprise. I've been saying it for years.

"There's nothing out there," Kelly says.

"There's *freedom* out there, Kelly. They have us trapped in here, don't you see? We are living *their* lives, the way *they* want us to."

"What's wrong with our lives? We have food. We have shelter. We have safety. We have each other. Isn't that enough?"

"That's all good, but I think there's more. I think they aren't telling us the whole story. I think they're afraid to go out farther than the deadwood for firewood. I don't know why, but I want to find out."

"They say the world was destroyed. It's toxic. It'll be a hundred years before we can go back out in the world safely."

"Kelly, I'm going. I have to." I can tell by the look on Kelly's face that she is deeply hurt, but not surprised.

"Then I'm going with you."

That, I did not expect. "You can't. What if they're right?"

"Make up your mind, Thomas. Stay with me here and try to be happy, or we'll leave together and do the best we can. I won't have it any other way. We're meant to be together."

I ask Kelly to think about it for twenty-four hours. She tells me she doesn't need to think about it. She says she has been thinking about it for a long time and already knows how this is going to play out.

"Oh yeah? How? Will we be alright?"

Kelly shakes her head. She looks so serious and sad I almost cave in.

"Well, I feel hopeful," I tell Kelly. I'm trying to encourage myself a little, too, if I must be honest. "It's a walk into the unknown. How exciting!"

"If we cross the creek, there's no coming back. That's the rule."

"They'll take us back," I say.

"No, Thomas, they won't. My father told me so, over and over. He says if I go with you and cross the creek, I cannot come back home. If I try, whoever is the watchman will have to shoot."

"He wouldn't shoot his own daughter!"

"My father said it in tears. He meant it."

"I suppose it might be dangerous. You don't have to come with me."

"I know that, you fool. But I'm going to stand by you. I'm going to walk out there and see what we might see. And I'm going to hope we turn around before we cross the creek."

"If that's what you want to do," I say, "but I'm not turning back."

"Maybe you'll change your mind."

I ignore that and tell Kelly we'll depart in the morning. She tells me she's been forbidden to leave.

"They can't stop you!" I say, indignant. "You're eighteen!"

"My father and mother both said they would lock me up if they had to."

"And what did *you* say?"

"I asked them not to worry about me. I assured them the right thing would happen. That seemed to satisfy them, but they're not going to let me just walk out the gate tomorrow."

"Then we'll do it tonight," I say. "There's only one watchman at night." My mind is reeling with ideas now that the plan has been set in motion and accelerated. "Gather whatever you can and meet me here after midnight. The sooner we get over the wall the bigger our head start, in case they come after us."

"If we cross the creek, no one will be coming after us. They'll be in mourning."

"Then we'll have to show them we're survivors, too."

"Or fools," Kelly says. She stands and gives me a kiss on the cheek before heading off to start her chores, the worried look never leaving her face.

The day is done, and everyone in the house is asleep. I tiptoe to the kitchen and pack a bag with all the food I can gather. I take one of the kitchen knives and our family's flint and steel. I put on my warmest clothes. I'm ready.

When I get outside, I sling the bag over my shoulder and go around to the back, where my ladder is leaning up against the side of the house. I carefully bring it down, trying hard not to make any noise. Then I head toward the north wall.

I stop well short of the wall and watch for a while. I see no movement in the north watchtowers, so I figure the watchman must be at one of the south-facing towers. Now I just hope Kelly doesn't change her mind.

She doesn't. Kelly arrives with her packed bag. She looks nervous and tense. We look into each other's eyes and draw each other into a long hug. I can feel her heart pounding. "Are you ready?" I say to her.

"No."

"Well, we have to get going if we hope to get over the wall

without anyone noticing. The north towers are clear for the moment."

Kelly nods. I grab one end of the ladder, and she grabs the other. We then head to the wall as fast as we can, keeping low and quiet.

A few minutes later, we are at the wall. We stand the old ladder up. It reaches nearly to the top. "I'll go first," I tell Kelly.

I take the first step onto the ladder. My heart feels like it will jump out of my chest. I can't believe this day has finally come! I take another step, then another, until I can reach up to the top of the wall to help pull myself up the rest of the way. When I put my hand on the top of the wall, I feel a sharp, piercing pain. "Ouch!" I say, louder than I would have liked. I look at my hand which is now oozing a bright red. "What the hell?"

I grab the edge of the top of the wall and stand on the last rung of the ladder to take a look. I see the problem. Shards of glass have been encrusted along the top. One final deterrent to anyone who would want to climb over. I climb back down to bandage my hand and think for a minute.

I tell Kelly we have to put something on top of the wall thick enough to cover the glass shards. We decide we need a mattress. "Stay here. I'll be right back," I say to Kelly.

I head back to my house as fast as I can. I sneak back into my house and take the thin mattress off the cot where I sleep. I almost knock a book off the nightstand but catch it before it falls and makes a noise. Carefully, I carry the mattress out of the house and slowly close the squeaky door behind me. I race back to Kelly. Time's a-wasting!

I find Kelly wringing her hands and rocking back and forth. "What's the matter?" I ask.

"Nothing. You took so long!"

"I got back as fast as I could. Let's go!"

I sling my bag over my shoulder again and step up the ladder, lugging the small mattress to the top of the wall. I place one end on the glass shards and fold it over. The shards help keep it in place but don't pierce through.

Now I throw my bag over to the other side of the wall. It lands with a soft thud. Then I look back to Kelly and tell her this is her last chance to ditch out. She looks at me, rubs her hands together, and starts her climb up the ladder. When she almost catches up to me, I swing my body over the mattress to the other side of the wall and let go. It's a longer drop than what I would have thought, but I fall to the ground and roll away. I stand back up to help Kelly.

Kelly grabs the mattress on top of the wall, steps up to the last rung on the ladder, and swings herself over like I did. Just before she lets go, panic crosses her face. But she closes her eyes and lets herself drop.

She falls in an awkward position. Her right foot hits the edge of a large rock at the base of the wall, twisting her ankle. She lands with her full weight on it and lets out a brief shriek as her leg snaps just above the ankle with a terrible crack. A piece of her shattered bone juts out through the skin, and blood begins to soak her sock and pant leg. She pounds her fists on the ground, grits her teeth, and fights back a scream.

"Kelly!" I call out. But before I can reach her, she passes out.

I am able to catch Kelly's unconscious head before it hits the ground. I ease her down and hurry to inspect her leg. I take off her shoe and use the kitchen knife to cut off her sock and pant leg. I use the material to tie a tourniquet around her leg to stem the bleeding, just like they taught us at the compound in case something like this ever happened.

A wave of nausea and dizziness hits me as I see the sharp point of bone jutting out through the skin. After a few deep breaths, I compose myself and decide to straighten her broken leg as best I can. I take good hold of her foot and pull, stretching the leg. The broken bones make a sickening, grinding sound as they try to align themselves. I wiggle the foot and ankle from side to side to help the process. Thank God, Kelly stays unconscious for that. I find two short sticks to use as splints and place them on either side of her leg. I take my jacket off, and then my shirt. I use the knife to cut lengths of material from my shirt to make long bandages that I wrap tightly around the leg and the sticks, applying as many layers as I have material for. This seems to keep the leg in place and to control the bleeding at the same time. I release the tourniquet and the wraps stay dry. She's safe! And suddenly I start to shake. It takes a while for my pulse and my breathing to slow down, and for the shaking to stop. I can't believe I did all that to her leg. I'm so glad they taught us how to help each other when we're hurt.

I look around to see if there is anything Kelly can use as a crutch, but I find nothing. My mind races as I try to figure out how we are going to cross the 200 yards of rough field to the creek now.

Kelly starts to moan. I hold her in my arms as she regains her senses. When she is awake enough, she becomes aware of her pain again and almost screams. She puts her hand up to her mouth to muffle the sound.

"Take some deep breaths," I say, realizing that's good advice for my own self at the moment. "Let's take a moment and see what we have to do."

"This is a sign, Thomas. We need to go back."

"No. We have to keep going. I'll help you. Things will look better when we get to the creek. You'll see."

Kelly grunts and grimaces as I help her up. She bears her weight on the good left foot and holds the broken right leg in the air. I have her put one arm around my shoulders and try to take as much of her weight as possible. We begin to hobble the 200 yards to the creek.

We have to stop frequently. Kelly is in a lot of pain and almost passes out again. But she manages to keep going when I ask her to.

About halfway through the field, we see the first dead body. The stench of decay is overwhelming. A bloody mark on the chest is probably where the bullet hit and killed him. The intruder's feet and legs are nearly disintegrated up to the knee, and I wonder why.

Just then we hear Kelly's father yelling through a megaphone. "STOP!" he says. "It's not too late. Come back and everything will be alright!"

I look behind me to see two people coming after us. They are moving slowly in their yellow beekeeper suits, but faster than we are.

"C'mon, Kelly," I say. We have to *move*! Now!

We try to walk faster, but the pain in Kelly's leg is just getting worse, and she looks pale and dizzy. We don't have far to go—I can see the stripe of green that I first spotted from the roof of my house. The creek must be right about there.

"Stop!" Kelly's father repeats. "You'll die if you go much farther."

I know Kelly's father will say anything at this point to get his daughter back, so I keep pushing us faster, willing us to get to our destination. I'm certain I'll find my answers when I reach the green lands beyond the creek. Kelly and I will be alright.

We are breathing hard now. I'm carrying almost all of Kelly's weight. We can't hold our breath or plug our noses as we struggle past the bodies of another few intruders.

The land now slopes gently downhill, and at the bottom I can see our destination—the infamous creek with the undrinkable water. Suddenly I understand. The green stripe is the creek itself! As we stagger closer and closer to it, I can see a thick green slime slowly oozing downstream. The bank on either side is a dead black.

We are twenty feet from the creek when Kelly's father and the other watchman catch up to us.

"Not another step!" Kelly's father commands. "It may already be too late, but maybe not!"

My mind is in a fog of confusion now, and I find myself saying, "I'm crossing the creek. I'm going to find out the truth!" I turn my gaze to Kelly, then to the creek and the lands beyond.

I want my freedom. I don't want to go back to be a captive in their prison, but I want Kelly to be safe.

"Come home, son, it's not safe" Kelly's father implores.

"No!" I take another step toward the creek, now almost dragging Kelly as I go.

Kelly's father sees his daughter wince in pain. She looks ghostly pale and her hair is plastered to the sides of her head in sweat. I'm worried she is about to pass out again.

"What happened to Kelly?" he says, a look of panic and concern taking over his face.

"She broke her leg going over the wall."

We both look down to Kelly's leg and notice a bit of blood starting to soak through the bandage.

"She could die from that injury! At least leave *her* with us. We can take care of her."

"No," I say again. I didn't know I could be so committed and persistent. *Or stubborn and stupid?* The thought crosses my mind.

Kelly's father makes a sudden lunge toward us. I try to pull Kelly into the creek with me but he is too fast. He latches onto Kelly's arm and pulls back hard. I lose my hold on her. She falls limply into her father's arms.

I lose my balance during the brief skirmish and take a couple of steps back, stepping into something soft and gooey. I look down and see I am standing in the creek.

Kelly's father brings his hands up to his mouth. "Oh no," he says. "What have you done?"

We stare at each other for a moment before Kelly's father and the other watchman lift Kelly up and start heading back to the compound.

I call out to Kelly and make an effort to go back to her, but her father turns around and pulls out the handgun he carries on his belt. Before I'm out of the creek, he points it at my chest. "Not another step," he says.

I start to feel a burning sensation in my feet and legs, so I quickly cross the creek and get out on the other side. My pant legs now have holes in them that weren't there before.

"I'm sorry, Thomas," Kelly's father calls out to me from across the creek. "I'm sorry we weren't enough for you."

"Why?" I ask. "Why did you have to keep us like captives? Why couldn't you just let us be free?" These questions were more of a lament than anything else.

"To keep you safe. You know that. So you could survive. So you could build a life."

"The life of a prisoner!"

"No, Thomas. Within the compound walls, you were free!"

He turns around, in a hurry to get Kelly back home to their loving care. A big part of me is very glad about that. But he turns around one last time to talk to me.

"You were always free. You were free to choose, and you chose this. Now make the most of it. Go explore the world and do it fast. You may not have much time. But you can't come back to us. We can't heal your contamination, and we can't allow you to contaminate the rest of us."

I look at Kelly's father and see both kindness and anguish in his eyes. I start to think that maybe I made a mistake.

"If you do decide to come back," he says, "if we see you cross the river and approach the compound, we will assume you *want* us to shoot you down, to end your suffering. It would be one of the worst things I'd ever have to do in my life, but I would do that for you."

The burning in my feet and legs is more intense now. I quickly take off my shoes, socks, and pants and wipe off the sticky green slime. By the time I look back up, the others are gone.

So now I'm free. This is what I have been dreaming about for most of my eighteen years. No one to tell me what to do, or where I can or cannot go.

I look down at the green creek and know I cannot cross it again. I turn around and go up the small hill on my side of the creek, to the unknown lands that lie beyond. My burning, bare feet make things difficult.

At the top of the hill I see another patch of deadwood. Broken branches litter the ground between the dead trees. I work my way around them, trying to keep a steady direction so as not to walk in circles.

I break out of the deadwood and stumble upon an old, deserted road. I walk the road for a full day, eating as little of the food in my bag as I can, trying to make it last. I hope to find something edible and drinkable along the way. Finally, I reach what was once a city, and it is not at all what I had imagined. Every building is demolished to rubble. There is no sign of life anywhere—no sound, no movement except for the dust being scattered by the wind. There is nothing growing, nothing green.

I realize my freedom has brought me to this point in my life. My food is almost gone. My feet no longer burn. Now they feel numb and have turned an awful, dark purple color. It's the rest of me that hurts—body, mind, and soul.

I sit for a while in the thin shade of an old, dead tree and I think. I was hoping to learn the truth, and it finally comes to me. *I didn't escape because I was never a captive.* I guess people like me learn the hard way—*limits aren't always bad things*.

I wish I could turn around and go back—to Kelly, to my family, even to the hard work. I wish I could say thank you, and I love you, and I'm sorry to the people who love me. I realize now I was always free to do and say all that.

ABOUT FERD CRÔTTE

Twitter @FerdCrotte

Ferd Crôtte is an Internal Medicine hospitalist physician and is the author of 'Captiveedom' in this anthology. His debut novel, Mission 51, is currently in production by Inkshares. Ferd and his wife Gail live in Winston-Salem, North Carolina.

THE GILDED TOWER

By Christopher Lee

"**The Year was 2098 when the veil was lifted between our World and the Void,**" his voice booms as the Warden recites the sacred liturgy of the Torr, the order of watchmen who keep the world of men safe from the terrible world of the magical.

"Our mother, the Earth, had protected our species from the dangers of the void; her loving nature had served as the vanguard until man's meddling revealed the true nature of the multiverse. The gods were not at all what we expected them to be, and our myths contained little in the way of road maps for us to follow as some of us might have hoped. Daimons flooded the streets, otherworldly beasts left corpses in their wake, and people went mad as magick coursed uncontrollably—our world transformed into a hellscape. When the forces of magick broke upon our plane of existence, no one was prepared. The ancients tampered with our genetics and breached alternate realities with super colliding particles, and in doing so, they brought down the wrath of the gods—at least, that is what our ancestors believed when the sky burned red with the flames of perdition. Had it not been for the emergence of a select few who were born with the ability to control the phenomenon of magick, the whole of human history might have been lost. A return to the dark ages would have been inevitable and our descendants would have been damned. Those who stood and fought for the people built the first Tower, and the charter of the Torr was born."

My name is Gwydion, and in your ancient tongue, I am a warlock: an oath-breaker of the sacred laws of the Torr. The world you know will pass into the shadow of myth and legend, and a new world will be born from its ashes—a world replete with magick. In my time, there were many threats: demons, old gods, egregores, and every manner of evil that your fear-stricken heart could conjure. I can only imagine that the time I am now sent to will be just as bad—more likely worse. I tell you this tale that you might in your own time rectify the mistakes that your descendants will make long before mine. What follows is the account of how a disgraced magician discovered the single most valuable truth in existence—that freedom is a lie, sold wholesale to the ignorant masses.

It began when I was released on parole into the care of the Torr.

"I, Gwydion, renounce and condemn the temptations of the black arts and pledge my body, my breath, and my spirit in service to the Torr until such a time that nature takes its course. I hereby swear to uphold its laws and its charter, and give my life and the lives of my brethren to make safe the lives of those whom magick is meant to serve. By my blood, by my soul, I surrender all. So mote it be."

Do you?

Her voice is tempting, sumptuous. It can belong to only one hellion, the daimon queen Lilith. I stop and gather my thoughts - is it her? Or is it simply the fragmented memory of the demon who possessed me before my incarceration?

Can someone as corrupt as you promise anything at all?

"Begone," I whisper under my breath. I shake my head and conjure a field of white light about my aura, my subtle bodies, the seven shields that encapsulate the human form. The white light surrounds me, banishing the darkness, putting the thought-form of the temptress on notice that I am indeed a changed man. Though I do not know how much good it will do, the demonic remnant of the evil spirit that once hijacked my soul has an unending thirst and hunger. I must hold true to my vow: that I am a man dedicated to preserving this world and all worlds from the forces that would seek to corrupt and destroy.

The portal flashes a blinding kaleidoscope of light before me. Freedom and a new lease on life exist beyond its rippling surface—if one can call it freedom. My mind lashes out, rebelling against the programming embedded in my consciousness. I have accepted the Torr as the reason why life still exists in this world, and yet a part of me senses the deceit in their dogma. The Torr, despite their altruistic facade, are little more than prison guards to those of us fixed within the confines of their walls. My heart battles my head. It is my choice now, to either live under their regime or be cast back into the void of Perdition, from which I will now emerge. It seems to be no choice at all, a double bind from which I shall never escape.

"You've been with us for six cycles. You came to us a broken man; a ship without a rudder lost on the placid waters of the damned." The Warden's voice is laced with ethereal reverberation. His glasses are thick, like the bottom of a high-heat phylactery, obscuring his piercing gaze. His sadistic grin flashes from beneath his curled mustache—it is a face I won't soon forget. More importantly, it's a face I vow to never look upon again. "May you leave this place and never return. If you have doubts in the power of your will, look to your markings, for they provide the way to salvation. Let them be a beacon against the darkness within your soul."

The sting of the enchanted needle remains, coursing waves of pain across the surface of my skin. It is a harsh but necessary reminder of the dark path I once walked. I close my eyes and feel the magick working within me—the sigils tattooed to my body will stand forever as a warning of the dangers of practicing magick beyond the oversight of the Torr.

"There will be those on the outside who will look upon the marks of the Waerloga as a disgrace. This is ignorance. For I know as you know that they tell the story of your deliverance. Wear them with pride, for you are far more deserving of your station than those who have never seen the abyss. Remember this! Recite your prayers, hold fast to the laws of the Torr, obey your Varth-Lokkr—and you cannot falter." His voice is hoarse but sure. "Go now, with light of the divine, for we are called as servants of the Divine Mother's greatness."

I bow my head in reverence and proceed through the portal. My body is twisted and torn as I cross through the liminal and re-emerge in the land of the living. The process of manifesting in the physical realm can only be likened to a bolt of lightning striking the surface of water. I ride the electric current and feel myself plunged into the depths of the living world, made anew like a freshly christened child. It takes a moment for my astral form to adjust to the physical body that it now calls home. I open my eyes and examine it; the memory of my old body crashes against my psyche, and in a flash of brilliant design I am reborn.

The first breath stings as it fills my freshly conjured lungs. Life burrows and burns its way into the corporeal form that has manifested, animating it in the glorious light of the divine. I allow my hands to caress the beauty of this form; my virgin palms slide across the smooth skin atop my bald head, and my eyes close in reverence of this new holy communion. It only takes a moment to process—the scent of the living, the warmth, the sound, the pulsing beat of a heart—so many take this wonder for granted. But I know the gravity of such a gift; I know because it was stripped from me over four hundred years ago.

The silence is shattered by a gruff voice. "Parolee number ninety-seven, you have been assigned to the Torr of the Nev Vork Megapolis. The year is 2757, and you have been without a physical form for four hundred fifty-seven years." I pause while the owner of that voice considers my form. "Much has changed since you were sent to Perdition. I trust that the warden has prepared your soul for this incarnation. We have much need of someone with your skills. Should you prove yourself useful, in time I may elevate you to a station fitting your talents. Until then, I expect you to serve without question or rebuke. Understood?"

Before me stands a colossus of a man, coated in the fine ceremonial armor of the Sentinels of the Torr. He is, without a doubt, the Varth-Lokkr: the guardian of this Torr. The fashion is unmistakable, no matter the time that has passed. He bears the mark of a daimon attack across his face, which tells me that he will have little patience for one of my kind. His eyes reflect his disdain. I find his openness strange; surely, he would know how to guard his thoughts. Yet this man lets me gaze deep beyond his irises to the sacred dwelling within—he does this without fear of my power. I can feel his disgust as he reads the markings upon my face, the ancient script telling him all he needs to know of my sins.

"A portal for the damned; your marks tell me that you will be a thorn in my side. Rest assured, you will find no leniency within the confines of my Tower, Waerloga," he chides. "Each step, each breath, each thought will be cataloged and reconciled against our laws. The warden believes you to be rehabilitated, Oath-breaker, but I remain unconvinced. It is your duty to prove to me, and to the rest of humanity, that you have put your dark ways behind you and that your life now belongs wholly to the Torr."

"I have done s—" I say.

"Your words mean nothing to me," he barks. "Your actions are the proof I require. I expect nothing less than perfection, as that is what this world deserves. From me, from you, and from everyone who calls this Tower home."

I bow my head and make the mark of the cross before my body, a gesture of respect and a sure sign that I am not only listening but abdicating to his decree. It is the least I can do, for it is due in no small part to him that I am here—I owe this man my life. Without his signature, I would still be a disembodied soul languishing in the depths of Perdition.

"You will report at once to your residence and make yourself known to your liberator," he says.

Liberator. I hear her familiar scoff, laced with a potent poison. *Was it not I who was your true liberator? I showed you the potential of your true power, unchained and unbroken.*

I wince and close my eyes. The lurid scent of her penetrates my mind, calling forth the memory of my past transgressions. I want to invite her in again to feel her strength and her desire, but to do so would be suicide.

"Is there some problem you need to divulge to me, Waerloga?" The Varth-Lokkr's eyes tear right through me.

I shake my head. "I just need time to reintegrate with this form. My memories are returning," I pause. "The things I've done... I..."

"Those things are in your past. Destroy the *old* you at all costs," he demands.

He looks delicious. I'm betting his flesh tastes just as sweet as his sin. Perhaps I'll save him for last.

The Varth-Lokkr's eyes linger for a moment, and his mouth curls into a disapproving frown. "Hmph, it will take time, but you will get your bearings. If anything seems amiss—anything at all—do not hesitate. Make your way to the isolation ward and seal yourself inside, in such an instance. I trust you remember your protocols?"

"I do, Your Eminence."

"Dismissed."

Time fluctuates in rapid succession when one incarnates, and I feel the walls of my bower close about me. This body is finally integrating with my soul, and things begin to slow down. The clash of my boots on the floor sound like the drums of war, the musky scent of ancient tomes caresses my nose, and my eyes feast upon the intricate patterns expressed by the manifested world. My gratitude for such things is distracting and wholly engrossing as my body and mind unite once more in holy union. Before I can call my attention back to the present, I come upon the end of a narrow corridor where an oaken door stands, carved with the seal of Solomon.

How quaint. She calls to me again, and I wonder if perhaps she is simply a manifestation of the transmutation from soul to body, an error in the metaphysical code.

They still believe the mark of that ancient fop commands the legions of the void? Had I been unleashed in that time, when he bound the weakest Prince of Hell I would have devoured this world whole, starting with the 'wise' Solomon; his father's precious blood would have been exposed for what it truly was.

I feel faint and press my hand into the cool stone wall beside me. Her voice licks at my spirit and I shake my head in an attempt to wipe her voice from my mind. I close my eyes and silence returns. I take a deep breath to center myself.

"She is but a memory," I whisper before opening my eyes.

The shock hits me like a bolt of lightning straight to my forehead as her form cavorts before me, as beautiful as ever: a daimonic queen, bathed in the pleasure of sin. Her eyes glisten as they feast upon my newly minted flesh.

Of course, my knight in shining armor had not yet been born.

She hisses gently in delight and licks her lips as her eyes devour my body.

Imagine what wonders we could have unfolded in that time. Perhaps you could find your way to that time, where together we might rule the whole of the cosmos. Can you see it? King Gwydion. Nay—Emperor Gwydion!

I close my eyes in prayer. "Archangel Michael, be my sword in battle. Part the ways of sin with your hallowed blade and carve a path for my righteous service. Dispel this ancient memory of my forgiven sin."

I open my eyes and watch her vanish; her face is painted with displeasure, and a part of my heart feels as though it has been singed with a hot blade.

"How long are these visions going to persist?" I mutter.

As long as you deny your fate.

The voice in my head fades.

"BEGONE!" I shout in agitation, twisting to-and-fro. My voice explodes in the corridor, echoing and shattering the silence just as the oaken door opens. Across the threshold steps an aged man with a crooked back. He carries several volumes of what appears to be ancient runic lore. He, too, bears the marks of the Waerloga.

"Excuse me, my son," his high-pitched voice chirps. "Are you lost?"

I straighten my tunic and my spine. "No sir. Name's Gwydion. I was told to report to the eastern wing for my first assignment."

"The Eastern Wing? Bookbinding, yes, my department. Strange." He peers over the rim of his spectacles. "Cannot recall ever asking the Varth-Lokkr for an assistant." He shoves the ancient tomes into my arms. "Very well, follow me. To the library, at once!"

He scurries past me, quicker than expected, judging by his age. It feels as though my body is still adjusting, because my mind makes no sense of why I would be called back from Perdition to serve as the assistant to an aging chronicler. In my previous life I was a front-line soldier, a spellcaster of the highest order deadlocked in an eternal battle with the daimon horde.

Could we have won? I wonder.

He turns around and catches me processing his request. "Now, now, come along. I don't have but hardly two years left in this form, and I don't need it being wasted by an assistant who can't follow simple marching orders."

I hurry to his side. "I'm sorry, sir. It's just that I thought I misheard you at first. I am glad to help you to the library, but I believe there must be some mistake. Did you say 'assistant?' As in your assistant?"

He hobbles with an apparent disregard to his old frame, and I struggle to keep up. "Now, young man—I assume you are young because of that ridiculous statement—surely someone with even a modicum of wisdom would know that the Torr, especially the high-and-mighty Varth-Lokkr, does not make mistakes. You are to be my assistant, wherein you will help me research and produce spells, wards, incantations, and magickal tools for those in the field to use."

"So we haven't won?" I mutter.

"By the gods, boy, are you deaf, dense, or some abominable combination of both?" he grumbles.

I hardly acknowledge his disgust; my mind whirls at the possibilities. *Might I once again cast balls of flame and lightning at enemy sorcerers? Might I once again rend unclean spirits from the flesh of the innocent?*

He drones on and on about the 'privilege' of service to the Torr and my new position as his assistant.

"But I am no bookkeeper!" I scoff. "Surely my talents are better suited elsewhere. The Varth-Lokkr would not have called me from Perdition to run errands for a crooked, ancient spook of a librarian."

He stops without warning and cranes his neck to glare at me.

I shut my eyes and mouth, wishing for the wisdom to turn back time.

"Perhaps you should tell the Varth-Lokkr how you feel about his decision?" the old man remarks.

"No, sir, I meant no offense. I am simply trying to understan —"

"You do not need to understand! You need to obey! Now, please follow me. We will go to the Varth-Lokkr's office and explain to him that he has made a mistake in his assignments. I am positive that he will see the error of his ways once you inform him that Gwydion, the murderer—" he points his wand at the corresponding sigil upon my face before proceeding to the others—"the rapist, the child-feaster, and oath-breaker, believes that he is deserving of a *higher* station. Please lead the way. I would like to see the look on his face when a fresh parolee tells him that he prefers the comfort of his cell."

"Sir, I beg of you, please forgive my indiscretion. I cannot go back there. I...this is my only chance to prove to the Torr that I am indeed cleansed."

He looks at me. For a moment, I feel the empathy seeping out of his carefully guarded auric field. "That's more like it. Now take these to the archives and retrieve this list for me. I need these texts within the next hour. I am crafting a spell that must be cast tonight under the hour of Mercury, and I have little time to prepare. Do this correctly, and I will consider keeping your misgivings to myself."

I nod and head toward the archives.

Days turn to weeks, and I begin to grow accustomed to the crooked old wart. He reeks of books, ink, and age. However, his presence and what might be considered "his company" acts as a soothing balm when compared to the utter absence of warmth in Perdition. I've seen only two other Waerlogae in my first weeks within the confines of the Torr. They pass without words, their noses ever-pressed to the grinding stone in the hope that, one day, they might rise above their station as a Warlock. I must admit that I, too, focus upon the dream that one day I might be so raised.

In a building as massive as the Torr of Nev Vork, there are only three people I have spoken to. I estimate there must be thousands who toil here in the service of mankind. Billions more scurry about the surrounding city blocks. This dreadful silence feels as though I am sequestered within some monastery upon a distant mountain in the sky. I long to hear the harmony of songbirds, to smell fresh grass again, and yet my mind discerns I may never enjoy the pleasures of such things again.

The old bookkeeper sends me to-and-fro, collecting all manner of magical items, tomes, and artifacts. The work is simple—his craft is crude but effective. I wish I could impart some of what I had learned from my time under the influence of the demonic presence of Lilith. Yet, I know, that doing so would only serve to embolden her return to this plane and renew her attempts to collect that which she desires most—my soul.

I watch the bookkeeper pore over ancient manuscripts day

in and day out, searching for something that eludes him. I nudge carefully where I can to aid him. Conversation is even more difficult than watching his rudimentary spell work. It took seven days for me to learn his name—only for him to tell me I shall not use it. Seven more days passed before I learned where he came from. Seven more still before he allowed me to ask him what his favorite color was, and yet I linger in the desert of ignorance about this man I am bound to serve until he draws his final breath. I want to ask him why he carries the marks of the Waerloga, but I cannot quite muster the courage. I estimate he is somewhere around the age of one hundred and twenty.

"One hundred twenty-two years, seven months, three weeks, and two days since I was released from Perdition." His outburst breaks our tense silence.

"I beg your pardon?" I ask.

"Your incessant attempting to unfurl my past transgressions was at first a minor annoyance. Now I can smell nothing but your dark odor rooting around my aura. Do you have any further questions you might ask me face-to-face? I'd be more than happy to illuminate any mystery you require if it will allow us to get back to work."

I sit back and relent. "Forgive me, sir, I sought only to understand the cosmic reasons why you and I were brought together in this time."

He laughs, his belly brimming with a guffaw. The old coot might actually have feelings after all. "Cosmic reasons? Good gods, you are a fresh one, aren't you? You are here serving me because you are a Waerloga; this is all you are fit to do in the eyes of the Torr. Forget whatever delusions you hold, you had your chance to be one of the Shining Ones. Only those who have lived without transgressions may walk upon the plains of Elysium. But you—" He snickers. "You wasted that opportunity."

My fist slams against the table. "I did not waste it!"

His sharp eyes pierce through me. I close my own and

breathe until my composure returns. "Forgive me, I only meant to say—it was taken from me."

He chuckles. "Well, that matters little now, does it not? Gwydion, if I may impart a bit of wisdom. I have served as a Waerloga for almost eighty years. My record has been perfect. I have not stepped one foot out of line, and yet not *once* have I been invited to so much as break bread with those who perform the great works of the Torr. Not *once* have I been called to do anything other than the drudgery of my station. I hope that it takes you less time to accept your place here than it took for me to realize. It has been, what? Two months since you returned to the service of the Tower? And you still have not grasped that the life of a Waerloga is hardly better than the life of a flea-ridden dog!"

"I do not follow," I respond.

"We are nothing more than slaves, Gwydion; all magick-born, all Waerloga, all who serve the Torr. What we do, we do not because of some grand mission; we 'serve' because we have no choice. We are given no freedom because of the curse upon us and we will die without any such pleasantries. This finely filigreed and gilded tower is but a prison—a cage from which there is no escape. You know something of cages, if I am not mistaken?"

I nod.

"Does it matter what shape or color the walls come in?" he asks. "One day, these walls will cease to exist. It is our job to make sure *that* day stays forever fixed in the future. It is a prison—a cage of servitude. This you must accept if you are ever to pay your penance."

He presses his spectacles from the tip of his nose to the bridge and breathes deeply.

"Does the memory linger?" he asks. "Does it speak to you still?"

My eyes close. "She speaks from time to time. Her sweet poison drips into my veins and it takes all that I am to keep her at bay."

“Well, at least you got a female,” he says with a chuckle. “I’ve got the voice of some hoarse water demon. Sounds like he’s gargling shards of glass. Makes reading a terrible task.” A brief, wistful look crosses his face. “Imagine that, a bookkeeper who has trouble reading.” I can see his faraway look as he imagines a life devoid of this curse. He straightens his back as much as he is able and he coughs, directing his attention back to the present moment, and his voice resumes its normal timbre. “As such, it is my penance, and one I am glad to pay. But trust that it will be with you forever. She will never leave you be, not until she gets what she wants. And that day must never come, no matter the cost. Do you understand? Not even to save someone else’s life!”

Even hours after I’ve retired to kneel and pray before the altar set within my quarters, his words stab and ache within my heart. My knees kiss the cold stone floor, and I raise my eyes to the visage of the Divine Mother.

“Divine Mother, full of grace and mercy, I ask that you grant me the wisdom to grasp what is is that I must learn. Why am I here?” I pause. “How can his words be so true to my own heart? I have seen the darkness and I know its true face, and yet this crooked old fool harbors such ill will to the only thing that stands against the darkness of the void. Can he be right? Is this a prison?”

For a moment, I am embraced in the light of the divine. I can feel the gentle caress of the Mother’s hands upon my face, and her forgiveness laps against my soul as waves gently caress the beach. But through the silent air, a hissing laugh slices through my concentration, attempting to end my nightly prayer rituals.

I release the breath from my chest and focus my energy.

You can focus your chi, you can put up walls, you can ward every space, but you will never be rid of me. We are bound by things beyond your meager understanding.

The daimon queen gazes at the altar before me, picking up

various artifacts and mocking their significance.

You will call to me again, and you will release me. It is only a matter of time. Go ahead and disperse me with your peasant magick again... I know that is what you wish to do. Know this: soon, very soon, you will see that I am your only friend.

I grind my teeth, "BEGONE, DAIMON!"

Then everything goes black.

I wake upon the stone floor, covered in a cold sweat. Each of my enchanted markings are humming, buzzing with energy. My skin feels like it is being dipped in acid and set ablaze. I howl in pain, stifling the noise as much as I can. I do not want to attract the attention of the resident ward.

Something is happening to me, something impossible. I look down and notice that two of the markings upon my arms, the sigils that bind my hands from committing harm upon another soul, have been carved from my flesh. What I first believed to be sweat is in fact blood, but there's too much of it to be mine alone.

I try to regain my wits, but my head is pounding like an anvil by a hammer. I look at my surroundings. I have somehow made it from my quarters, past the guards, the wards, and all security measures into the office of the Varth-Lokkr.

My eyes strain to discover the genesis of the pool of blood I am lying in.

You won't find it here. In fact, no one will find him for quite some time.

I manage to rise to my knees and begin to pray, "Mother, divine light, guide and protect your servant, your child, in this time of darkness."

The white light rushes to my aid, enfolding me in the love of the divine, but the respite is fleeting. I feel the cold hard sting of the temptress' unholy hand across my cheek.

Stop this! You debase yourself!

My eyes follow her curvature, kissing her physical form as she stands before me. By some form of madness, I have lost my mind! "No, you were cast down. You are nothing but my splintered mind, an echo of my sinful past. I will not grant you power over me!"

The sting returns as her hand strikes me again.

You cannot believe that, not after all you have seen, after all you know! Release yourself unto me and end this!

The prayer of the light of the divine fills my mouth once more, and my lips begin to make the motions.

You have no choice!

She grips my chin. Her razor-sharp claws tug at my skin as she turns my head, and my eyes fall upon the mangled corpse of what appears to be a fellow magician of the Torr. His body appears to have been mauled by some fiend, an abomination of the void.

"What? What has done this?" I cry.

You! You have killed again. And you did so enjoy it. I could feel your pulse racing. Each blow felt as pure as unchained lust. Soon your comrades—your precious magicians—will uncover what you have done. You will be sent back to Perdition. This time for good, never to incarnate again.

I stagger whilst raising myself to my feet. My wrists ache where the skin has been flayed by a ritual dagger strong enough to break through the runic wards tattooed on my skin. I focus my energy and place my right hand upon the wound on my left wrist. "Divine Mother, show mercy to me; heal the wounds of the past and empower me to do your will upon this, your divine creation of the Earth."

My flesh itches and burns as the light from my hands heals the wound. I do the same on the other side.

Amidst the calming light of the Divine Mother, I hear Lilith's sinister siren call. The cackle permeates the room, darkening the candlelight in the putrescent fade of the void.

You can heal yourself, but you cannot place the ward back upon your body. If I must, I will take your protections from you one at a time until you do exactly as I will.

"NO! No you are not real; this is a test. A test. I must not falter," I whimper.

A test? Look around you! How else did you slip past every unbreakable layer of security and arrive here with another's blood upon your hands? How will you explain that to the Varth-Lokkr? He and his men are on their way here now.

I scramble to collect my thoughts. There is no way I can clean up this mess and return to my quarters undetected.

"No, I will not capitulate; this is a dream—nothing more."

I recite the prayer. As I do, I hear the approaching footfall of marching boots.

Do you think they will believe you? Will you blame me? I have all the time in the world, and you have very little. Allow me some modicum of space within your heart. Trust me once again, and I will clean up this mess for you. Grant me that which I ask, and I can make this all go away.

Her words are sweet like candy; they entice, they cajole, and they call to me because I know in part that something about this vision, this dream, is true. Fear begins to grip me, and because of it, my resolve crumbles. The tattoos upon my skin light up in a brilliant flash, their rudimentary attempt to dispel the darkness.

"I am Gwydion, magician of the Torr. I am not your puppet. I am not your toy, demon."

She laughs, her cackle careening off walls.

I am no mere demon; you know very well who and what I am. Search your shattered mind and tell me: did you really think these wretched old fools could bind me, rend me from your flesh, and destroy me?

I look away from her, hiding my face from her penetrating gaze. I know all of her words are true. The Torr, for all of their power, did not know all.

LOOK AT ME!

Her banshee wail explodes from her lips, and her elegant ram horns glow white-hot.

Do you want to die, here, like this? A Waerloga forever locked in a tower?

"Who has done this?!" I bellow.

My dear, sweet Gwydion. You have. You killed because it is an intrinsic part of your own nature. You have always been this way because you are my devoted child. Do you not remember our pact? When will you grasp the truth of it all? You are not like other men, because your veins flow with the blood of my own.

She pauses and grips my chin once again, gazing into my eyes. Her tender lips kiss my own, and I feel something within my core dance in elation.

Yes, there it is. Do you feel it?

I nod as tears stream down my face, guilt and shame mix with pleasure and pain, sending my emotions swirling down into the whirlpool of desire.

Allow me a small accommodation within your heart. Place your lips upon mine. Feed upon your lust once more, and I shall make this all disappear.

Fear cascades against the walls of my heart, and panic strikes true. I rise to my feet, grab her by the waist, and press hard against her cursed lips with my own, promising to allow her some form of control within my own walking corpse. Her skin burns against mine, sending shivers, sparks, and sin careening through my flesh. It is a lust, nay, a fervent longing to lose myself in the darkness of the abyss. My spirit elates, twisting and turning in desire and, in a flash of blinding light, I am returned to my quarters.

My eyes open upon the solitude of my room; the candles upon the altar are lit, and a wave of calm falls over me. I look to the wards placed upon my body and watch as the illumination fades.

"It was a dream," I sigh. "A vision—only a dream."

I remain in prayer until dawn breaks upon the world, grateful that I have once again defeated the darkness within my soul. Renewed by my faith, I scurry about my morning tasks. I go straight away to my apprenticeship under the crooked old bookkeeper.

He's already hard at work, minding and binding a tattered old tome with the mark of the *monad* upon its cover. He looks over the rim of his spectacles at me and remarks, "You've the look of a man possessed." He pauses. "That is of right and just faith. Did an angel come to you in your dreams?"

I smile. "No angel, least none that I saw. And yet my faith is renewed by the morning light. What tasks shall you set me upon this morning? Binding? Cataloging? Transcribing? Name your task, sir; I am ready to do the work of the Torr."

He chuckles. "So eager, to boot." He sighs, "And yet, unfortunate timing."

"What do you mean?" I ask.

His eyes tell me more is afoot, "The Varth-Lokkr has requested you to report to his office."

Sweat begins to bead upon my brow, and my clammy palms grip at my tunic and straighten my robes. "Did he say why?"

He's back at the books, enthralled by his meager tasks. The memory of my pact with Lilith floods my mind, and anxiety takes hold.

Does the Varth-Lokkr want to see me because of the body? It couldn't be. Did Lilith hold up her end of the bargain? It was just a dream, Gwydion; relax, all will be well I am sure. The Lokkr would have detected a daimon the moment you passed from Perdition onto this plane of reality. I wonder, my mind racing with probabilities and potentialities.

If she deceived me, it would be no great surprise. If they have found the body, soon the boots of the Lokkr will fill the corridors, looking for the person responsible, and that person is undoubtedly me. I look at the old bookkeeper, who remains oblivious to what is about to transpire. I want to yell at him, to tell him to get out of here. He has no idea what is coming, no clue about what Hell is about to be unleashed. His only cares in the world are books. I have to protect him.

I close the cover of the book he is examining. "Alright, listen to me. You need to get out of here."

He scoffs, "Excuse me?"

My eyes lock on his, and I whisper, my intent fixed on convincing him. "Something is happening, something huge. I do not know who it is, or when it is coming, but there is something amiss about this entire operation."

He takes my hand off the book and flings it aside. "Now, I do not know what tonics you've been taking, Waerloga, but I *do* know that if you don't control that paranoia, the Varth-Lokkr is going to send you straight back to Perdition. From what I hear, he doesn't like you much, anyway. Now I suggest you leave me to my work and begone!"

I feel my teeth slide against each other. "Look, I don't have time to explain; all I know is that something is coming, and you are the only one here who doesn't deserve its wrath. If you do not go, I promise, you and everyone in this tower will die!"

"You have lost your mind, haven't you? I sure hope the Varth-Lokkr finds a way to fix you before he saddles me with you again. Now leave my study at once."

I grab the book and toss it across the room. The cover comes flying off, and the pages detonate into a dazzling shower of runic symbols and flying shreds of paper. "Goddamnit, you old fool! I said leave!"

He stands up in defiance; his voice is shrill. "Guards!"

The hate billows within me, and I feel the dark energy of abyssal magic rise. My pupils widen, and my vision goes red. I try to fight it. "I told you to run!... Gahhhhhh... Leave before it is too late!"

Muscles convulse, teeth pop and snap as they grind across each other, croaking in ecstasy as I feel the familiar caress of Lilith. I look down and notice my feet are roughly two feet off the ground. I wrestle with her in the depths of my soul, bound in an eternal match of wits and whips. I catch the horror in the crooked old bookkeeper's eyes. "AHHH! Run, you fool!"

Her whispering voice fills my ears with demented laughter in delectable harmony with the sound of Lokkr boots in the hall behind me.

You know what will happen if they see him with you, don't you?

He will be just as guilty as you; you've failed again, and now another's blood lies upon your hands.

She cackles.

Your pathetic will is so wonderfully delicious.

I hold on with every bit of my strength, fighting her at every turn, but her seduction enraptures my mind. I can feel the lurid call of hate and anger within, coaxing me to unleash the infernos of Hell upon this holy place. Amidst the struggle, I see the old wart coiled up in the corner, holding a book and chanting a flailing attempt to dispel the daimon queen who now uses my body as her own personal playground.

Damned fool, he won't stand a chance—either my flame or their blade will claim his life today.

I turn within. In my mind's eye, I look upon her foul, cursed form. "What do you require to save his life?"

This time?

She manifests before me, and her lips curl.

Everything...

I close my eyes and say my goodbye to the realm of the free, and I feel her take the reins of my soul. My vision goes foggy and dark; the last thing I see clearly is the old bookkeeper vanishing from sight. For all of her deception, the daimon kept her end of the bargain. My only hope is that he is clear of the Torr, somewhere far away from the Lokkr.

No, don't close your eyes, Gwydion. I want you to see. I want you to see the truth.

Lilith maintains her hold over me and forces my eyes open.

The Varth-Lokkr and his guards stand in the doorway, their bodies poised to do battle with the devil himself. Two of the men soil themselves in abject horror before they are reinforced by the overpowering will of their staunch commander.

"By the command of the Torr, by the power of the old gods and the new, I will vanquish thee, demon! May you find your proper place in Hell!" he wails as he charges forward toward me, blade unsheathed and bathed in the light of the divine. The blade ignites in flame, and he shoves it straight through my chest.

I can do nothing but watch, and I mutter a slight prayer, "Forgive me... Divine Mother... Forgive me..."

Lilith cackles as she grips the blade with what once served as my hand. The steel melts in her palm, and she grips the throat of the Varth-Lokkr, lifting him off his feet. I fight her with all of my might, and for a split second I win. She releases her grasp, and the Varth-Lokkr falls to the floor. His guards come to his aid and pull him back beyond the door frame before forming a shield wall in front of him.

Lilith cracks my neck, moving my head from side to side, exerting her power over me once again. Inside my own mind, I am bound by the chains of my sin. I am aware of all that transpires outside , but my soul is restricted to this empty void. There she meets me, face to face, as her carnage ensues outside of this inner realm.

Well, that was fun now, wasn't it? Are we done yet, Gwydion?

I whimper like a child as I feel the weight of her corruption fall upon my meager shoulders.

Good, I'm glad that is settled.

She leans down and caresses my cheek.

Don't worry my love, I promise you will enjoy this...fully.

She stands up in full control of my body and my magick, empowered by her fiendish rage. She brushes off her hands and sets her sights on the guards. I can feel her sadistic smile spread across what was once my face.

Now, let us begin.

ABOUT CHRISTOPHER LEE

Website: http://www.christopherleeauthor.com
Twitter @ChristLeeEich

Christopher Lee is the independent author of Nemeton and Bard Song. Outside of his gig as an author, he is an avid history buff, amateur mythologist, bardic poet, Holistic Life Coach, Reiki Master/Teacher, Mindfulness Practitioner, and keeper of the old ways.

SOMETHING IN MIND

By Mike Donald

The Gwaithian lay under the glare of the high intensity lights. The hovering scan-bots floated above him, reading his vital signs... probing deep into his brain, measuring the echoing thump of his triple interlocking hearts. If he'd understood the concept of time, he would have realized he was billions of years old, and for all intents and purposes, immortal. But as the nano-repair bots traveled through his reptilian structure, he wasn't thinking of anything other than the fact that he was in mortal danger.

Their civilization had existed on Gwaith since the beginning of time. The Gwaithians were powerful and gray-skinned, with reptilian features and sharp jaws. They were massive and employed a 360 degree eye-slit that gave them phenomenal visual clarity. Using two or four legs, they were able to move with astonishing speed. Their land was unending, and no one had ever bothered to map it. The sky was always a fluorescent white above them, and the temperature remained constant.

War was unheard of, food was plentiful, and they spent their infinite lives producing works of art, which adorned the hundreds of palatial galleries alongside the wide marbled streets of their capital, Gwaithopolis.

The vast operating space was crowded with top specialists in their field. No one had ever ceased to function before, and they struggled with the concept of losing one of their kind. Death was just a concept talked about by their philosophers... of which there were many. When time has no meaning, talking can go on for a long time.

The understanding of pain was another thing they battled to comprehend. Japod had tried to explain what he was feeling to the scientists that studied him. But having no framework of time or pain, he just kneaded his head between his hands and whimpered softly. Now, his "condition," as the specialists were calling it, had become too severe to be ignored. They'd narrowed the problem down to his brain. The Gwaithian brain consisted of a sophisticated mix of electrically conductive organic gases, which gave them enormous intellectual and artistic scope. Whatever Japod's condition was, it interfered with his thought processes... the simplest of tasks such as walking, talking and eating were becoming too much for him to cope with.

Whatever was going on inside his brain was getting stronger while he became weaker. The scientists scanned his brain with nano-bots, closing in on the source of the problem. The bots returned from their travels through the billions of synapses in his cortex, where the sparking thought neurons flickered in the dark. Having collected the necessary data, the bots were ready to concentrate on the source of his "condition."

The scientists had to form a whole new cadre of specializations to deal with their own bodies... with no hospitals, surgeons or medical skills, they were in uncharted territory. If Japod stopped functioning, he would be the first Gwaithian to do so. Scientists pored over their data-filled screens. Analysts measured the chemical and electrical balances of Japod's physiology and compared them to a sibling—it was the only way they could work out what was different in Japod, and that helped them narrow the problem down to Japod's brain. As they processed the information, it became obvious that the level of electrical activity in Japod's brain was growing exponentially.

As the last of the nano-bots disgorged its data into the computer, a picture began to take shape. Something alien was living inside his head.

An unknown creature was moving across his cerebellum toward the cortex—too fast to be a virus, it appeared to be a living organism with its own source of energy. Japod's "condition" had taken a turn for the worse. If the scientists couldn't halt the alien presence, he was likely to become the first Gwaithian in their eternal history to cease functioning.

In the star-filled darkness of deepest space, a loud hum filled the interior of the steel cryo-deck on board the spacecraft *Edge.* Massive pumps drew the freezing gas from the stasis pods lining the sides of the deck, while warm, filtered air was circulated and injectors forced low levels of adrenaline through the sleeping crew's circulatory systems.

The pod doors swung open. The crew members hauled themselves out, disengaging the cannulas from their arms... essential equipment for keeping their blood filtered and oxygenated while in cryo-stasis for over a decade.

Captain Victus looked around at the bleary-eyed crew members. They'd made three hyperjumps, and even though stasis halted aging, his body was telling him otherwise. He nodded to a muscle-bound black man, Keno, a giant of a man, and his second in command. "Something must have tripped the alarms. Could we finally be near the edge?"

Keno shrugged. Like the Captain, he'd seen false alarms before. "Who knows? Last time it was a black hole, time before that an exploding sun. The computer's not as discerning as a human."

The Captain nodded to his crew. "To the bridge."

The crew headed up the walkway leading to the control bridge. Keno turned to the Captain. "I don't know about you, but it feels different this time."

Captain Victus smiled. "You telling me it's third time lucky?"

Keno chuckled, a flash of startling white teeth. "Naa, I'm on my fourth marriage. No... I don't know, just something..."

Victus nodded. He felt it too. The engine noise had slowed and quieted, as if the reactors weren't working as hard as usual. The latest development of cold fusion propulsion, melded with plasma, generated over a million times more energy than engines of the past. They were so powerful it was considered too dangerous to use them within a million miles of an inhabited planet. The crew relied on their warning scanners to switch to conventional power if any signs of life were detected ahead of them during their voyage.

The crew headed slowly up the walkway, their protesting muscles making progress slow and painful. Their mission to reach the edge of space had lasted over a decade. Though the space agency had cited the mission as a search for new worlds to colonize, its real purpose had been known to only a few: to discover if space was truly infinite or, as theorists had suggested, or merely the starting point for something greater.

The Captain and crew reached the bridge. A glass observation window spanned the width of the vessel and was protected by a foot of titanium alloy during their trip as a precaution against meteor storms. The Captain always liked to look at the reality before he fired up the many electronic versions of what was out there.

The steel shutters slid clear of the glass. "Jesus..." Keno stared through the glass as the Captain engaged the bio-plasma scans.

Vanya, his statuesque communications officer, looked at the instrument readouts as their ship hurtled through a milky white vapor. It blotted out the canopy of stars that had been visible during their previous awakenings. She pointed to the monitors. "No infra-red signatures, no radio signals, no radiation... nothing."

The Captain and crew stared at the white opaqueness visible through the observation window. The Captain shook his head as Vanya ran through every sensor available... and gave up. She turned to him. "Billions of stars, black holes, white dwarfs... everything puts out some kind of signal... they can't all have disappeared."

Keno voiced the thought in everybody's mind. "Maybe this is the edge?"

Victus kept quiet. He knew the same as everyone else —which was nothing. The communications officer tapped on her computer tablet. "It's getting denser... we're slowing down." Victus stared through the viewing screen.

The milky fog was thicker now. "Go to full power... something's holding us back." Keno engaged the drive. The craft shuddered as its massive plasma engines pulsed. The deck groaned as the full force of the drives kicked in.

Vanya studied her displays. "If we keep this power level up, the cores will overheat."

Victus stared at the milky mass as it streamed past the observation window. Moisture started to cover the glass. Keno turned to him. "Could be a dense gas."

The Captain nodded. "A gas giant like Neptune..."

Vanya looked at them askance. "With no heat signature...?"

"Could be a dead star?" Keno guessed.

Vanya glanced down, checked the readouts. "No radiation, no magnetic field, nothing..."

An alarm blared. Warning lights flashed. Keno's fingers flew across the control surfaces. The warning lights winked off. "Primary core's down."

The captain nodded. "Take us to half power on the secondary."

Keno tapped at the controls. The ship's engines became quieter. "We're barely moving. Could be the effects of a gravitational field..." His face showed something the captain hadn't seen in Keno before...fear.

The crew all looked to him. Victus furrowed his brow.

He was descended from a seafaring family. His father and grandfather had all been captains, and as long as he'd known there had always been stars to navigate by. But now there was nothing—less than nothing. All of his instruments were useless. Down to his secondary plasma engines and with nothing to guide him, he felt helpless and insignificant. "Launch the shuttles."

Keno looked at him. "But Captain, if we have to abandon the mission..." He trailed off. His face sad. They had been traveling through deep space for so long the power cells in the shuttles would never be able to get them back to Earth.

Victus locked eyes with him. They'd been friends their whole lives, but he was still the captain. "Whatever's out there the shuttles will meet it first. We'll get readings from their systems before they're out of range."

Vanya punched instructions into the computer. "I've linked all of their sensors into the distress beacons. Whatever happens the data will be streamed back to our receivers."

Keno tapped icons on the control surfaces. A monitor displayed three schematics of the shuttles. "In three, two, ONE." The icons on the screen dropped away from the outline of the ship, accelerating ahead of them.

Vanya linked a loudspeaker to the audible tracking signal from the shuttles. Each of them emitted a different tone... like an old-fashioned sonar signature but with fewer echoes. She studied the readouts. "Nothing." The beeps echoed around the ship. Three electronic heartbeats.

Suddenly, one disappeared. The captain looked at Vanya. "No trace of any impact or even a distress signal... whatever happened must have been instantaneous."

The second signal died. Now there was one mournful beep as the final shuttle continued through the whiteness enveloping it. Victus stared at his crew. "Initiate the self destruct sequence on that shuttle."

Vanya hesitated for a second... then entered a series of numbers. A tinny speaker squawked into life.

"Self destruction sequence initiated... T minus five... four... three... two... one." The icon of the third shuttle winked out. The spacecraft rocked as the shuttle's nuclear reactor detonated with the power of a small sun. A pulse of white light flickered through the dense vapor streaming past the observation window.

Victus looked to Vanya. "Anything?"

Vanya studied the readouts streaming across her screens. "There's a reflection off the electromagnetic pulse wave."

Victus leaned toward her. "What does it mean?"

Vanya pointed to a spectral shape on the monitor. "When the core of the shuttle detonated, it put out a wave of electromagnetic energy. Anything in front of it that alters its speed shows up as an obstruction and generates an image."

Keno nodded. "Like sonar."

Vanya touched an outline on the screen. "Yes. Only instead of sound, it uses magnetism. This shape here is our ship." She tapped the ghostlike outline of the spacecraft, which filled the lower half of the screen.

Victus touched a semicircle of energy at the top of the screen. "What's this?"

Vanya zoomed in until it filled the screen. "Looks like the outline of a planet."

Victus shook his head. "But it's concave? So..."

Vanya nodded. "We're leaving it."

Suddenly, the ship juddered. An unholy rending sound filled the control deck. Like giant fingernails tearing down a steel blackboard. Overloaded electrical circuits belched sparks. The observation window spidered with cracks. Victus grabbed his seat for support as the spacecraft was tossed and turned like a leaf in a storm. Keno frantically worked the controls. "The secondary core's overloading—it's *gone*!" The lights flickered and died. Emergency lighting winked on. The sound of the engine ceased. The hull buckled under unimaginable forces as if they were caught in a monstrous vice. And as their ship started to come apart, the last thing Victus and his crew saw was a wash of fluorescent light and a vast reptilian eye-slit.

The Gwaithian scientist known as Gorgolia studied the smoking metal object through the electron microscope above the tray next to his patient, Japod. He looked at the two twisted pieces of metal already on the tray, which were magnified over a million times. He switched to an image manipulation bot hovering over the object. The buckled piece of smoking metal came into sharper focus as he watched. He noted markings etched on the side of the metal parasite... they spelled out "EDGE." Of course, the symbols meant nothing to him.

Japod stirred on the steel surface beside the scientist. He looked up at him with his reptilian eye-slit. The operation had been a success. They had managed to extract the parasites from Japod's brain without serious damage to his functionality. There was localized burning from one of them, but they had managed to control the heat it emitted with a superconducting freeze bot.

Gorgonia dropped the remains of the metallic parasites into a cryo-controlled specimen jar, sealing it with a vacuum lid. He was sure he'd seen a smaller parasite moving inside the thin metallic tube, and he wanted to investigate further. As he helped Japod out of the investigation room, he marveled that such tiny parasites could have become such a big problem.

ABOUT MIKE DONALD

Website: http://www.touchwoodpictures.com/
Twitter @smokingkeys

Mike worked for the BBC as a sound mixer, wrote for comedy sketch shows, and developed sit-com ideas. Brought up in Scotland and England, he worked as a script analyst for gap finance company Aramid Capital, and has written many award-winning screenplays.

COWBOY FOR A DAY

By Christopher Hinkle

Clint has issues with his memory. Yesterday, he was an undercover US Marshal. Today, he's a cowboy. The problem is, yesterday's adventure isn't finished yet. And to get out of this mess, he'll need to become something different again.

The questions came to me at 4:37 in the afternoon. They were the same two questions I asked myself every day, at the same time—*who am I* and *what the hell am I doing here*?

A brief survey of my surroundings proved mighty helpful. I rode a horse and appeared to be somewhere in the Badlands. And to top it off, I was wearing a wide-brimmed cowboy-style hat. As easy as that, the answer came to me. I must be a cowboy and this must be the old West.

As for the second question—*what the hell am I doing here*—that one was going to take time to unpack.

I was okay with that. Besides, most other details, such as the names and particulars of those traveling with me, remained entirely intact. Of that, I was sure.

"Clint, let's make camp here," Miss Kitty called from behind me and motioned back to a girl squirming in her saddle. "Skeeter needs to pee."

At twenty-two years old, Skeeter was the youngest in our group. She was thin and tattooed and wore a dishrag of a shirt with the words *Ozzfest 2018* written on it.

Ozzfest. I wasn't familiar with that tribe.

I took off my hat and wiped the sweat from my forehead. Around me, there was nothing but rocky cliffs, scrub bushes, and pancake-style cacti. The environment was as hostile as those who traveled it.

"Snap out of it, daydreamer," Miss Kitty said, trotting her horse closer to mine. "We're making camp."

There was a bite to her voice, but I let it wash over me.

Meanwhile, Skeeter darted into the bushes, while the Chinaman ducked behind some boulders closer to the cliff.

I found it difficult to reconcile Skeeter's presence. She was a dainty sprig, and entirely out of place in this rugged environment. I couldn't help but feel sorry for her. What business could she possibly have out here and with this rough bunch?

"Something's bothering you, Clint. What is it?" Miss Kitty said.

"Ain't nothing," I said. "Just keeping an eye out for... you know—dangers and stuff." *And wondering what the hell I'm doing out here.*

I pulled the reins to the right, but Miss Kitty grabbed them and held fast. For a woman of her age, she had a powerful grip and lightning reflexes.

"You best not be holding out on me," she said in a voice as kind as Christmas. "You're here for only one reason. You negotiate this deal for me, and we all go home happy. But if you fuck this up, I *will* kill you myself."

The woman possessed an appetite for power. She stared at me about ten heartbeats too long. Inside, my guts twisted like a sack of rattlers.

"Ain't no problem," I said.

"Best not be. I won't tolerate slip-ups."

Miss Kitty was a right piece of work. She let go of my reins and trotted off, but I knew my response hadn't satisfied her. Not by half—and again, I wondered what I'd gotten myself into.

That's when I heard Skeeter calling my name—like the desperate whimper of a child who'd fallen and cried for their parent.

Lord, no. I bolted through the thicket, images of rattlers and scorpions passing through my mind. The thorns lashed at my skin and clothing, but I plowed through them with a furious determination.

On the other side, Skeeter appeared fine. She was also topless. Grabbing me by my shirt collar, she yanked our bodies close and held me so I couldn't pull away.

"What the hell are you doing?" She hissed in my ear.

I wasn't entirely comfortable with her rubbing against me, so politely tried to pull away.

"Stay," she demanded and started kissing on my neck. "If they see us, we'll play it off like we're making out."

I had absolutely no idea what she meant by that. But in my defense, having topless twenty-something-year-olds rubbing up against me tended to be distracting.

"I don't think we should be doing this," I said.

"Too late for that. Just play it cool or you'll blow our cover. If Kitty suspects either of us—"

"What are you doing?" a voice said.

Startled, both Skeeter and I jerked around to find the Chinaman strutting down the bank toward us. He eyed us suspiciously.

"A girl's got to have fun," Skeeter proclaimed, diving for her shirt and pulling it over her head.

I just stood there like a startled deer, trying not to look guilty, but failing miserably. The timing of his arrival was unfortunate, to say the least.

"And you get the rest, after the job," Skeeter said playfully and hightailed it back to camp.

I didn't want the rest of it. Heck, I didn't want the first part. I'd only come to help.

"I was afraid a snake bit your butt when you were peeing," I called after her, but realized that didn't improve matters.

She disappeared up over the bank, leaving the Chinaman and me in an awkward standoff.

"This isn't the time, and you know it," the Chinaman said.

Hell, what did he know? I snorted and tried to walk away, but he grabbed me by the arm. What was it with people grabbing me? I could feel my temperature rise.

"Get off me, Chinaman," I said.

His eyes bulged, and he barked some reply about being Korean. But I'd had enough. I didn't have to answer to him.

Jerking my arm free, I turned to storm off. The motion pulled him off balance, and he fell against me. I went to push him off, but my reflexes kicked in and instead, I sucker-punched him in the side of his head.

The Chinaman dropped and wallowed on the ground. Covering his face with his hand, he cursed me in Chinese.

Eventually, though, he staggered to his feet and stomped back up the bank toward camp. I wondered if he was going to tell Miss Kitty. I hoped he wouldn't—expecting that would make the intolerable old coot even more unpleasant to be around.

My head throbbed. Miss Kitty and the Chinaman had rubbed me up the wrong way, and to complicate matters, I still didn't know what the hell I was doing here. As for Skeeter... I didn't know. She was confused and making herself vulnerable through childish naiveté. Sexually, I was too damned old for her. But I'd be lying if I said I didn't feel some sort of connection.

By the time I returned to camp, a false calm had settled over everyone. Miss Kitty unrolled her sleep sack away from everyone. I had no doubt she'd bite my head off if I came too close. Skeeter had formed a ring of stones on the ground and was filling it with chunks of dry wood. I could tell she was making a deliberate effort not to look at me. And as for the Chinaman, he'd dumped the contents of his satchel onto the ground and was sifting furiously through it. He scowled at me, crow's feet forming at the corner of his eye. I scowled back, resisting the urge to march over and smack him again.

"Clint," Miss Kitty said and nodded toward the horses. They'd been tethered away from the cliff, which dropped a fast fifty feet. "Unsaddle the horses."

It wasn't a request.

"Ah-right," I said while still glaring daggers back at the Chinaman.

Apparently, he'd not mentioned our altercation to Miss Kitty. Otherwise, she'd be on us both like ugly on an ape. Neither of us needed that. But I could see in his eyes that he wasn't going to let this go.

"Saddles, Clint. Saddles."

"Yes'm."

I made my way toward the horses, stewing. Miss Kitty was a thorn in my backside. The Chinaman was...well, a thorn in the other side of my backside.

I'd be better off working a ranch in Montana, driving cattle across the lonely prairie, or whatever I wanted. There was plenty of work for a cowboy if one knew where to look. Anything would be better than this.

I wanted to go. And yet, I wondered if Skeeter would be alright without me. Clearly, she needed someone to watch over her—to keep her out of trouble. Or more importantly, to keep trouble away from her. There were evil people in this world, and they lived their lives preying on the young and naïve.

I didn't know what to do.

I couldn't remember unsaddling the horses, but they were all neatly lined in a row behind me. It was dark, and I sat on the ground beside the campfire, transfixed by the embers dancing in the flames. Across the fire, and on either side of me, Skeeter, Miss Kitty, and the Chinaman sat eating.

"That was disgusting," Miss Kitty said, nodding toward her plate—which was white and thin as parchment. "Where did you buy this crap?"

Across the fire, the Chinaman shrugged. "Wal-Mart."

Wal-Mart? Sounded like an offshoot tribe of the Shawnee.

Miss Kitty discarded her plate into the fire. And within seconds, it was taken by the flames, burning as if made of paper. Skeeter and the Chinaman followed suit. But when I looked at my own plate, there wasn't a lick of food on it, and I reckoned the Chinaman must have taken it when I wasn't looking.

"We'll meet Rico tomorrow, at noon," she said. "We'll cut a deal and then we'll leave. Simple as that."

"I still think that coming all this way to meet in *neu-*

tral territory makes us look desperate," Skeeter said and then snorted. "I wonder if Rico knows how desperate we really are?"

Miss Kitty lurched forward, slapped Skeeter, nearly batting the poor sprig off the side of the cliff.

I was dumbfounded. My jaw dropped and hung slack. Skeeter cowered back, and I was about to protest when I looked again at the fear in the sprig's eyes. *It's okay,* they said. *Don't say or do anything.*

It wasn't okay. It boiled my blood. But I remained seated and kept my mouth shut.

Across the flames, Miss Kitty glared like the devil down at Skeeter and me.

"Yes, we're desperate. Rico knows it. And tomorrow, he's going to screw us slow and hard. And you know what, we're going to take it." Her gaze shifted toward me, and I resisted the urge to cower. "I don't like it, but that's the reality of our situation. Our one saving grace is Clint. Think of him as a walking bottle of lubricant. He's going to negotiate on our behalf."

In terms of my earlier question—*what the hell am I doing here*—I realized Miss Kitty had just spelled it out for me. But to be fair, I still didn't understand.

"This isn't the sort of job you walk away from," Miss Kitty continued. "Either you grow or you die."

The conversation carried on much the same—a circular mystery spiraling downward into mind-numbing ambiguity. I didn't bother to listen. My tolerance was depleted, and I had other matters on my mind.

Tomorrow, at first light, I was leaving and taking Skeeter with me. I'd not abandon the sprig to these heathens.

I slept with one protective eye open, watching over Skeeter. I didn't trust Miss Kitty or the Chinaman not to harm her. And if they tried, I wanted to be ready. But as the night passed, I was whisked away across the grassy plains of dreamland.

I was galloping down the prairie—hooves pounded like drums as a herd of buffalo scattered before me. I trailed the largest of them, the butt of my rifle pressed into the crook of my shoulder. Once I had it in my sights, I curled my finger snugly around the trigger and...fell off my horse.

I thought so, anyway. I felt like the ground was plain whipping the shit out of me. But upon waking, I realized it was just Miss Kitty. She was standing over me, relentlessly stomping me like the pistons of a runaway steam train.

"Ouch, damn it! Get off me, you ol' coot!" I yelled, fighting my way to my feet. "What the hell's got up your goat, anyway?"

That's when the Chinaman stepped into my field of view. His face was swollen and the color of dawn before a storm—a mixture of overlapping black, orange, and shades of blue.

It hurt to look at.

"You want to tell me what the hell happened?" she demanded.

It was a loaded question if I'd ever heard one. She didn't want to know what happened. She was looking for a fight. So, I disarmed her with simple indisputable logic.

"You can't trust him. He's a Chinaman. Ain't none of them can be trusted."

Miss Kitty's face contorted in some majestic display of indignation. She lashed out, wheeling her fists toward me.

"You will not fuck up this deal!"

I covered my face and head with my arms, but she didn't hit me a second time. Instead, she stormed off past Skeeter, toward the line-up of saddlebags.

Skeeter tried not to appear frightened, but it wasn't working. And I could tell that inside her, fear and terror were doing a number on her.

Enough was enough. I marched over to Miss Kitty, who was tearing through her saddlebag like a coyote in a chicken coop. I didn't know what she was looking for. I didn't care, either.

"Listen, whatever deal me and you have—it ain't working

out. I think it's time we just went our separate ways." I made a point of not mentioning Skeeter just yet. Better to test the water before jumping straight in.

"So that's it. I'm done."

I should have seen it coming. Miss Kitty was vicious—a coiled snake.

"I warned you, Clint," she said. "This isn't the sort of job you walk away from."

She turned, brandishing a revolver. The gun was like none I'd seen. It didn't appear to have a cylinder and was small enough to fit in the palm of her hand. Skeeter must have seen it too. She screamed. The scream made Miss Kitty jump. Her attention faltered. And that was when I made my move.

Like every true cowboy, my instinct was faster than lightning across the prairie. Before Miss Kitty's attention could refocus, I swatted the gun from her hand. It flicked end over end into the distance and over the side of the cliff.

At the same time, Miss Kitty lost her balance, and I used her momentum to drive her to the ground. She landed with a *whoof*, the impact pounding the air from her lungs.

Throwing myself on top of her, I pinned her with my knees and began to pull my belt free. If she was going to behave like an unruly animal, then I was going to hogtie her. Simple as that.

But before I could do that, the Chinaman appeared at my side. He thrust his palm forward, revealing a small canister cupped in his hand. The canister hissed and spat like a snake, its venom burning my eyes and lungs.

I stumbled away, gasping and frantically rubbing my eyes—but that only made it worse. Blinded, I tried to scream. But the venom burned my lungs to where I couldn't speak or breathe. I was vulnerable, utterly helpless.

And then I was falling. Someone had just shoved me off the cliff.

Shiiiiii—

The sun trudged across the sky like a mule knee-deep in mud. From its perch, it looked down on me helplessly lying at the bottom of the cliff. Its heat bore down, reminding me that I was alive.

But any comfort at that realization was overshadowed by my failings. The Chinaman had overpowered me. Miss Kitty had outsmarted me. And now, Skeeter was left, unprepared, unprotected, and powerless against these two villains. What sort of cowboy was I? A piss-poor one, that's what.

I could feel tears forming in the corners of my eyes.

Overhead, a buzzard circled. The predator's shadow danced over me, subtly marking my battered and bruised body as its future meal.

"Hurry up and die, so I can eat you," it said.

Frankly, I didn't care anymore. I deserved to die. At least I'd be doing the buzzard some good.

"Buzzard," I said. "Before you eat me, tell me. Have you seen Skeeter? Will she be alright?"

The buzzard landed beside me, small pebbles shifting under its clawed feet. It dipped its head low and then back up again. Then it danced closer to me, so it could speak into my ear.

"Without you, she is doomed."

The buzzard's words were gunfire through my heart, exploding my chest and stringing my despair wider than I ever thought possible. What could I do?

The buzzard danced back a few paces, stopped atop a chunk of shiny metal—Miss Kitty's gun.

"Time is short, Clint. You can do this. You *are* a cowboy."

I hurt too damn much to cry, but I did anyway. I couldn't help it. And by the time they'd stopped, my tears had washed away my fears and my pain. And all that remained was stone-cold determination.

Hang on, Skeeter. I'm coming.

There was no mistaking the saloon when Kitty came to it—

a dilapidated relic from years past. Rico had chosen it as neutral territory. And as much as Kitty hated to admit it, the saloon was exactly that.

With Clint out of the picture, negotiations fell to her. It was part of being the boss—if there was a gap, then she filled it. But negotiating was the least of her worries. She had more pressing matters, like not shooting Rico.

"It was unfortunate what happened to your supplier," Rico said. The smoke from his cigarette trailed the flippant motion of his hand while his meathead entourage stood by like watchdogs.

Idiots—all of them. Especially Rico, with his pretty-boy scorpion tattoo on his neck.

"Risk comes with the job," Kitty said as flatly as possible, careful not to allow too much condescension in her voice. It didn't help to bite the hand that might, in the future, feed you.

The incident had made headlines across the world: *Plane carrying two tons of Dust shot down over Colombia.* Technically, it was only 1.8 tons, but the media always rounded up.

Rico smiled and laughed out loud. "The risk comes with the job. I like that."

He began pacing the floor.

"Speaking of risks, my dear Kitty. There is a little something I've been turning over in my mind. And I was hoping you could help me assess the risk of a particular situation."

Here it comes. Or at least Kitty hoped so. She was quickly tiring of this little prick.

Rico held one finger up in the air.

"First, you have thousands of dealers depending on you to supply them Dust to sell." He held up another finger. "Second, you have no Dust to sell them. It was seized, and you have no way of getting more. Third—and this is a really important one—some of these dealers will lose thousands of dollars a day when they run out of Dust."

Rico paced the length of the bar in an infantile show of contemplation, but then stopped and shifted his gaze to his three upheld fingers and then back to Kitty.

"Tell me, what do you consider the risk will be, to you personally, when your dealers run out of Dust?"

Tolerance was not one of Kitty's strongest attributes. But what made this particular instance worse was that Rico was right. It was just like she'd said to Clint. 'This wasn't the sort of job you walked away from. Your business either grows or dies'—*and if it dies, I'll die with it.* Rico may have been a smarmy ass, but he held the power to save Kitty's business. And her life.

"You called me here to make an offer," she said. "I need a supplier. Can you hook me up with one? Or, is this a social visit?"

Rico swaggered to a rickety wooden chair. He made a show of scrutinizing its structural integrity before setting it to one side.

"Kitty, you misunderstand. I didn't ask you here to connect you with another supplier. I asked you here so I can buy you out."

The impact of the offer was like a tidal wave. It collided with Kitty, indifferent to her presence. But as it washed away, what remained was clean and appealing—and better than anything she could have imagined.

Mentally, Kitty updated her mantra. *This wasn't the sort of job you walked away from—unless you're bought out.*

"Tell me more," she said, unable to hide her delight.

Dehydrated and sunburnt, I staggered through the Badlands, where endless miles of rock raised like blisters across the land. What few bushes grew out here barely qualified as scrub. And where the scrub wouldn't grow, there were sparse stands of cacti. I cut through them, weaving this way and that until, hours later, I stumbled upon a saloon.

The saloon was dilapidated, clad in rough-sawn wooden planks and rusted sheets of corrugated iron. Had a strong wind blown through, it might have toppled the structure. As I approached, I imagined that whoever had built it had simply given up prior to its completion.

A few yards from the saloon, a barn offered half a dozen horses respite from the sun, and between the barn and house sat a watering trough. In a past life, that trough had been a clawfoot bathtub.

As quietly as I could, I made my way to the trough and sucked down the water as if it were the last on Earth. Each gulp sent another mouthful of warm viscous liquid down my throat. I couldn't decide if I should throw it up or keep drinking.

Voices from inside the saloon pulled me from my dilemma, and I darted quietly onto the front porch. Crouching beneath an open window, I peered through sun-yellowed curtains to see six people.

My heart fluttered at the sight of Skeeter and boiled at the sight of Miss Kitty and the Chinaman. Luckily, they didn't appear to be harming the wee sprig. There were three other people there too—a fancy-dancy rancher with a scorpion tattoo on his neck, and some hired muscle.

Skeeter sat on a rickety chair beside a card table. Both were covered in dust. And there was a book on the table before her. It was opened sideways so that half of it stuck straight up in the air, as if its bindings were too tight. I could just make out the vague outline of an apple with a bite taken out of it, on the cover of the book.

The six of them appeared to hold a single conversation, Miss Kitty and the tattooed man as the dominant speakers. I couldn't quite make out what they were saying. But I reckoned it didn't matter. As long as they kept talking, I'd take care of the rest.

The time had come to save Skeeter. Turning, I glanced back at the barn, to the horses, and then to the clawfoot watering trough. A plan slowly began to form in my mind. I'd need some rope too. And I wondered how long it would take me to crawl up under the saloon.

Negotiations lasted more than an hour—from the larger details of how the transaction would take place down to the minute details of data validation and handover period. When they'd finished, the agreement was simple and without ambiguity. In exchange for all her contacts—names and details of almost a thousand street dealers—Rico would pay three million in cryptocurrency. All that remained was to transfer the file, the funds, and the data key. That was where Skeeter came in.

"It works like a satellite phone, except my laptop *is* the phone," Skeeter said, booting up her computer as everyone gathered behind her. "For our purposes, we don't need to make calls—we need the data connection. And to be on the safe side, I've added another eleven layers of security. So, our connection is entirely uncrackable."

Rico stood with his arms folded across his chest. "With enough time, anything can be cracked," he said.

Still typing, Skeeter snorted. "Not if the security algorithm changes every eight seconds."

Kitty's interest in technology was limited to whether or not a device worked. Beyond this, she didn't care. So, she'd hired Skeeter to worry about these sorts of things for her.

"You ready?" Skeeter asked.

Rico nodded his consent. "Yeah. Let's do this," he said, and Kitty nodded in agreement.

Leaning over her laptop, Skeeter mashed keys faster than Kitty's eyes could follow. "I'm pulling the data file through the back door of a car wash website. And now through the coding of a steam train enthusiast forum. And now via a university student's unofficial blog on Don Quixote—it sucks, I've read it. And voila."

Skeeter turned in her rickety wooden chair to face her audience. "Congratulations, your data file has now arrived safely in its final destination, via the most untraceable route money can buy."

She was showing off. Normally, Kitty would have put the

girl in her place, But she let it slide this time.

"Satisfied?" she asked.

Rico nodded. "I'm impressed. And I don't say that lightly. If your Skeeter needs a job after we're done, I'll happily poach her from you," he said.

Kitty rolled her eyes. "For another three million, I'll sell her to you," she said flatly and nodded for Skeeter to step away from the laptop.

"Your turn."

Taking his cue, Rico sat in the rickety chair in front of the laptop. And within a matter of minutes, he'd transferred the full amount, in the form of cryptocurrencies, into Kitty's specified accounts.

When he'd finished, Rico turned and smiled at Kitty, flashing his pearly white teeth. The deal was almost done. It was almost over. And that didn't feel right.

Kitty had been in this business long enough to know nothing this good ever happened. And if it did, it would take time. That was the reality of the business. But this transaction was too good and too fast, and that worried her.

"The money's there," Rico said, stepping back from the laptop. "And now I want the encryption key."

At this, Joon-woo stepped forward. He was Kitty's right hand in all dealing—a Korean immigrant and trusted friend. He took center stage in front of the laptop.

The encryption key was his part in all of this. The key was nothing more than a random code generator. But it was unique in the sense that its code was required to unlock the data file Rico had just spent millions to purchase. Once he gave Rico the encryption key, the transaction would be completed, and Rico would have the full details of thousands of drug dealers across the US.

Before touching the laptop, he turned to Kitty and waited. But she didn't nod.

The tension in the room ramped up. Eyes widened and Rico subtly took a step back.

"You've got my money," Rico said, wearing a thin veneer of charisma atop palpable anxiety. "Now, give me the key."

Kitty hadn't made it this far in life by playing the fool. She had a solid rule: if the deal didn't feel right, then the deal could wait until she was certain again. Over the years, her little mantra had kept her from making many mistakes, many of them potentially big. Now, on the brink of cutting the biggest deal of her life, all of her instincts told her to stop. Until she could figure out what was bothering her, she wouldn't—

"How did you know Skeeter's name?"

As quickly as the question left Kitty's mouth, the guns came out.

My plan was far from ready. Ten yards behind the saloon, I hunkered behind a thorn bush, tying off the rope to the saddle. I'd taken three horses from the barn. The one beside me whinnied as I jerked the knot tight.

I heard a commotion inside the saloon—furniture scooting across the wooden floor and then crashing, followed by the booming proclamation, "US Federal Marshals!"—then gunshots followed.

Ready or not, it was time.

"Hah!" I called, whipping the horse's flanks with the flat of my palm.

Startled, the horse bucked and lurched forward, pulling the rope tight. What followed was a crashing groan as sheets of corrugated iron peeled away from the saloon. One after another, they flung haphazardly over the ground like cards on a poker table, launching the odd shard of wood in the process.

What remained was little more than the structural framing and the occasional rough-sawn plank. The saloon looked like a behemoth carcass, with people scurrying like rats inside its ribcage.

Skeeter dove behind an overturned card table, Miss Kitty darted behind the bar, and at least one person lay dead on the floor.

More gunfire followed, spooking the horse I'd left on the far side of the saloon. Like the first, I'd tethered the other horse to ropes. But where the first had been tied to the saloon's sheet metal, the others were lashed to the clawfoot trough via the underside of the saloon's raised floor.

The horse bolted. The slack in the rope vanished, and the clawfoot trough, which had likely not moved in fifty years, jumped up like a jackrabbit. A moment later, floorboards inside the saloon rose in a quick splintering line, like the world's largest prairie dog burrowing its way beneath the floor.

The distraction exceeded my expectations. Everyone inside the saloon scattered in opposite directions and I drew the gun, squeezing off six rounds in quick succession.

Click, click, click, click, click, click.

It didn't fire. Not even one shot. But it diverted everyone's attention toward me.

Ah, horse's tits!

Shoving the gun down the seat of my pants, I picked up a piece of splintered wood—it had fallen off the saloon when the sides peeled away. Screaming like a lunatic, I charged straight through the side of the saloon and then swung the club for all I was worth.

My first victim was one of the strangers, a beefy man with a thin mustache and overbite. I corrected his dentistry problems, cracking the club into his jaw hard enough to remove it from his face. He dropped like a ten-cent sack of taters.

My momentum turned me completely around in time to see the Chinaman leaping from behind an overturned card table toward me.

"Clint, watch out!" Skeeter called.

But I was prepared. Yanking the worthless piece of crap gun from the seat of my pants, I chucked it at him as hard as I could. Missed by a mile.

The gun slammed into a plank of framing behind the Chinaman and fell. But the second it hit the floor, it fired. The Chinaman staggered forward two steps and collapsed. He had, I noticed, a rather large hole in the back of his head.

Behind me, Skeeter called again, "Get out of there, Clint. Chopper's on its way."

Miss Kitty peeked out from behind the bar long enough to squeeze off a round. The shot splintered just above my head, dropping termites onto my shoulders.

"I'm going to kill every one of you!" she screamed.

What the heck? She has another gun? What kind of woman carries two guns?

"Not if I don't kill you first, you ol' coot!" I yelled back.

On the floor, a flash of light caught my eye. Picking it up, I turned it over twice. *The badge of a US Marshal.*

"Don't kill her, Clint!" the tattooed man said. "We haven't got her encryption key yet."

I hadn't a clue who that man was or how he knew my name. Likely some sort of trick.

"Oh, for fuck's sake. You mean Clint's a Marshal, too?"

"And me," Skeeter said.

A Marshal? A rare moment of clarity washed over me. And at that moment the words *undercover agent* crossed my mind. Somewhere in my memory, I knew the words and they held meaning. But for the life of me, I could not reconcile them.

"Figures," Miss Kitty said, as she launched from behind the bar and grabbed Skeeter.

Time slowed to a molasses pace. My heart lodged in my throat, and I took a half step back, using a wooden vertical pillar for cover. Skeeter tried to struggle, but Miss Kitty had tangled her fingers through the sprig's hair, holding her fast and pressing her gun against the back of the poor girl's neck.

"Step out here where I can see you, Clint," Miss Kitty said in a whispering sing-song voice.

Given her fury, this new slower pace chilled me to the bone. It was pure evil and carried a malice. She was backed into a corner with no escape and nothing left to lose. Only the question remained—how many people could she take out on her way down?

The reality of the situation set in, chilling me to the bone. I had no cards left to play—no trick up my sleeve. There was no cowboy move I could think of that would get Skeeter or me out of this jam.

Oh, Skeeter. Why did you have to get caught up in all of this?

The time was 4:36 in the afternoon, and my time as a cowboy was at an end.

As my internal clock slowly ticked closer to 4:37, I encountered those same two questions I face every day—*who am I* and *what the hell am I doing here*?

"Step out here, Clint," Miss Kitty said again. "Three seconds or she dies!"

Who am I? My eyes drifted from the US Marshal's badge cupped in my hand to the dead Chinaman, who lay like a fallen kinsman.

"Two."

Was I Chinese too? What the hell am I doing here? I didn't know. But what I did notice was the tin star in my hand wasn't a badge any longer. It was a Chinese throwing star.

"One," Miss Kitty said and pulled her finger tight around the trigger.

That was when the answer came to me. I was a ninja.

Drawing upon the courage of my father, and of his father, I faced the viper. She who called herself Kitty, she who was coiled and ready to strike.

"Clint, you are one stupid son of a..."

Using dragon's speed, I loosed the throwing star from my hand and guided it with my mind. The star sailed across the saloon, flicking end over end, and lodged in the corner of her eye—just as my master had taught me to do.

Kitty wavered as if uncertain as to the absolution of her demise. In her eyes danced a lifetime of confusion, and regret, and anger. They were eyes of a woman who'd once been powerful, but whose power had come to an end.

"You were a worthy opponent, Kitty," I said, stepping forward and kicking her gun safely away.

Five minutes later, a mother dragon appeared, flying across the sky. She landed a short distance away and opened her womb, spilling out my fellow ninjas. Skeeter named the dragon *Helicopter*. It was a fine name.

"It might take a few days, but we'll make her talk. And from there, we'll link-in with the DEA and make the biggest sweep of drug busts in US history."

Skeeter was truly wise beyond her years.

My fellow ninja gathered the honored dead—those who fell at the hands of Kitty and would walk the warrior's path no more. As for the viper, Kitty, she too was escorted to Helicopter.

"Why don't you come with us, Clint?" Skeeter said, motioning for me to join her inside the dragon. "We can send someone else after the horses."

I declined, respectfully.

Skeeter boarded Mother Dragon, and I waved farewell as she took to the sky. Twice, Mother Dragon crossed the path of the sun, and each time, its shadow passed over me. It was a good omen.

I left shortly after, leading the horses back across the Badlands. I traveled with a perfect knowledge of who I was, and the certainty that this would not change—at least for the next twenty-two hours.

ABOUT CHRISTOPHER HINKLE

Born in the backwoods of West Virginia, Chris Hinkle is a country boy down to his molecular structure. He now lives in New Zealand where he works for the Government and puts forth a reasonable effort at masking his inner-hick for the benefit of those around him.

BREACH

By Evan Graham

"We're a million miles away from Samrat. How did you even manage to find something to run into out here?"

"I'm just that good, Maya," Helmsman Roy joked over the comm. "I don't think you appreciate the sheer level of skill it took to hit a target that small in the literal middle of nowhere. I deserve a medal."

Maya Prasad nudged the controls on her suit's EVA rig. A few short puffs from her back-mounted propulsion pack guided her along the port side of the *Chandrakanta's* monolithic hull. Crewmen Rajiv Singh and Maureen Conover followed her.

Maya swept her searchlight across the craft's metal skin, illuminating the ship's name written in Colonial Hegemony English and Devanagari script. Her searchlight caught an ugly, crumpled hole right at the corner of the blocky letter "C" at the *Chandrakanta's* foresection.

"Found it. Singh, Conover, set down here."

Maya and the two crewmen maneuvered toward the gash in the ship's hull, activating magnetic clamps in their boots as they came near enough to touch down. The crewmates were minuscule compared to the thirty thousand-ton behemoth on which they stood, itself infinitesimal against the backdrop of deep space. It really was remarkable that the *Chandrakanta* had managed to collide with another object in that vast nothingness.

"Get this plate off," Maya ordered. As they worked, she moved to the hole, inspecting the shattered ceramic fragments radiating out from the crater-like opening. She plucked one of the larger chunks from the rim of the hole, glared at it, then flung it away into oblivion.

"You hit that rock really hard, Roy."

"That rock hit *me* really hard," Roy objected over the comm.

Maya flicked a few more chunks of fragmented ablative plating from the mouth of the hole and shone her headlamp into it. She reached in halfway to her elbow and yanked a softball-sized iron meteorite from the gash, tossing it to Singh.

Singh almost fell backwards from the rock's surprising mass. "Wow... this is heavier than it looks."

"It's solid iron." Maya held her soldering gun up to the wound in the ship's hull and started to work on repairing the damaged wiring inside. "Not worth a lot on the ore market, but it's a nice souvenir. Just a little something to memorialize Roy's bad flying, since he's definitely not getting a medal."

"Hey, now." Roy's voice took an indignant tone. "Let's be fair. All the charts say the Mahatma System isn't supposed to have any notable debris fields. There's nothing here but Samrat and its moon. Hitting a meteor way out here is, like, a one in a billion chance."

"It's probably a free-floating rock," said another voice over the comm. It was Dr. Hashida. Maya wasn't sure why he was on the comm at all. He wasn't a member of the crew, just some egghead academic who had chartered passage on the *Chandrakanta* to get to one of the research outposts on Samrat. "It's likely a fragment of a rogue planet or some other interstellar body that drifted into the system from elsewhere."

"Yeah, so like, one in a trillion chance, then," said Roy.

"Let's not waste any more talk on the odds of hitting the rock we hit, alright?" The new voice was that of Captain Pariva Yadav, a rare hint of irritation working its way into her eventoned, soft-spoken voice. "It doesn't matter how unlikely it is. It happened, and it's put us behind schedule. We should be on Samrat by now. Prasad, how is it coming out there?"

Maya paused her soldering, shining her helmet's light into the hole. "It isn't actually too bad, Captain. The plating dispersed most of the impact force, so it didn't penetrate that deep. It shredded the control cables for maneuvering jet seven, but that's one of the redundant ones. I can patch it now, or we can go on without it."

"Alright, Prasad. Go ahead and patch it, then get back in here. I don't want to waste any more time," said Captain Yadav.

"Got the bolts free, ma'am," said Conover.

Maya nodded, jetting away from the hole while Singh and Conover pulled the fractured plate free. A few gravel-sized chunks of ceramic dislodged from the hole in the middle of the plate as the crewmen pulled it away from its mountings. With a grunt, they hurled it away from the ship, watching the slab tumble end over end into open space.

"Go ahead and get the replacement," Maya said. "I'll stay here and keep working. See if I can get any functionality out of that thruster."

With an exchange of nods, Singh and Conover turned and floated back toward the airlock. Maya set back to work soldering wires.

An incongruous glint of light in the corner of her eye took her attention off her work for a moment. She turned to the starry abyss beyond the axe-head shape of the *Chandrakanta's* bow, but saw nothing. It could have been nothing more than an errant reflection off her faceplate. Or....

"Hey, Roy?" Maya said hesitantly. "Can you check the prox sensors again? I thought I saw something."

"Yeah, give me a sec." The comm was silent for a few moments as Maya continued scanning the empty sky around her for signs of movement. "Well, short-range doesn't show anything interesting. Expanding it out to mid-range, I see a handful of rocks about the size of the one you just found. Other than that, nothing of note."

"That's unusual, isn't it?" Maya pressed. "If they're just fragments that drifted in from past the edge of the system, shouldn't they have dispersed farther apart than that?"

"It is unusual," Dr. Hashida answered. "Even if we're seeing debris from a larger rock that recently broke apart, the energy needed to fracture a rock of that size would have also been enough to spread the debris over a much larger area than this."

"Dr. Hashida, please get off the comm," Captain Yadav said, stifling a sigh of exasperation.

"No, Captain, I think this is important," Maya insisted. "Roy, can you please check the long-range sensors? I really think I saw something, something bigger than a meteoroid."

There was another prolonged moment of silence as Roy checked the readings. Finally, his voice came over the comm once more, this time carrying a note of urgency. "Captain, she's right. There's a large object headed our way, outbound from Samrat. Thermal signature. Looks like a ship. Must have just come out of superluminal drive, 'cause it definitely wasn't there during the last sweep."

Maya's heart thumped hard in her chest. The Mahatma system had no natural debris fields, but it did have something much worse: pirates. Many of them were disgruntled former prospectors who had flocked to Samrat back when precious gems were first discovered in the desert planet's vast sand oceans, only to find the gems were spread too far and thin to be effectively mined. Some of those prospectors had bet everything on hitting it big, only to end up stranded on the desert world without the means to get home, eking out a meager living by robbing transports like the *Chandrakanta* or raiding the smaller scientific research outposts in the pinnacle canyons.

Some Samrati pirates were much more dangerous, though. Maya had heard rumors of everything from Aftothysian eco-cultists to Expansionary Coalition privateers prowling the Samrati space lanes in combat-ready ships to harass, board, or destroy Hegemony ships. This far away from Earth and the other colonies, anything could happen. And nobody would be there to see it.

"Hey, Prasad?" Captain Yadav's voice was calm and even, but carried a subtle undertone of urgency. She was likely thinking the same thing Maya was, but didn't want to alarm the crew. "Bring everyone inside for a minute. Hopefully this is just an outbound transport passing by, but…let's play it safe."

"Copy, Captain," Maya answered. "Heading back to airlock now."

Maya jetted back along the *Chandrakanta*'s hull toward the airlock, doing her best to seem calm while pushing her thrusters just a bit past their specs. She could hear her breathing getting harder in her helmet's air cycler, despite the fact she wasn't exerting herself. *Don't let yourself panic. This whole thing is probably nothing. Stay strong, set a good example.*

Maya finally reached the protruding cylinder that served as the ship's primary airlock and docking ring. With a few carefully timed puffs from her maneuvering jets, she slowed down enough to grab onto one of the external handrails ringing the lock. A circular hatch slid open, and Conover and Singh helped her climb inside, shutting the hatch behind her.

"We're in, Captain. We're all in," Maya said. She nodded at Singh, who activated the airlock's pressurization procedure.

"Alright," Captain Yadav replied. "Strap yourselves in. Roy's going to try and get us some distance."

Maya took a seat on the bench sandwiched against the wall between the inner and outer hatches, while Conover and Singh sat down on the bench opposite. "Is it still coming our way?" Maya asked, fastening a safety harness over her lap and chest.

"Yes. We are in a main trade lane, so it's most likely just another freighter. I still want to get some distance, though." The concern in Yadav's voice undermined the optimism in her words.

"Shouldn't they have hailed us by now?" Conover's large, blue eyes and the errant wisp of red hair tickling the inside of her faceplate made her look very young, and the tremble of fear in her voice made her sound even younger. She *was* young, too: twenty when she joined the crew on Showalter a year ago. She'd only been on two flights since then, and if Maya remembered correctly, she'd never been on an interplanetary flight before enlisting on the *Chandrakanta.*

"They probably don't know we're here," Singh said. "We only picked them up because Maya asked us to search for them. If they're not checking long-range sensors, they probably haven't seen us yet." The twinkle in Singh's deep brown eyes and the warmth of his confident half-grin seemed to put Conover at ease. But the beads of sweat forming on the dark skin of his temples and the way he held his meteorite with a nervous death grip reinforced Maya's sense of looming danger.

A rumble rose up through the ship, sending vibrations through the floor and walls in the cramped compartment. The ship lurched, and Maya's body fell forward against her harness as Singh and Conover were pressed against the opposite wall from the force of the ship's acceleration. "We're underway," Roy announced over the comms. "New heading: thirty degrees starboard, thirty degrees downward pitch."

"Give me drive engines two, four, and six at forty percent for a twenty second burn," Yadav ordered.

"Aye captain, forty percent burn," Roy answered. The rumble swelled to a roar as three of the ship's massive thrust engines flared to life, pushing the gargantuan vessel forward on its new heading. The heavy G-forces of the ship's acceleration pressed Maya even harder against her harness, pushing the air out of her lungs in a heavy grunt.

"Captain, the other ship has changed heading," Roy shouted. Each word he spoke showed the effort of fighting the G-forces on his diaphragm, but even with the strain in his voice, there was no mistaking his panic. "Intercept course! They're coming at us!"

"Crispin, full power to the mass de-simulator. Roy, set a nav point for an in-system superluminal jump. Anywhere but here."

"Charging de-sim," Machinist Crispin answered. "Forty seconds to full mass de-simulation."

Maya cursed under her breath. Normally, running the ship's

mass de-simulation generator was her job. Without the physics-masking sheath of exotic pseudomatter the de-simulator could create around the ship, the *Chandrakanta* couldn't activate its superluminal drive for a quick getaway. Crispin was a fine machinist in her own right, but Maya knew she could have gotten the de-simulator running at full power at least ten seconds faster.

"Unknown ship is at 0.021 AU and closing." Roy said.

"Sixty-degree yaw rotation and standby engines one, three, five and seven for sustained burn. All hands, brace for high-G maneuvers."

Conover gripped her harness with both hands, eyes squeezed shut as tears of fear trickled backward across her temples. Singh's eyes were also shut, his mouth moving in a silent prayer. Maya looked at the iron meteorite Singh still held in both hands, pressing heavily into his stomach with the continued G-force. *We should have secured that...*

"De-sim at fifty percent charge," said Crispin.

"Shots fired, shots fired!" shouted Roy.

"Fire all engines, full power!" screamed Yadav.

For a second, Maya could feel another surge of acceleration as the freighter's engines flared, trying in vain to push the lumbering behemoth out of the path of the incoming shots.

Then, the *Chandrakanta* exploded.

A perfectly aimed rail shot had pierced the ship's hull with surgical precision, slicing through five decks and striking the mass de-simulation generator square-on. The partially coalesced pseudomatter sheath that had been forming around the ship instantly collapsed, dispersing its collected energy into a violent detonation that ripped the *Chandrakanta* apart. Massive, multi-ton chunks of hull plating and superstructure supports flew apart in all directions as a fireball swelled at the site of the detonation, then quickly receded as the inferno burned off all the air and fuel the explosion released. The white-orange glow of superheated metal illuminated an expanding debris field of ceramic shards, heat-warped bulkheads, shredded engine cowling...and one tumbling airlock chamber.

Maya fought to stay conscious as the uncontrolled G-forces of the airlock's spin and velocity threatened to overcome her. Conover had already passed out, and Singh looked like he might join her any second. Maya's eyes darted to the meteorite in Singh's lap: it was pressing so hard into his stomach he probably couldn't breathe, and the G-force had pushed his arms back against the wall. He wasn't even holding it anymore.

"Oh God, no..." she mumbled through gritted teeth.

The disk-shaped airlock yanked against a set of trailing cables anchoring it to a larger piece of debris, putting an end to its spin and arresting some of the G-force on the airlock's inhabitants. Inside the chamber, the meteorite flew forward from Singh's lap, impacting the wall next to Maya with enough momentum to leave a three-inch dent in the metal. Maya attempted to reach for the rock, but her arm felt like a two hundred-pound weight.

A secondary explosion from a chunk of one of the ship's engines knocked the airlock backward in a sideways spin. The meteor flew diagonally across the chamber, striking the window in the outer hatch, creating a spiderweb of cracks in the reinforced glass.

"Wake up, wake up!" Maya screamed at the two crewmen opposite her. Conover and Singh stirred lethargically, struggling to regain their wits and not quite succeeding.

Another impact sent the meteorite flying back toward Maya's side of the chamber. She managed to reach out for it this time, but the rock hit her outstretched hand like a cannonball, pinning it to the wall with a crunch of breaking bones.

Maya cried out in pain, and this proved to be enough to rouse the other two from their torpor, just in time for another impact to send the rock flying across the chamber one more time.

The meteorite careened directly into Singh's faceplate,

shattering the glass into a rain of transparent gravel that skittered across the wall behind his head. With a sickening *shunk*, the iron ball imbedded itself in Singh's face, crushing the bones of his skull as it pressed halfway into his helmet.

Maya looked on in horror as blood gouted from the crater in Singh's face, pooling in the back of his helmet like a bowl. Conover screamed as red flecks pelted the side of her helmet.

Suddenly, one more collision righted the airlock's spin, putting an end to its tumble and reducing the G-force inside the chamber to a tolerable level. Blood from Singh's shattered helmet splashed against the other walls, but the meteorite remained lodged solidly in the wreckage of Singh's face.

Conover's screams shifted into an endless repetition of panicked curses. Maya forced herself to focus on the situation at hand.

How are we alive?

They had been lucky. They had been *extremely* lucky. The chamber hadn't been fully pressurized yet, or the compression wave from the initial explosion would have turned their organs to jelly. The two heavy bulkheads on either side of the airlock had made it strong enough to withstand the blast, and the airlock's position on the outside of the ship meant it had been ejected from the explosion instead of consumed by it. They had been *incredibly* lucky.

Or at least two of them had.

"Conover," Maya snapped. Conover had devolved into a weeping babble that no longer contained words. "Conover, pull it together!"

Conover stopped, choking back a sob. The inside of her faceplate was fogged with panicked breathing. "They... they're dead. They're all dead!"

"And we're not. Not yet. Let's keep it that way, huh?"

Conover turned slowly toward Singh, another sob escaping her. Maya held out her arm and snapped her fingers in Conover's face. Between her bulky gloves and the thin atmosphere in the airlock, no sound came from the gesture, but the movement caught Conover's attention.

"Don't look at him. Look at me."

Conover looked at Maya and nodded silently.

Maya unstrapped herself from the harness, wincing as she tucked her shattered hand against her chest, and moved to the airlock's outer hatch. Or rather, the hatch designed to be the outer one, as now both hatches opened into empty space. She peered through the cracked window, heart sinking as she watched the steadily expanding field of debris that had been the *Chandrakanta* only seconds ago.

The devastation was shocking. The ship had been absolutely shredded by the blast. Of the thirty thousand-ton, two hundred eighty meter-long spacecraft, Maya couldn't see a chunk bigger than a small car. Warped metal plates bounced off twisted girders and tangled together with shredded clusters of loose wiring everywhere she looked, all while a constant hailstorm of gravel-sized bits of ceramic rained against the outside of their accidental escape pod. Only the occasional flash of plasma from a secondary explosion or surge of sparks from a somehow still-powered electrical system gave any indication that this debris field had ever been a spaceworthy vessel. A vessel thirty-one people had called "home."

"Sur.....kanta, can you hear...?"

The static-garbled transmission surprised Maya so much, she let out a little yelp. Conover's red-rimmed eyes widened. "Survivors!"

"....vivors of the *Chandri*....a, can you hear...?"

"That's Dr. Hashida! We have to contact him!" Conover said, fumbling with the comm settings on her gauntlet. With a sudden blur of movement, Maya grabbed Conover's hand and yanked it away from the comm controls. She made eye contact with Conover, silently mouthing a "shhh" behind her faceplate.

"....Hashida here with crewman...and....scape pod. Are there any other....vors?"

Conover began to protest, trying to free her hand from

Maya's grip. Then, outside the window, an invisible lance pierced through the haze of dust and mangled metal as if slicing through space itself. It struck something on the far side of the debris field, and another fireball flared into brief existence. Half a second later, the transmission from Dr. Hashida ended with a shriek of static, then silence.

Conover stared in shock at the glittering bits of debris from the distant obliteration of the escape pod. Maya, still holding her arm with her one good hand, turned Conover to face her. "No comms. They can track them. Not even close range comms. There's enough air in this chamber to carry our voices, even with the suits. Turn it all the way off."

Conover nodded, switching her comm off with a shaky hand. "Who...who would do this? Who would shoot escape pods?"

"Pirates." Maya turned her gaze back to the window, searching for something beyond the edge of the debris field. "System's got a big pirate problem. I've heard rumors about them doing things like this. They take a few dozen tons of loose rocks like the one we hit, seed them out in a trade lane, then attack ships that hit them when they stop to make repairs."

"But...why would they just...kill everyone? What do they gain from this?"

"That's a good question, actually," Maya mumbled. "Not sure what they hoped to get from scuttling the ship like that."

As if in answer, a gargantuan shape drifted into view. The pirate ship was at least twice the size of the *Chandrakanta*, built like an upended tombstone. The ship's bow opened into a huge maw: a colossal bowl-shaped net made of a chain mail-like material that rippled with the impacts of a thousand fragments of *Chandrakanta*. Debris scooped up by the net funneled inward in a series of waves as timed electromagnetic pulses in the net's fabric drew the refuse toward a gaping orifice at its center. Hundreds of robotic arms, mounted like insectile mandibles around the "mouth" of the ship, probed the constant landslide of debris for larger or more interesting pieces. The arms then tucked them away into sorting compartments as the rest of the captured material merely sifted into the black mouth at the center.

Maya watched in awe and dread as the huge starship slowly plowed through the debris field, leaving a clear path behind it as it inhaled the *Chandrakanta*'s wreckage one pass at a time. "It's a comet chaser. A *Bowhead*-class, I think. They probably stole it from rock jockeys mining the Kuiper belt."

"Comet chaser?" Conover asked.

Maya nodded. "See that big mouth-thing on the front end? These ships are designed to collect the debris that sloughs off in comets' tails. Some of them have rail guns for shattering comets into tiny bits they can scoop up. That's what they hit us with."

"That's why they scuttled us," Conover said, a look of horror on her face. "They didn't even care about our cargo. They're just going to scoop up what's left of our ship and sell it for scrap!"

"Not scrap. Ingots. That ship's got a built-in refinery and processing plant. They'll melt everything down and process it into neat little bars. They won't even have to sell it on the black market. They can claim their cargo is a year's worth of hard mining finally paid off. Nobody will ever know it used to be a ship." Maya closed her one good hand tightly into a fist. "Cowards. Absolute cowards."

Conover blinked at her. Maya didn't like the expression on her face—it looked like Conover could go into a breakdown at any minute. There would be time to go into shock later, but to escape this catastrophe, Maya was going to need her to keep it together.

Maya put her hand on Conover's shoulder, forcing her to stay focused. "I have a plan. I think I can get us home. But I'm going to need your help. Can I count on you?" Something in Conover's vacant gaze sharpened a little, and she nodded at Maya with something almost resembling confidence.

"Good." Maya turned back to the cracked porthole, watching the pirate leviathan make another lumbering pass through the debris field, leaving eerily vacant space in its wake. "Now, that ship is huge and terrifying, but it's not as bad as it seems. Ninety percent of a *Bowhead's* interior is ore processing machinery and cargo space. Most of it isn't even pressurized. All the ship's living quarters are on one deck. The crew complement isn't even that big—it can accommodate maybe ten people, and most importantly, two people can fly it."

"We're going to board it?" asked Conover, barely contained panic in her voice.

"How full are the tanks on your EVA harness?"

"Eighty-one percent, ma'am."

"Okay. Here's what we're going to do. We're both going to top off our EVA tanks from Singh's suit. Then, we're going to open the airlock. I'm going to grab one side, you'll grab the other. When the *Bowhead* comes close enough, we're going to use our maneuvering jets to pull the whole airlock toward the *Bowhead's* docking ring. We're going to manually dock with the pirate ship."

"We're going to...how? I don't know how to dock with a ship the right way, let alone like this."

"This will be easier than docking a whole ship," said Maya. "We don't have thirty thousand extra tons of mass to move, and we'll be able to see all the minor course corrections we need to make right up close instead of from a console on the bridge. All we have to do is line up our mooring clamps with theirs. I can engage them manually. The pirates are flying nice and slow right now, so we'll be able to catch up."

"Okay..."

Maya didn't like the uncertainty in Conover's voice, but it was all she had to work with. "Okay. We're going to top off our EVA tanks now. Don't look at Singh, just look at his harness. Got it?"

Conover nodded weakly as the two of them moved to

the corpse of their crewmate. Maya pulled the body forward against the straps that still fastened him to the seat, giving them easier access to the compressed nitrogen tanks that fueled Singh's maneuvering jets. They hooked their own harnesses up to ports on his, a soft hiss assuring them that the transfer was underway.

"Conover, tell me what an airlock bridge is."

Conover closed her eyes in concentration, to Maya's satisfaction. *Good. Keep your mind occupied. Focus on problem-solving instead of just the problem.* "It's... ummm... normally one door in an airlock is always closed, but when there's an airtight seal between two ships, you can open all four doors to make an open corridor."

Maya nodded. "Good. That's correct. You can only form a bridge while both airlocks are fully pressurized, and you can't un-dock from a ship while a bridge is in place. Why can't you do that?"

Conover's eyes went wide with sudden understanding. "If you un-dock from another ship while a bridge is open, all your air vents out into space."

"Yup." Maya disconnected from Singh's tank and moved to the airlock door. Conover followed, and they watched out the cracked window as the pirate ship loomed toward them on another pass. "I'm going to open the hatch. Stay as close to the airlock as you can. Keep an eye out for wreckage." Conover nodded with a faint look of hopefulness.

Maya opened the hatch. Immediately, a torrent of gravel-sized debris began pelting them from all sides, though the gust of air from the now-decompressed airlock blew some of it away. Maya tucked herself against the side of the airlock, gripping one of the handles tightly. She couldn't see Conover from her position, which was worrying. She'd have to trust Conover to hold on and keep her wits entirely on her own.

Maya sought the huge bulk of the pirate ship amid the maelstrom of wreckage, and with a jet from her EVA harness, she began moving the airlock toward it. It was torturously slow getting started—the airlock had to weigh close to a ton, and her EVA harness was not designed to propel that much mass. She wasn't even fully confident that she'd have enough fuel to get to the pirate ship, even on a full tank.

Slowly, they closed the distance. Maya could actually hear the deep thrum of the *Bowhead's* engines as it approached, the sound waves carrying through the cloud of dust particles and trace gasses surrounding them. She felt a sharp pain in her leg as a piece of shrapnel pierced it, but a quick glance down confirmed the damage was minimal, and the auto-sealant foam in her suit quickly closed the breach. She huddled closer to the airlock.

The gauges on her wrist said her fuel was down to forty percent. The pirate ship was close enough now that she could see the texture of the matte black paint on its hull. They were keeping pace with it, but the *Bowhead's* airlock was still quite a distance away.

Something slammed hard into Maya's back, knocking the wind out of her and sending her tumbling away from the airlock. She struck the *Bowhead's* hull with a breathless grunt, and she struggled to regain control as she tumbled into space. With a few carefully controlled bursts from her maneuvering jets, she righted herself, then sped back toward the airlock that Conover was now clumsily trying to pull forward on her own. She gripped her handhold tightly once again and helped steady the heavy load.

At last, the hatch of the *Bowhead's* airlock came into range. Maya turned around and fired her jets in the opposite direction to slow their approach, hoping Conover had the presence of mind to do the same and that they weren't pulling uselessly in opposite directions. She was relieved to feel the airlock slow down as intended—Conover was pulling her weight.

Now came the tricky part. With barely any fuel left in her maneuvering tanks, Maya had to guide the one-ton chunk of metal to perfectly align its docking clamps with those of the *Bowhead.*

Delicately, tenderly, she nudged the metal hulk into position. She felt it shift out of alignment as Conover fumbled on the other side, but slowly she eased the bulky chamber back. She felt the last of the propellant sputter from the jets of her maneuvering thrusters. In desperation, she slipped her broken hand under one of the rails on the outside of the *Bowhead's* airlock and began pulling the two airlocks together with brute muscle.

Blades of pain tore through her wrist and arm. Black flecks circled in her vision as she forced herself to work through the agony, focusing intently on the clamps that slowly slid into the receiving slots on the *Bowhead's* airlock. Finally, with a satisfactory clang, the two locks socketed together.

Maya climbed one-handedly around the airlock to the exposed hatch that had formerly been the door to the *Chandrakanta*'s interior. She heaved the lever for the emergency manual clamps, and the two airlocks were finally secured.

Conover crawled around her side of the airlock to meet Maya, gripping a large sheet of paneling that she'd picked up at some point to use as a shield against debris. Maya gave her a thumbs-up, mouthing a "good job." Conover smiled weakly.

Maya engaged the manual unlock for the hatch and heaved it open with Conover's assistance. They tucked inside quickly and slid the hatch shut again, re-engaging the lock. Maya took Conover by the shoulder and pulled her close, touching their faceplates together in an incidentally intimate gesture that brought Maya a surprising degree of comfort.

"Can you hear me?" Maya asked. Conover nodded. Even though the airlock was still in vacuum, the vibrations against their touching faceplates were enough to carry her voice. "Okay. We're going to open our lock to theirs, and I'm going to override their lock's safeties. We have to pressurize this chamber first, or their airlocks won't open. There should be enough air in Singh's tanks to do that, but if we still need more, we can dip into our own air in a pinch. I need you to do that while I work, okay? Get the air pressure in this chamber up to one atmosphere."

Conover nodded and immediately went to work opening the valves on Singh's suit with a surprising degree of confidence and engagement. *That's my girl. Good job.*

Maya opened the hatch with the cracked porthole and drifted over to the *Bowhead*'s sepulchral black hatch. It opened without difficulty, a gust of air pushing past her as it equalized with the low pressure of their airlock. She crept up to the *Bowhead's* inner airlock and set to work switching it entirely over to manual control.

As air from Singh's tanks slowly filled the chamber, Maya could hear the steady thump of rowdy South African throbcore music blaring through the ship's intercom. That was an unexpected windfall. Even with the noise of the constant clatter of debris against the *Bowhead's* hull, she'd been afraid the noise of their makeshift docking maneuver might attract attention.

Several minutes passed. Maya finished switching the door controls to manual and was now waiting anxiously for the compartment to fill with air. Finally, Conover gave a thumbs-up, and a look at the gauges on Maya's suit confirmed they had successfully pressurized the chamber.

Maya grinned and yanked the door lever, sliding the inner hatch to the pirate ship open.

Her grin vanished immediately. Floating on the other side of the wide-open door was a tall, heavily built man. He looked at her in open-mouthed shock, one pale, tattooed hand gripping the handrail on the opposite wall and the other clutching a case of beer bottles. They stared at each other in frozen disbelief for almost a full second before either of them moved.

The man pushed the beer case to the side, letting it drift down the hallway as he lunged for Maya. She tried to pull away, but she was weighed down with a cumbersome space suit and EVA harness, while the man was clad only in a black tank top and cargo pants. He easily outmaneuvered her. Maya made it only halfway into the *Chandrakanta's* airlock before the pirate seized her broken hand. She cried out, and seeing the pained response, the pirate squeezed harder, a look of sadistic glee on his face.

Maya's mind filled with a dreadful certainty that this was the end. After all they'd been through, they'd been caught just inches from the finish line, defeated by this final hurdle. The pirate dragged her backwards, shouting out in a language or dialect she didn't understand as he pulled her into the hallway, laughing at her attempts to break free.

Then the laughter stopped, replaced with a loud crack and a pathetic gurgle as a softball-sized iron meteorite slammed into the man's skull, crushing it like a ripe melon. The pirate's grip released immediately, and he tumbled backwards into the corridor with blood pooling across his face in a crimson bubble. Maya looked back at Conover in shock, the other woman standing at the final closed hatch with her jaw set in grim determination. She held out a hand, stained red from gripping the blood-soaked meteorite.

"Come on, ma'am. We're almost there."

Maya grinned and pushed herself forward, taking Conover's hand. She could hear shouts echoing from inside the pirate ship, blending with the blaring noise of the music as they approached. They gripped the release lever together and turned the latch. With a roar of hurricane wind, the door blasted open, sending them once again into space.

Maya's arm was nearly yanked out of its socket as she struggled to hold on to the free-swinging hatch. She thought for certain she'd lose her grip, but Conover clung tightly to her, and the two hung on with all their combined might. Maya watched debris fly out the airlock in an endless torrent: random garbage, tools, the beer case the pirate had been carrying. Most of all, though, she took notice of the flailing bodies as half a dozen men were hurled into open space without any protection. She tried to convince herself she couldn't hear their screams mixed with the roaring wind.

Just when Maya thought she wouldn't be able to hold on

any longer, the rush of air slowed to a trickle. The ship had been depressurized. It was empty. It wouldn't be for long, though. The *Bowhead's* atmosphere recycler would have more than enough reserve air in its backup tanks to keep its two new owners alive.

Maya hugged Conover with both arms, finally allowing herself to weep tears of relief. She paid no attention to the steady metal rain that still pattered against her suit, or to the throbbing pain still shooting up her arm from her fractured hand. She drank in this moment of triumph, holding Conover in a tight yet tender embrace as she sobbed in pure, elated relief.

"Are you alright, ma'am?" Conover asked softly.

Maya nodded, laughing between sobs. "You did so well, Maureen. You were amazing."

Conover smiled at her. "We were amazing."

Maya smiled back, stifling a sniffle. "Let's check out our new ship."

The two climbed back through the open hatch, swinging it shut behind them for the last time.

ABOUT EVAN GRAHAM

Evan Graham is the author of upcoming science fiction thrillers Tantalus Depths and Proteus. He has a Bachelor's degree in Education Studies from Kent State University, where he triple-minored in English, Writing, and Theatre. He currently lives in rural Middlefield, Ohio and is extensively involved in local community theatre, both on the stage and behind the scenes.

THE FAOII OF ASHWOOD

By Tahani Nelson

Eilan hung on the back of the chair, watching his mother practice her needlework. She scowled, her eyes narrowed in concentration at the lopsided triangle and vague spiral before her. She grumbled under her breath. "Give me a sword and I could find someone's kidney with a blindfold on. With an arrow I could pierce an eye without touching the lid. But this? This is impossible."

Eilan's father smiled from across the room as he tugged on his boots. "You don't have to learn it, Erika. The baby won't mind."

Erika briefly put a hand to her slightly swollen belly at the mention of their unborn daughter, then brushed a strand of blonde hair away from her face with a frustrated gesture. Determinedly, she narrowed her cerulean eyes and returned to her needlepoint. "*She* might not mind, but *I* will." Erika hissed as she jerked the needle through. "Rebecca from across the square has already taught her girls advanced patterns. The young one can even make a blade-blessed cat. I will not be outdone by a simple housewife!" She inhaled sharply as she pricked her finger yet again, then sighed. After a moment she continued, her voice calmer than before. "That wasn't fair. Rebecca is a good person, and I value her friendship. But there are things that a girl expects to learn from her mother, Terin. I want our daughter to have those things."

"She'll have more than Rebecca's daughters could ever dream of, my love." Terin leaned over the chair and planted a kiss on Erika's forehead before reaching over to tickle Eilan's ribs. Eilan's squeals and protests momentarily drowned out his mother's grumblings.

"Do your chores, Son," Terin said kindly as he finally relented, still smiling. "I'll see you this evening."

"Yes, Father." Eilan helped to gather his father's fishing nets and opened the door, waving goodbye until Terin turned the bend that would lead to the river on the other side of town. Behind him, Erika inhaled sharply again and cursed under her breath.

"Mother," Eilan ventured as he resettled himself on the back of the chair. "Will you teach the baby how to use a fantoii, too?" He looked at her beautiful sword hanging on the wall, his own practice blade hanging underneath it.

"Of course." Erika answered as easily as if she'd just explained that the sun would rise again the next day. Eilan pondered for a moment.

"Will she be better at it than I am?" Eilan spoke quietly, and his mother stopped her work. After a moment, she set it to the side.

"Come here, my son."

Eilan came around the chair and settled on her lap, laying his head on her shoulder. He had a little more trouble fitting there these days, and he wondered if he'd fit better again after Imir was born or if he was getting too big to be held by his mother. Erika pet his hair as she spoke.

"No one can ever determine your worth but you, my dear one. That will go for your sister as well. I will train you both equally, and how good you become will depend on how hard you try and nothing else. Do you understand?"

"Yes, Mother. But Imir... Imir's a girl. So she might get to be Faoii one day, right?"

Erika shook her head. "We are not going to leave her at one of the monasteries to train. She will live with us—her family. She will know her father and will learn from her mother...and her big brother." She smiled at him. "You will both become fine warriors if you choose to be, even without titles or Oaths. And you will have each other no matter what happens. She will be Imir, daughter of Erika and Terin. That's all the title she needs."

Eilan smiled down at his mother's stomach, then frowned. "If Rebecca ends up teaching Imir how to sew because you can't, will you teach her daughters how to fight so it's fair?"

Erika's eyes darkened half a shade, but the door swung open before she could reply. Eilan turned to see who was there.

"Father! You're back already!"

Terin didn't seem to hear him. "Erika," he said, his voice strained. "There's a Faoii outside. I met her on the path and led her back here. She says... she says she's looking for you."

Erika deposited Eilan on the ground and rose with one fluid motion so quick it surprised him. She normally moved slowly around him so he could see each step, learn each motion. But sometimes, when she was scared or worried, she moved with a swift, flowing grace that was nearly inhuman. Eilan was going to ask his mother what was bothering her, but she was already striding across the room. He frowned as he realized that the air felt different—almost like it does right before a lightning storm.

"Eilan. Stay inside." The air crackled when she spoke, and the hair on Eilan's arms stood up. He nodded, but his parents were already out the door.

Once he was sure he wouldn't be noticed, Eilan rushed to the window. He had never seen a true Faoii before. He knew his mother had been Faoii once, but that was a long time ago. He couldn't imagine her as one of the soldiers from the stories, with their singing blades and magic voices. But the woman who stood standing in the square—she was everything he thought a Faoii should be. Her bronze breastplate shone in sunlight, and her sharp fantoii rested easily on one hip. Eilan knew that they were the same, but somehow hers looked better than the one his mother kept on the wall. Even the warrior's long braid had iron rings woven into the pleats, making his mother's simple braid look drab and listless in comparison.

The Faoii stood straight and proud, and her dark eyes glinted like obsidian in the sunlight—so much more powerful than his mother's pale, blue, *boring* eyes.

Erika reached the Faoii and fisted her hands one over the

other, like she was grasping an invisible hilt. She bowed her head, and the other woman mirrored the greeting before speaking. Eilan wanted to hear the magic voice the stories spoke of, but he was too far away, even after he opened the window. Still, the Faoii seemed to speak quickly and with an urgency that was uncommon in Ashwood, and she moved her hands often as she spoke, only stopping periodically as Erika replied.

The two women spoke for a long time, and people began coming out of their houses with curious or annoyed expressions as they stood to watch the two Faoii hold their heated discussion. Soon a small crowd had formed, and Eilan could make out the sounds of incredulous laughter and shouted denials from their neighbors. He didn't know why they were arguing, but he didn't think they should disagree with a Faoii. He was even going to go out and tell them so, but before he could muster the courage to disobey his parents' orders, his father stepped forward, raising his hands in a placating gesture. Eilan smiled. Father always tried to make things easier for everyone.

But Father made a mistake. His hand briefly brushed the Faoii's bronze breastplate as he tried to talk down the gathered townsfolk. The Faoii reacted immediately, drawing her sword with a swift movement, dark eyes sparking angrily. Even from across the plaza, Eilan saw the sudden fear in his father's eyes. Eilan wanted to go out and help—how could a stranger make his father look so small?—but his mother was already there, standing between her husband and the Faoii with such an air of indignation that Eilan took an involuntary step backwards, surprised by the strength in his mother's stance. Erika planted a firm finger on the other Faoii's chest as she spoke, and the other woman finally relented, resheathing her blade before bowing her head and saying something with lips that barely moved.

Eilan gasped. The rest of the crowd had dispersed at the sight of bare steel, but his mother had stood up to a Faoii, even without a blade. And *won*.

Erika said something else, still jabbing a finger into the Faoii's chest, and Eilan leaned as far out the window as he could, straining to hear. He was too far away, though, and was forced to duck back inside when his parents turned back toward the house. The strange Faoii stared after them from the square.

Eilan had barely grabbed the broom and begun sweeping the hearth when his parents reentered, trying not to be obvious as he watched them out of the corner of his eye. He'd learned long ago that if you pretend you don't know what grownups are saying, they'll keep talking where you can hear. Terin pursed his lips while he shut the door firmly, then turned to face his wife with uneasy eyes. She was already pacing back and forth in front of the fireplace.

"Erika, you can't."

"Don't you think I know that?" She ran her fingers through her hair agitatedly, but only managed to pull more strands from her braid. "I know, Terin. I know. But you heard her—they're tracking down Faoii. If we stay here, they'll destroy everyone in Ashwood just to get to me." She cast a worried glance at her belly and at Eilan, who pretended to sweep a new spot on the floor.

"But, Erika. She wants you to go to Cailivale? Where there's an entire group of Faoii to target?"

"If that's where they're gathering an army, that's the safest place. I won't join the ranks. I'll be too far along by the time we get there to be useful, anyway. But if we can find a place to live near their barracks, we'll have more protection than in any other city in the empire."

"We don't even know if what's she's saying is true! I've never even heard of these... Crowli? Crueli?"

"Croeli. And no one has. They're the Faoii's most ancient enemies. The only people in millennia that even posed a threat to the Order. They're supposed to be more monster than man, but with magic that rivals even our own." Eilan noticed his mother's hands shaking and could not think of a time he'd ever seen that before. "But the Faoii defeated them centuries ago. Now they're just stories for the unascended. I didn't think there were any left."

"She could be mistaken, Erika. Ascended Faoii or not, she looks young. She might not even know what she's talking about."

Erika shook her head. "It's taboo to even mention the Croeli outside of the monasteries, Terin. It's not a rumor that would spread lightly. And the way Faoii-Sarai said it...you felt the power in her voice when she commanded everyone to get out of Ashwood. You felt the command in your bones, right? You don't use that kind of power on a whim. This is real. It's happening. And if she found us here, they will too. Ashwood isn't safe."

Terin wiped a hand across his face. "Then let's go stay with my brother in Riventide. No one there will know you're Faoii. We'll be safe until...until they stop looking."

Erika put her head in her hands, and for a moment she looked more tired than Eilan had ever seen her. But when she looked up again, her gaze was fierce.

"No. We can't just leave everyone here, Terin. You heard the way they argued with her. How they called her insane. They offended her—that's why she was so quick to draw steel. I might have been able to convince her that that was a mistake, but she's still Faoii. Arrogant and proud. She'll leave everyone here to die if they don't choose to leave on their own."

Terin frowned thoughtfully. "I'll try to convince the others to leave, too. Maybe they'll listen to me." He fidgeted with the clasp on his shirt as he spoke, and Erika rolled her eyes as she reached up to fix it for him.

"My love, you are the bravest and most honest man I know, but if Faoii-Sarai out there wasn't able to convince them with the magic voice of the Order behind her words, nothing you say will be able to change their minds." Erika looked up and met her husband's eyes. "If the Croeli really are coming, they'll tear Ashwood to pieces. We both know there's not a decent blade in this entire village, and definitely no warriors. They'll be slaughtered. But I—"

"No, Erika." Terin grasped one of her hands and laid his other one on her belly. "There are other lives to think of now. Imir needs you to be safe. Eilan and I need you to be safe."

"These are our friends. We can't just leave them." Erika brought his hand up to her lips and kissed it gently. "We'll figure it out. Illindria provides, my love."

Eilan tried to sleep that night, but his mind was racing. His parents had done their best to explain the situation to him the day before, and he was nervous. Mother said the Croeli were bad men that had destroyed all the Faoii temples. His mother had never lied to him before, but Eilan didn't know how to believe her this time. Everyone knew that the Faoii were invincible. No one could defeat Illindria's greatest warriors. But somehow the Croeli had, and now they were tracking down whoever was left—pulling out the remaining "weeds" by the roots wherever they could.

The people of Ashwood wouldn't leave their homes in the face of impossible rumors, and there was no one to protect them if the Croeli came. Eilan had watched his mother pace around the house for hours as she tried to come up with a way to help everyone. There was an army forming in Cailivale—a whole army of Faoii that could fight the Croeli. Faoii-Sarai said it was being led by Faoii-Kaiya and Faoii-Lyn, but his mother didn't know either of them. They were supposed to be powerful Faoii. But they were too far away to help the people of Ashwood.

At last his parents had come up with a plan that made them both feel a little easier. They were going to leave in the middle of the day. That way, if they were being watched, the Croeli would leave the town alone and follow them, instead. His mother said that an army can't move very quickly, so they'd be safe if they kept to the river. They could go to Riventide and lie low until the Faoii army came and saved all the small towns like Ashwood. And, until then, their little family would warn everyone they could.

Eilan liked the way his mother's face filled with pride when she told him that he would help her and Father save people as they told everyone about the Croeli. And he liked the way the hair on his arms stood up when she prayed in front of the Illindria statue above the fireplace that night:

"Blessed Illindria, Wielder of the Eternal Blade, I thank You for my family and for the sisters that call to me again. May the blades of those that fight in Cailivale sing with the voice of every throat that has cried out against injustice and dance with the steps of every innocent child. May they lead the choir, and the voices of their swords deafen the ears of our enemies. And, as they do, allow me to join their song once more, in whatever way I can. For my sisters. For my family. For You. I am Faoii."

Eilan prayed, too. His mother always said that Illindria listened when you prayed. He prayed for his parents and his friends. He even prayed for Rebecca and the two girls that made his mother sad because they were better at sewing than her. He prayed that everyone would be safe.

He knew that Illindria listened to prayers, but he was still scared when he finally fell asleep.

Eilan felt like he'd only closed his eyes for a few moments when suddenly there was pounding on the door, loud and insistent. Eilan was out of bed even before the final knock finished ringing through the house. He rushed to his parents' bed on the other side of the room, and his father picked him up as they watched Erika pull her fantoii off the wall. She held it differently now than she did when she was training him. Her grip was the same, but something changed in her movements, in her stance—and for the first time in his life, Eilan felt an unnatural fear of his mother as she glided to the door.

Erika swung the door open and lunged forward with her

blade, but the woman on the other side of the opening ducked below it and countered with her shield before shoving Erika back inside and slamming the door behind them. Her piercing eyes flashed with the light of the fireplace's low embers.

"Faoii-Sarai. What are you doing?" Erika hissed as she lowered her blade a few inches.

"I smelled them on the wind. They're here, Faoii. We need to go now, and even then we still might have to fight. Where is your breastplate?"

Erika froze in place, her entire body rigid as she cast a glance back at her husband and son. Their eyes met for a moment, and then she was moving, her motions fluid as she pulled a sturdy chest out from beneath the bench across from the fireplace.

"How close? We sent the Omtir brothers to scout the roads, and neither saw anything at all. They can't be here already."

"Closer than should be possible. The Croeli can cover entire leagues in a single night, and we don't know how they're doing it. It's beyond even what the Order is capable of," Faoii-Sarai whispered as she glanced out the window. "That doesn't matter now. My orders are to bring you to the barracks alive. You can ask Faoii-Lyn whatever questions you want about the Croeli when we get there."

Eilan watched Faoii-Sarai buckle on his mother's bronze breastplate with quick, practiced movements. Sarai had to punch new holes in two of the straps to make them big enough to fit over his mother's slightly swollen belly. He wondered what she would have done if the baby had been bigger. But then the thought disappeared as Eilan watched his mother transform into a warrior he'd never expected to see. In that moment, as Faoii-Sarai fastened the last strap, he thought his mother might be a goddess.

Erika shook her head. "Terin and I aren't going to Cailivale. You should return to your superiors, alone. As quickly as you can."

The dark-eyed Faoii reacted as though Erika had landed her a physical blow.

"But we need every warrior left! Even with your...condition, you are necessary. There are only a handful of ascended left in the entire country now." She stepped in front of Erika as the older woman turned away to help her husband gather some hastily packed supplies.

"There are no hard feelings amongst the Order that you chose a different path, but this is bigger than all of us. We are the strength of the weak and the voice of the silent, Faoii. You cannot hide from your duties. We are called." Faoii-Sarai didn't talk any louder than she had before, but Eilan's teeth rattled at the last word, and the hair on his arms stood up.

Erika didn't even look up from the cloth sack she was shoving provisions into. "I have made my peace with both myself and the Goddess, Sarai. My oath to my husband and my children is more important to me than my Oath to Illindria, now. Your words will not sway me."

Faoii-Sarai looked like she was about to say something, but there was a sudden scream from outside. Her eyes darted to the door.

"There's no time. We can argue about this later, but first we have to get out of here alive." Another scream, followed by a sudden chorus of cries in the darkness. Eilan whimpered in his father's grasp as Terin slung the last of their supplies over his other shoulder. Erika cupped his cheek with the hand not holding her blade.

"Be brave, my son," she whispered. "Everything will be alright." She then planted a kiss on her husband's lips and moved to the door. "Meet me at Jodhan's barn across the cornfield. I'll meet you there when it's safe."

"Momma! Don't go!" Eilan had never been so scared before. For a moment he was terrifyingly certain that if his mother went through that door, he'd never see her again.

Erika smiled softly at him. "I have to get Rebecca and the girls. We can't leave them behind, can we?"

Eilan thought of the woman who actually was good at needlework and her two daughters who lived across the square. Rebecca was the only woman in town his mother ever talked to. And he *had* prayed for them the night before. Slowly, Eilan shook his head.

Terin shifted Eilan in his grasp. "Go get them, Erika. We'll meet you at the barn."

"No, Faoii." Sarai's voice was emotionless and icy as she stepped between Erika and the door. "Faoii-Kaiya and Faoii-Lyn need you in Cailivale. We can't afford to bring a house-wife and children with us. There's no room and they'll slow us down."

Eilan saw his mother's eyes fill with steel and ice as she swept a hand up in front of her and backhanded the younger warrior with enough strength to make her stumble. Eilan gasped. His mother was the gentlest person he knew, but now, as she drew herself up to her full height, he hardly recognized her.

"What happened to 'we are the strength of the weak?' Come with me and save those girls or go with my husband and protect my son—but do not get in my way again. You want to know the call of Illindria? This is it." She didn't wait for a re-sponse as she shouldered the door open.

It was unnaturally hot outside. The air was thick with smoke and screams. Eilan burrowed into his father's shoulder even as Terin's long legs carried them toward Jodhan's field in a sprint. Eilan got only a glimpse of his mother's shining breastplate in the night as she flew across the empty square, followed closely by Faoii-Sarai. Then she disappeared behind houses as his father carried him in the opposite direction, darting between buildings and through gaps in fences, scaring livestock who were already skittish at the sight of the growing flames.

The screaming from town got quieter, and for a moment Eilan felt safe. He hoped they'd escaped that easily and it was over. But then, just as he remembered to breathe again, his father stopped so abruptly Eilan almost fell from his grasp. Eilan let out a small yelp of protest and raised his head to ask his father what was wrong, but was shocked into silence by the monster in front of them.

A huge man with a scowling demon-like helmet stood in front of them, his jagged sword glinting in the firelight. The Croeli took a step forward, giving his dripping blade a quick flick of his wrist. Crimson drops splattered across the ground in a wide arc. Eilan choked back a sob as he felt his father straighten, afraid of what would come next. Terin didn't know how to fight, had never lifted a sword. He wished he'd grabbed his practice sword off the wall when his mother had grabbed hers. He wanted to protect his father. But he was afraid.

They froze like that for a moment, the flames from a nearby house reflecting in the invader's monstrous faceplate. Then he took another step forward, bringing his jagged sword up. Eilan heard his father's heartbeat increase to a rapid pace just before he suddenly moved.

With a sort of strangled yell, Terin whipped the heavy bag of food and supplies toward the towering Croeli and took off in the other direction before it could strike. Eilan barely heard his mother's favorite bowl shatter as it crashed against the Croeli's helmet.

Eilan tried to keep track of where they were, where they were going, but everything was moving too fast. His father changed directions several times, and even jumped over a fence once, though he never loosened his grip on Eilan as they ran. Eilan looked for his mother and cried for her as he wrapped his arms around his father's neck. But the Croeli were everywhere with their barbed swords and horned helmets, and Terin was struggling to evade them all.

Finally, Terin skidded to a stop, and Eilan raised his head. They were in the big barn at the edge of Jodhan's farm, with its giant painting of Illindria on the far wall. The Goddess's smile was bright and beautiful, but it was her breastplate and shining fantoii that made him feel better. The Goddess once protected the world from real demons. She could protect him and Father from the Croeli until his mother came to get them with Rebecca and the girls. He was about to open his mouth to say so, but as he looked around, Eilan suddenly didn't feel very safe at all.

The barn was filled with sobbing, terrified people. A few prayers to the Eternal One struggled to rise above the din, but mostly there were only wailing cries. The sound and the scent of fear was nearly overwhelming. Eilan tried not to cry as his father whispered quietly into the night. He'd never heard his father pray before.

Eilan didn't know how long they'd been in the barn, surrounded by fear and heartache, when suddenly the background noise was pierced by shrill screams. A glint of fire on steel flashed near the entrance, and a throng of people pushed their way to the back wall. The people of Ashwood wailed for mercy, but there was no response other than a low chuckle and the crackling of straw catching fire. Then the great barn doors slammed shut, only briefly covering the sounds of screams that echoed across the rafters.

Eilan clutched at his father's chest as the mob pressed them against the back wall of the barn and the cries grew louder. People scrambled at the door, only to draw away as flames licked their hands from the other side. They pounded against the walls, sobbing and screaming. Several people prayed to Illindria in desperate tones, their voices rising in pitch as the seconds passed.

Eilan couldn't see anymore as the smoke thickened. His eyes and chest hurt, and he couldn't feel anything else as his father cradled him against the ever-growing howls. He wanted it to stop. He wanted to go home. He wanted to get on the boat and go save all the people his mother said they'd save.

He wanted his mother.

Just when Eilan thought the people and the smoke and the

fear would suffocate him, there was a sudden and terrifying *crack* above his head. Terin spun toward the sound and let out a relieved cry at whatever he saw there. A distant voice tried to raise itself against the terrified screams.

"I'm coming! I'm coming! Hold on!"

Eilan jumped involuntarily as the head of an axe splintered the wall in front of them again, but he could now see his mother on the other side. He screamed at her to hurry, to get them out. His chest hurt. He couldn't breathe. His mother raised her axe again.

Eilan remembered that his mother had said the Croeli had magic, but he didn't think that even a Faoii could appear out of thin air like the man that suddenly formed behind Erika did. He stepped from out of nowhere like there had been a door, his sword raised above his head. Eilan was so surprised that he couldn't even speak, but his father recovered more quickly, screaming out in fear and desperation.

"Erika! Move!"

Eilan's mother dropped low immediately, barely dodging the Croeli's blow as he let his sword fall. Without enough time to draw her fantoii, she rolled to the side and reversed the grip on her axe instead. The Croeli's blade had barely finished its arc when Erika shoved upward with her calves and swung the axe with all her might. There was a sickly *squelch* as the invader's torso slumped over his drooping intestines.

Erika yanked the axe from the lifeless body and brought it back to the wall again. Blood splattered Eilan's face as it struck.

People tore at the hole and pried boards away with their bare hands. Erika flung the axe aside, unable to find purchase without cleaving fingers, and yanked at the splintered wood. Her fingers bled with the effort and her face streamed with sweat.

"Terin! Help me!"

Eilan was surprised by how quickly his father let him go in order to rush forward. But he followed, too, scrambling to pull at boards and pieces of wood that cut into his hands as he yanked. It hurt, but he refused to give up, yelling to his mother that they were coming. Others responded to the call, too, and the people of Ashwood were mighty in their desperation. As the flames behind them rose higher and closer, the citizens of the tiny town pressed forward with a final, powerful determination. The splintered boards of the barn cracked beneath their weight, pried apart by the pulsing bodies. Eilan was lifted and shoved from the oppressive heat into the chilled autumn air.

"Run, Son! Go!" cried Terin above the din.

Eilan stumbled across the grass outside, trying to cough the smoke from his lungs. He tried to look for his parents but couldn't see anything through his tears. When he tried to stand, the scrambling bodies behind him only pushed him forward. He was swept away from the barn almost immediately.

Eilan scrubbed at his eyes until he could see. There were people everywhere, cries and screams and the sound of swords clashing nearby. He forced his way back through the crowd, trying to follow the sound of an axe striking wood. He hoped his mother would be at the end of it. He wanted to help her. But when he arrived, it was only Gavin the butcher busting through the side of Jodhan's tool shed. Hands grabbed for pitchforks and scythes, and the burnt, soot-covered faces of Ashwood's citizens glowed in the light of the fires as they turned on the invaders that had just tried to burn them all alive.

Something about those faces reminded Eilan of his mother when he'd watched her put the breastplate on not long before. They were not Faoii, but in that moment the people of Ashwood were more than they'd ever been before. And for the first time Eilan understood why his mother would want to stop being Faoii, why she'd give up the world he'd heard about in stories so she could live in this little town and prick herself with sewing needles in front of the fireplace. This was her home. Their home. And he wanted it to be okay.

Eilan picked up a shovel. It might not sing like a fantoii would, but his mother said that a sword was just a tool. If that was the case, he didn't see why a tool couldn't also be a sword.

Just then, someone grabbed his shoulder, and Eilan spun around with a yelp, swinging his shovel hard. He briefly hoped that it sounded like his mother's war cry and not like a regular scream.

Rebecca's youngest daughter, Elizabeth, shrank away from his scream and the shovel that flew above her little head. The doll she hugged was dark with tears and soot. Eilan's heart clenched in shame as he dropped his shovel, raising both his hands like his father had in the square.

"I'm sorry, Elizabeth. Don't be scared. It's okay. It's okay. Come on." All thoughts of fighting forgotten, Eilan pulled Elizabeth toward the cornfield. She sniffled and looked up at Eilan with round eyes.

"Have you seen my mommy?"

Eilan whispered a word his mother wouldn't approve of, and his cheeks flushed red even though he knew she couldn't hear. "Was your mommy in the barn?" Elizabeth shook her head.

"I lost her in the corn. She said to go to the shrine."

Everyone knew Jodhan's Illindria statue in the middle of his cornfield. No one ever understood why he'd put that there instead of a regular scarecrow, and a lot of villagers had laughed at him over the years. But they'd laughed at his mother, too, and look how that turned out. He could almost hear his mother's words on the wind. *Illindria provides, my Son. Even when no one else understands how.*

Eilan tried to smile for Elizabeth and pulled her deeper into the cornfield. "Let's go look for her, okay?"

Eilan heard Rebecca's strained and desperate whispers before they'd reached their destination. He was about to let go of Elizabeth's hand, but when Rebecca's frightened voice bordered on shrill, they heard someone else shush her, and he pulled Elizabeth back.

"Let me go!" Rebecca whispered hysterically through the corn. "I have to go find her! She was right behind me!"

"You go out there and they'll find all of us. Stay put." Eilan drew his eyebrows together as he crept forward. He saw a huddled group of villagers gathered around the Illindria statue. Rebecca was sitting on the ground with two men gripping her shoulders. Elizabeth saw them too, and broke free of his grip, rushing forward.

"Mommy!"

"Oh, Elizabeth! My baby! You're safe!" The relief in Rebecca's voice was palpable as Elizabeth collapsed, sobbing, into her arms. Rebecca wrapped her arms around both of her girls and rocked back and forth, crying into their hair. "You're safe. You're both safe. We're okay."

Eilan looked at the grownups gathered around the statue in the corn. They sat or crouched in a huddled mass, their faces dark.

"You're hiding," he said accusingly.

"We're surviving, boy," someone hissed back. "We're not fighters. Sit down and stay with us until this is all over."

Eilan looked back and forth between the faces, wondering how he could have ever considered his mother something less than Faoii. Even before he truly understood her old Order, he could not imagine her hiding like this while her friends and neighbors fought for their lives. He shook his head, then smiled at Rebecca. He wasn't going to be like that. He'd be better than they were. His mother said that he would be a warrior.

"Keep the girls safe, Ms. Rebecca. I'll make sure no one finds you." He thought he felt one of the hiding grownups grab for him, but he was already dashing back toward town.

Now that the surge of adrenaline from the barn had worn off, Eilan knew he wasn't ready to stand next to his parents in the heat of the battle that sounded from the town square.

But he could make sure that those who were too afraid to fight were at least protected. He spent that night patrolling the edge of Jodhan's cornfield, his reclaimed battle shovel in hand. He gathered the few townsfolk that broke away from the fighting, wounded and weary, and pointed them toward the shrine.

At one point several people were pushed back from the town proper by a particularly powerful Croeli, who roared so loudly it rattled Eilan's bones. For a moment Eilan was paralyzed with fear, just as he had been in the barn, but he remembered the way his father had warned his mother, and he broke through it, rushing to help. The townsfolk had felled the armored monster before he'd reached them, but they seemed proud of him, anyway.

"Keep doing what you're doing, lad. We'll tell your parents you're okay." Eilan's heart soared when he heard those words. His parents were still fighting. They were alive. He smiled up at the men and thanked them for the news. Then he clasped his hands like he'd seen his mother and Faoii-Sarai do.

"Illindria watch over you. I'll be at my post."

Finally, just before dawn, the sounds of fighting coming from town stopped. Time crawled by in an eerie silence, broken only by the crackling of far too many dying fires. Eilan clenched his shovel and watched the paths that led to town. He almost didn't believe it when he heard the sound he'd been praying for hours.

"Eilan! Eilan, where are you?"

Eilan finally abandoned his field and its hidden survivors, dashing out into the open, his heart racing. He'd planned to let his parents find him there, looking like an adult, protecting the fields. But he forgot about that immediately at the sound of their voices.

"I'm here! I'm here!" he screamed at the top of his lungs as his parents came around the corner.

Erika's tears of joy caught the first rays of the morning sunlight as she sprinted toward Eilan, sliding on her knees before him and gathering him into her arms. The tears washed away a layer of soot and grime, matting parts of her disheveled braid to her cheeks as she pressed him to her. She smelled of smoke and blood as she sobbed into his hair. Terin followed a bit unsteadily, a deep gash across his forehead still dripping blood into his eyes. But he beamed and laughed as he embraced Eilan.

"They told us what you did. You were so brave, my son. We are proud of you."

"There are people hiding in the corn. I sent them to the shrine of Illindria. I kept them safe, just like you taught me." If his parents responded, Eilan didn't hear, so elated was he to be back in his parents' arms as the last few tendrils of smoke curled into the morning sky.

The survivors of Ashwood met at the shrine of Illindria at the center of Jodhan's cornfield. Hours of confusion and sobbing pleas had eventually given way to a sort of order as the survivors were tallied and the remains of families reunited. Far too few had loved ones left to embrace as the sun slowly crept toward the middle of the sky.

The Croeli had eventually been overpowered by the desperate citizens of Ashwood, true, but it was at a high, high price.

"Farmers do not easily win fights against warriors," Eilan's mother told him quietly as they sat at Illindria's feet. "I am honored to have fought amongst those here, but there are always so many to be buried afterward. Remember that when we tell others about what's coming. They will want to fight, too, and we will have to help them understand."

Eilan nodded solemnly. He wasn't sure his mother would have said that to him a day ago.

Faoii-Sarai took control of the survivors quickly, giving orders with barking commands that were filled with power. No one questioned her anymore, and people moved quickly to obey, helping to organize families and tend to wounds.

Sarai warned that other Croeli would come to find out why their soldiers had not returned. Ashwood was no longer safe. But as the few remaining citizens of Ashwood huddled around the solitary statue in the middle of the cornfield, reflecting on their loss, few believed it had truly been safe to begin with.

Faoii-Sarai might have taken control with a brutal efficiency, but as the huddled mass of farmers and housewives began to drift away from the shrine, preparing to gather what they could of their broken lives, each stopped in front of Faoii-Erika for a final farewell. They showed her a level of respect Eilan had never seen, and he thought he understood. In all her years in Ashwood, they had not known his mother for what she was, and now they bowed their heads and made the inverted triangle of Illindria with their hands in her presence. She only smiled at them in return and wished them well.

"Where will you go, Faoii-Erika?" Faoii-Sarai asked Eilan's mother after all the other survivors had moved on. Her voice held more reverence now as the two Faoii stood looking at the Goddess statue. Eilan and his father stood back, watching the two warriors converse.

Erika considered for a moment. "I know that the Faoii are gathering an army in Cailivale to counter this threat. I know that my skills could be useful there. But you saw what happened. The common people are helpless. They can't all make it to the cities before the threat is upon them, and most don't even know how to try. They need to be warned, and if possible, trained. They need hope."

Eilan's mother placed a hand on her belly. "The Faoii are not my only people, Sister. I can give hope to those our Order cannot—or will not—reach."

Faoii-Sarai thought for a moment and nodded before turning and fisting her hands in front of her. "May the Goddess guide your battles, Faoii-Erika. You carry the future inside you. I'll help to ensure she has a bright one." She paused and looked to Eilan. "Them. Both of them. This is not just the world of the Faoii, anymore."

"No." Erika replied. "And we will all be stronger for it."

Two days later, Eilan and his parents boarded his father's simple fishing boat and watched the now-abandoned town of Ashwood disappear behind them. His mother slowly, carefully, worked on her needlework, barely affected by the river's gentle current. Eilan couldn't help but notice that it finally looked like a proper triangle.

ABOUT TAHANI NELSON

Twitter @TahaniNelson

Tahani Nelson is a Writer, Teacher and Nerd in rural Montana. Her debut series, *The Faoii Chronicles* focuses on strong female warriors in epic fantasy.

CONVICT 45

By Michael James Welch

Prisoner #4582645, or Convict 45 as his cellmates knew him, stood uncomfortably close to the front of a line that stretched nearly to the limits of his vision. Each reeking man shuffled slowly toward a huge, raised wooden platform. The government of Asluggoth had erected it recently on the dirt patch which passed for a town square. The massive wooden stairs were empty—each of the condemned waited at the bottom in turn. A hulking slab of a man stood on the platform, close to the high block upon which each neck would be laid. Shirtless and sweaty, the executioner hefted an intimidating axe that was easily five feet long, with its double-bladed head another two feet wide. Already there was gore at the edge of it, a crescent moon of red cratered with bits of viscera. Small chunks of flesh nested in the graying chest hair of the axe man, who tugged at his black cloth hood in a fruitless attempt to unblock his vision.

It had to be uncomfortable, Convict 45 considered as he stood. It was at least eighty degrees today—too hot for a hat. He wiped his sweaty hands on his baggy prison garb and succeeded only in making both filthier.

In due time, the grunt of the executioner split the air, followed by a *thunk* that caused the entire platform to shudder. What little crowd had bothered to show up was no longer reacting. They'd seen dozens of deaths already today and were busy talking amongst themselves in small knots of neighbors, friends, and coworkers. Their murmured conversations would pause with each swing of the axe, then pick up again soon after. Far from the town square, a lone dog barked continuously. The prisoner to 45's rear shouldered him forward impatiently.

Convict 45's lip twitched. He turned to survey the line of condemned behind him, carefully ignoring the annoyed gaze of the antsy guy on his flank. Beyond the mass of the stinking and doomed, he spied the rear gate of the city. There were no fewer than four heavily armored guards standing by it. Convict 45 deemed it impenetrable, and a frown consumed his angry face.

Then he formed a plan and dropped to his knees, falling out of line.

Prisoners murmured curses and questions about what could be wrong with Convict 45, but he ignored them and screwed his eyes shut, hissing pained breaths and holding his shins.

Once he'd counted forty footfalls, he rolled to his knees. Most of the damned were shambling forward without a glance at his prostrate form. Convict 45 rose to his feet and inserted himself back into the line, smiling at having duped close to twenty men.

Convict 45 turned to the man behind him, who was elderly and frail. "So, what're you in for?"

The ancient, emaciated man parted his stringy gray hair and replied, "Me?"

"Yes, you."

"I shot and killed a boy who was walking down the street too close to my house," the old man said, his eyes squinting a bit against the sun. "We've had this conversation befo—"

"See, this is what I'm always talking about. You were minding your own business, and this guy assaulted you, right?"

"I was sitting near my window, looking for suspicious people," replied the old man in a weary tone.

"Right, like I said, minding your own business. This guy—let me guess, he was one of those Acirfan types, right?"

"I'm not sure if he came from Acirfa or if he was born in Asluggoth, but yes." The old man's demeanor brightened.

"And he's walking up and down your street, probably looking into your windows, right?"

The old man considered this for a moment, and then his bearing straightened. "That's right." He shot his fist out, punching the air awkwardly. "And you know what else?"

"What else, my friend?" Convict 45 leaned forward conspiratorially.

"His head was covered. One of those things those... those... Acirfans always wear. You know what I mean? So, you can't really see their heads?" The old man's eyes squinted in query.

"That's exactly what I figured." Convict 45 straightened to his full height. "So, you shot this guy—"

"Kid," the old man interjected, his eyes turning down slightly.

"You shot this guy, and you got in trouble for it, didn't you?"

"Well, yes. I'm in line along with you for the axe man." The old man's head bowed.

"I'm so glad I was able to meet you before you died. You're a true patriot!" Convict 45 thrust out his hand.

The old man slowly gripped the proffered hand, his voice lowering in confusion. "You and I have been cellmates for two ye—"

"I'll tell you what—why don't you go ahead of me? Take my place in line. It's the least I can do for a patriot." Convict 45 shook his hand aggressively, pulling the old man into place ahead of him.

"But... doesn't that mean I'll die sooner?" the old man asked, his hand still trapped.

"Look, it's the least I can do. I will sing your praises." Convict 45 beamed magnanimously.

"Won't you be dead three minutes after me?"

"Maybe. Maybe so. And for those three minutes, I will sing your praises at the top of my lungs, friend. It's my honor." Convict 45 made a show of bowing his head to the old man, then finally released his hand.

The old man thought a moment, then straightened his spine and said, "No, sir," extending his recently freed hand back to Convict 45, "the honor is all mine!"

Convict 45 was in the process of wiping his hands on his

pants once again, but stopped and clenched the old man's hand again. It was much larger, and 45's grip was comparatively limp.

"What was that all about?" asked the man now standing behind Convict 45.

"A true patriot. Someone who was truly inspired by me," Convict 45 replied proudly.

"Inspired by you," the man repeated. "What did you do?" He was furiously scratching at multiple points on his body, such was his lice infestation.

Convict 45 took a measured step back. "What *didn't* I do, my friend?" He paused as if waiting for an answer.

In reply, the itchy man furtively scratched at his genitals, then the back of his neck, then his genitals again.

"I put the pride back into Asluggoth, that's what I did." Convict 45 crowed, "We were the laughingstock of the world for many years."

"I don't remember that. Dammit!" The itchy man reached behind himself, his face contorted, trying desperately to scratch the small of his back.

"Believe me. Here, let me help you. Let's trade places in line, and I'll scratch your back." Convict 45 suggested.

"But that means I'll get axed sooner," the itchy man thought out loud, then began scratching both armpits desperately. "You know what, that works for me. Go ahead."

Convict 45 smiled widely and changed places with the itchy man. He said to the man now behind him, "That guy's got food in the back of his shirt," indicating the itchy man with a thumb. The next three prisoners overheard this and surged forward, clawing at the itchy man's torso.

Convict 45 turned to the back of the line and craned his neck, bobbing it to-and-fro to see something in the distance. A scowling prisoner standing to the rear of him asked, "Something going on back there?"

After another moment of distraction, Convict 45 answered, "No, that's really the problem, friend. There's nothing going on back there. All the action's up front!"

"Near the dude *executing* everyone?" The man asked, a scowl encompassing his entire face.

"That's the one—near all the lucky ones up front." Convict 45 locked eyes with the scowling man.

"Lucky?" a man further back asked, peeking his head over the shoulder of the scowling man.

"Back off," the scowling man said, scowling.

"Lucky!" Convict 45 proclaimed. "Believe me, you *wish* you were at the front of that line. Here's why—"

"I know I can't wait to get up there," the itchy man interjected from ahead, scratching furiously and showcasing a vividly bruised eye.

"—because when the axe man brings that axe down on your neck, a couple of things happen," Convict 45 said. The men listening raptly now somehow numbered nearly a dozen.

The scowling man replied, "Right. Your neck detaches from your head. You soil yourself copiously at that moment, and then a minute later, you die."

Convict 45 paused, considering this for a moment.

"You mean a second later," one of the prisoners behind the scowling man corrected.

"No, I mean a minute later. Your head stays alive after it's severed." The scowling man turned and admonished his corrector. "Your brain's alive. You can see and hear."

"Aw, that's hogwash! You can't hear no screaming in that basket, with them heads," another man added.

Convict 45 held his tongue. Despite maintaining his smile, a vein on his temple pulsed. He was not used to holding his tongue. Allowing others the opportunity to speak was nearly unbearable.

The scowling man turned fully to the doubters behind him. "Look, I didn't say that they scream, now, did I? I said they can see and hear. Without lungs and breath flowing from your lungs up your throat—which is now severed—you can't talk, can you?" He let his sarcastic query hang in the air for a moment before finishing his lesson. "That's just science."

"Ah, *science,* you say?" Convict 45 pounced, pointedly avoiding the eyes of the scowling man, who had turned at 45's pronouncement.

"Yes, that's a well-known—"

Convict 45 cut off the scowling man, who became less a scowling man and more of a confused man. "Here's some *science* for you: When the axe man drops his blade, that blade gets duller with each man."

A volley of low gasps emanated from the gathered crowd.

"I suppose that's true," the confused man admitted, a hint of his scowl returning.

"So, each man in front of you is taking away your chance for a clean, painless cut!" Convict 45 declared, his voice rising.

The confused, scowling man's attempt at a reply was drowned by the rising murmurs of the crowd behind him.

"And I'll tell you what else is science!" Convict 45 elevated his voice further, exhorting the crowd's murmurs into outright grumbling. "The more men in front of you, the more of their *shit* you have to kneel in!"

That was all the rest of the line needed to hear. They surged forward, even the confused, scowling man, who had resumed exclusively scowling. Convict 45 moved neatly aside to let them pass.

In no time, he found himself standing alone at the back of the line, which now resembled more of a mob. Pushing and shoving began in patches throughout the crowd. There were men jumping up and down, trying to catch a glimpse of the gallows in the near-distance. The condemned were jostling each other for a closer position. At one point, a fistfight erupted on the platform itself, and the executioner had to break it up. The four guards at the back gate shared mystified looks, then abandoned their posts and waded into the crowd to restore order.

Convict 45 slowly walked backward, watching his handiwork. When he found himself at the unguarded rear gate of the city, he quietly let himself out.

The setting sun warmed his back as he strode away from the city-state of Asluggoth. His work here was done—the country was restored to the same chaos that had defined his tenure in charge. Convict 45 had heard that Arclantic City was faring well these days. He figured it could use a little greatness too, and he aimed his steps in that direction.

ABOUT MICHAEL JAMES WELCH

Twitter @mikexwelch

Michael James Welch is a proud Western New Yorker, an even prouder snowflake, and above all, husband and father to a wonderful family. His first novel, PrOOF, will be published by Inkshares in 2019-20. He feasts on your derision and bathes nightly in your disdain.

ART IMITATES

By Cari Dubiel

Pete Patterson was a bestselling author, but it wasn't because of his talent, as he had none to speak of.

His success, rather, came from the fortunate confluence of his last name's association with those of several other bestselling authors. Pete had wondered, when he sold his first book, if he should use a pen name, but his agent said no. "It's your name. Take advantage," Claudia told him. So he did, and it worked.

He rested his head on the train window and watched the American West go by.

"Leave it, Pete," his ex had said. Anastasia—he could still see her pretty, fake face. "You're making money, aren't you?" That was why they were exes now. She could have soothed him, reaffirmed him, told him the book was good on its own merit. But she hadn't even read it. The truth was that she did not read. She spent her free time scrolling through Instagram and cooking elaborate meals based on the posts in her feed. Pete considered this a valid pastime, especially when he became the recipient of said meals, but he couldn't help feeling disappointed at his latest launch party. She talked about herself the whole time, trying to dazzle his editors as he faded into the background.

His first book sold so many copies that he contracted for another, and another, until he built enough courage and money to leave both Anastasia and his soul-sucking job. Pete told her he'd pay his half of the rent for the rest of the lease, and then she'd need to find a new place. This seemed fair. Anastasia seemed indifferent, and he wondered if he shouldn't have bothered with the courtesy.

So he was homeless now, but not in a bad way. He was, for the moment, a resident of this Amtrak train, bound toward Wyoming. He was kicking around this idea for a Western—

so far he'd written thrillers, like those other guys named Patterson. He didn't know what Claudia would think of the new idea, but he had the money and time to experiment.

Wyoming would be his taste of freedom. He'd flown to California, sure, and had stopped in airports along the way, but he'd never traveled west of the Mississippi on the ground.

Pete had always dreamed of this. He felt like Paul Sheldon in *Misery,* before all the bad things happened. He was disappearing, going off the grid, becoming part of a different world. He imagined it: up each day at sunrise, contemplating the vast landscapes before him, mesas and mountains and primal energy. Fueled by nature and coffee, he'd write for several hours, lulled into peace by the sound and feel of his fingers on his laptop keys. He'd read—the classics, the new masterpieces. He'd disappear for a few hours, then walk into town and eat an expensive dinner every night. He might meet a woman, but if he didn't, that would be okay. He might learn tai chi, but probably not.

The best parts of life, Pete thought, as he ignored the snuffling and shuffling of the other passengers on the train. He hurtled toward happiness. Where the real Pete Patterson, man of talent, would emerge.

When Pete did emerge—from the train—he wandered the station. He hadn't realized that it was difficult to get anywhere in Wyoming.

One must have access to a car. No public transportation, and few towns were walkable. The towns were also hours apart. He didn't want to rent a car—he had money now, but he wasn't made of it. Uber and Lyft were nonexistent, as was the signal on his phone. So Pete ended up taking an expensive taxi to a motel instead of to that remote cabin. He ate dinner every night at the Denny's next door.

He did like being free of the day job, that endless slog of hours sacrificed to the gods of industry. Before the bestsellers, he had written briefs for technical manuals—each word he typed sucked more creativity from him. At night he'd tried to stay awake to work on his fiction, his vision swimming as he beat back exhaustion. It had taken months to complete that first novel.

Here, in the motel, he had the time to spend on the new project. He should have drafted quickly, effortlessly, pages filling almost of their own accord.

Except they didn't. Which was how he found himself at Keara's table.

He noticed her the first night at the Denny's. She wore a name tag that read "Becky," so naturally, Pete assumed that was her name. "Thanks, Becky," he said when she refilled his Coke.

"Don't believe everything you read," she said. "It's Keara."

Pete could tell when people were damaged. Keara was on the clearance rack. Her black polo was discolored at the sleeves, and her shorts were frayed. He thought it was the same outfit every day, washed maybe once a week. Pete liked her raw scent, though—it wasn't body odor so much as body character. Keara wore her challenges like armor.

As time went on, she started jutting her sharp chin at him when he asked for things. "You're here enough, you ought to get it yourself."

Her skin was sallow and white, papery-thin, her hair a sick but natural blonde. Pete thought she was beautiful. Or she was beautiful once, maybe in a different way.

Maybe Pete only wanted sex. It had been a long time. Anastasia had lost interest in him long before the official breakup, and he'd been writing intense stuff. Sexy scenes. He was glad his mother would never read the final product—not because she was dead but because she thought his writing was trash. And she was right, of course. Mothers are always right.

Pete was thinking of his mother the night he asked Keara a personal question. "You have kids?" He immediately regretted it—heat crept up his neck—and then he tugged at his collar.

She stopped, holding her coffee pot as if to pour it on his lap. "No," she said, crisp, and moved on.

God, he thought. *Peter, you are a fuckup.*

A few days later, Keara slid into the booth beside him. Her skin stuck to the pleather, came free with a snapping sound. Wyoming was hotter than Pete had reckoned. He was in the West, so he was trying to use words like "reckon."

"My name's not Becky," she said.

"I figured." Pete swiveled his straw in his empty Coke glass. "Sorry I asked about kids."

"Figured that was a roundabout way of you asking about my marital status." She wiggled her hand. "You haven't noticed my naked finger."

He shook his head, mumbled.

"You noticed?" She perked up.

"I'm a writer. I notice stuff." Burning collar again. *Shut up, Pete. You are not important. Stop pretending you are.*

"Whatya write?"

"My books are on the Publishers Weekly list." He had to rationalize. Always.

"Don't know what that means." Keara sat back, appraising him. "Doesn't mean I'm stupid, though. I read. Just don't know about lists."

"Lots of people bought it." Sweat beaded on Pete's forehead.

"Tell me what it's about. I like to read. Helps me escape from this shit." She waved her hands around.

Pete's legs twitched. "I'll do you one better." He reached into his satchel. "I'll sign you one right now."

Keara clapped once. "Joy. Now I can check out the back flap."

He scribbled in the book—his latest—and handed it to her. She examined the cover, the summary, his photo. "You spelled my name wrong."

"Sorry." Pete figured he should start pricing train tickets. He could go to San Francisco. That was where his parents met.

She shut the book and stood. "I'm not kidding. Next time you get your own coffee."

Pete didn't want to get his own coffee.

He didn't want to like Keara. He did and he didn't. She was rough but precious, like a dirty gem. He wondered if things would be different if he could take her to a bar, get her liquored up. Take her out of this place. But she seemed relieved to be rid of him each night when he paid his check.

So he decided to leave. Wyoming had been an interesting detour, but it was time to move on. He could write his next book somewhere else.

But on the night before he planned to check out of the Rodeo Motel, he noticed a long, pink welt on the back of Keara's thigh.

It ran all the way up under her black cargo shorts. He stopped himself from imagining the rest of it, how it continued. *Everything ends,* he thought. *Everything begins.*

Pete made eye contact with Keara as she approached him at the high bar. "What's up with your leg?" he asked her.

She startled, as if no one had ever noticed that piece of her anatomy before. "It's fine."

"Clearly, it's not."

"Kitchen burn. Don't worry about it."

"Not worried. Just wondering if there's a story."

"You're always looking for the story." She blinked. "Some crazy shit in that book of yours. You related to that other Patterson guy?"

"Nah." Question of the day. Maybe he'd write the next one under a pen name despite Claudia's objections.

"Well, I liked it. You're a good writer." She reached for the coffee behind the counter, but he shook his head.

"Just Coke is fine, thanks." *You're a good writer.* Words he'd never heard from Anastasia or his mother.

"Okay. I'll keep this pot for me." She winked. "Maybe I'll tell you tomorrow."

"Tell me—" He was about to say *what,* but she walked away before he could finish the sentence.

That evening, Pete extended his stay. One more night wouldn't hurt. He could get in another solid eight hours of writing before the train ride to San Francisco.

The next day in the motel, he drummed his fingers on his laptop, staring ahead at the generic painting stuck to the flat white wall. His lead female seemed off somehow. Too close to the ones from the other books. Flawed, yes—all characters were, they had to be—but his women were flawed in the same predictable ways. He wondered if, as a man, he could truly write from a woman's point of view. What did he know about being inside a woman's mind? Most of his readers were men, and did they care?

Maybe he needed to stay longer. Talk to her more. Get into her psyche.

That evening, he slid onto the bar stool beneath the lemon lights. Keara was freshly washed. Laundry day, it must have been. But she said nothing to him beyond the usual niceties.

"I'm leaving in an hour," he said, as he scribbled in a generous tip. "Taking the train to San Francisco."

"You just got here." She winked.

"Yeah, well. Gotta get on to the next thing." Pete waved, then stepped into the night.

With nothing better to do, he sat with his bag on the bench outside the Denny's. The warm breeze brushed his cheek. *You should be writing, you asshole time-waster. God. You throw time away like you'll get it all back. You get one chance.*

Keara came outside, lit cigarette in hand. "It's not goodbye yet."

"Apparently not."

She sat, her smoke trailing into the open air. "I need to tell you something, Pete. It's important."

Her voice had changed timbre. Not as jokey or twangy as before. Pete sat up straighter. "Are you looking for a woman who wants to be saved?"

She leveled her gaze at his. Didn't blink. He couldn't hold it, and he looked away.

"That's what I thought." Keara lifted her cigarette away from her lips. "If you want my story, you better be willing to take a risk."

His heart picked up speed. Did he care that much? He wasn't sure what he cared about at all. He'd thought he was better alone, but maybe that wasn't true. He just needed the absence of Anastasia.

"I'll ask you again," he said, nodding to her leg.

She grimaced. "Look. The man I live with—it's not good. I work so far away, at least I can get away for a few hours. I keep thinking one day I won't go back."

"Of course not.". It was so simple: why stay with someone who would burn your skin—literally? He pictured a lick of fire running along the back of Keara's thigh. "Come with me. I'll get you out of here."

"I knew you wanted to rescue me." She grinned, maybe for the first time. He saw that her face had kindness in it, a soft patch behind the rocks. "It's tough to be a woman. Men make so many assumptions."

"Sounds like an assumption."

Keara flicked her ash onto the ground. "If you want to know what I'm about—come home with me. You wanted a real Western experience, right?"

He did want that.

"You ride home with me tonight and I'll tell you everything." She turned to him, and her face was open and hollow. Pete felt her desperation. "Maybe you'll put me in a book."

He called Amtrak and said there was a family emergency, and they bought it. He wasn't about to lose money on this... whatever it was. He changed the ticket to Wednesday—maybe he'd be the white knight she needed, and they'd consummate a torrid affair in the motel he'd come to know.

Pete shook as he climbed into her car. With excitement, or maybe the secondhand smoke was giving him a buzz. The '89 Buick stunk with it. A primeval navigation screen dominated the center console. She fired it up. "It runs clean," she said. "Most people drive trucks, so cars go cheaper."

The night was pitch here, no streetlights. Winding, signal-less roads. Keara took the curves with practiced ease. She breathed hard, and Pete gripped the molded plastic of the passenger door.

"So, the thing is, I'm taking you to Trading Post. Where I grew up."

"Okay," Pete said. *It's all material,* he thought.

"It's a real Western town. With real Western shitheads." She rolled down the window and spit. "Pete, it's not cool there. I need you to help me."

Pete wasn't good at helping anyone besides himself, and even then, he wasn't what he'd call competent.

"Okay," he said again.

"I've been living with my best friend and her boyfriend, but it isn't working." They rolled around another corner, and Pete shut his eyes. Would it be rude to fall asleep? "They keep me locked in the basement. If I don't come back by curfew every night, they torture me."

Her leg. "How do you mean?"

"Whatya think?" Keara gritted out the words. "Do me a favor. Light me a cigarette. Pack's on the center console."

He'd noticed. She was never far from her cigarettes.

Lights came on, slowly, as the mountain road gave way to a semblance of civilization. Keara's cigarette tip flared in the dusky dark. He pressed his hand to the glass, looking out like a child. They slowed on the main drag. Pete saw saloons—honest-to-goodness saloons. This wasn't a real place. Pete had imagined this, and it had come to life, complete with the girl to save.

"So what do you need?" It made no sense. If they were torturing her—why did she go back? He could have taken her to the motel room just as easy. Taken her away on the train.

Keara pulled the Buick into a gravel lot between two huge-ass trucks, the kind guys pimp out to show the world how big their dicks are. She turned off the ignition. "Shotgun in the barn." She pointed. A lone, warm lamp burned inside a compact stable. Pete heard the agitated stamp of a hoof.

He frowned. "Continue?"

"It's not rocket science. You're a smart man. Shoot when it's time. Then run away, take the Buick. I'll leave the keys." She hoisted herself out of the driver's seat, turning the last of her cigarette to ash under her heel. "You'll be gone, I'll be gone. We'll never see each other again. No different from a few hours ago, right?"

He eyed her across the top of the car. "You haven't convinced me. Why come here at all? Why not just run away?"

"Trust me. It will be worth it." She sashayed toward the house, jutting her hip back toward him.

He crunched across the gravel to the tiny barn. It wasn't even a complete shelter for the animal inside. The horse was a pony, really, and not well-fed. Its ribs stuck through, poking at its fur.

It neighed at him—*interloper!*—and he scrambled to find a place to hide, something to duck behind. A stack of hay and farm implements. The animal musk surrounded him. He grabbed a handful of straw and offered it to the small horse, to make peace.

It chewed. Perhaps it had gotten used to being hungry. But why, when there was so much hay here?

Pete thought of Anastasia, making so much food, eating hardly any of it. She was probably at home in their apartment on her own, entertaining male company. Some guy was sitting at their glass-block table, chowing down on so much meat, while she ate a grape and a lettuce leaf.

He eased himself up on an elbow. The shotgun hung on the

wall, as Keara had described, and maybe it was loaded. He couldn't be sure. His experience with a gun was limited to one time in high school when his buddy had dared him to shoot his dad's pistol. He hadn't been able to figure out how to load it, so the gun had laid there, silvery and unimportant—an object.

Pete crept to the wall and lifted the shotgun away from its hook.

It had a nice weight, a heft, and he did feel a bit of that excitement he'd hoped for when he got on that train. Maybe, probably, it was loaded?

Pete felt, suddenly, like a prisoner.

He swallowed. He wanted to go home.

He took the shotgun to the outside part of the stable, where an awning extended over a concrete slab. The slab faced a house, a large single-panel window, where he could see into a kitchen. Keara sat at a table beside a slight woman and a bulky man. This must be the couple holding her hostage.

He watched for a few minutes. Mostly, he watched Keara. Did she look scared? Her range of emotion had befuddled him from the beginning. She'd gone from bitchy to warm to bossy to back again. Maybe she was a sociopath. Maybe she'd lured him here for some other purpose. It was stupid of him to think he could save her, anyway, even if that was the reason he was here.

Pete heard his mother's voice. *What are you doing, reading again? What kind of little boy reads all the time? Are you ever going to learn to be a man?*

Keara stretched her neck, swiveled it back in his direction. Maybe she'd seen him.

Pete took a big breath and slung the gun up to his shoulder.

Something about this didn't add up.

Did Keara really think he would shoot someone he didn't know? To be some kind of vigilante, some knight in armor? A cowboy?

Anastasia had wanted him to be there for her, but that was it. Like an ornament, a decorative water feature. Something she could say she had, something she could look at. She didn't care what he did with his time, what they talked about. Her reaction to his departure had been lukewarm at best. He supposed that what he wanted was a woman who paid attention.

Keara was not that. Her plan was half-assed. Why had he let himself get drawn in by her Western allure? She wasn't his muse. She was herself, an individual, and this wasn't a rescue. This was something else.

Pete looked back into the barn, with his twitchy pony. He put the gun down.

He imagined what would have happened if he had fired. Glass spraying everywhere, yelling from the house. His shoulder aching from the blowback.

Pete loped to the Buick and slid into the driver's seat. He fumbled for the keys.

Then he heard shouting. A man raced toward him, his face twisted. Keara was silhouetted in the dim light, her blonde hair a waxy halo. "Coward!" she screeched, shouting at his back.

Pete reversed and pressed the pedal to the floor. The car spun out, wheeling back along the road, his only way to the next thing.

He found a road, and another, and another, driving wherever he could find roads, following them wherever they went. Drove until he found a gas station, where he rested until the sun peeked over the horizon.

In a way, he got off easy.

His stuff was all in the car. He hadn't gotten shot. And he wasn't the type to kill a man, besides on the page. Not on the word of a flimsy waitress, anyway. There was the welt, but she'd probably burned her calf on her own, and it wasn't enough evidence for revenge.

He only wanted to go home... but he was homeless. At least for the moment.

Pete got gas and directions to the Denny's. Then he left the car there and got on a new train. As if Trading Post had never happened.

He had been trying to figure out what really had been going on at that house, under that awning. What that shot was really supposed to accomplish. He wasn't sure—maybe he'd figure it out—but he didn't believe anyone was holding Keara captive except herself.

Pete went to San Francisco and rented a place month to month. He couldn't afford this city forever. He wasn't looking too far ahead, though. He explored the Wharf, Chinatown. He took a tour bus across the bridge. The wind was surprisingly cold.

He typed in the new apartment, sitting at the window, looking out at the steep hills, the tiny expensive houses. He was focused.

Pete completed the new manuscript and turned it in. In a subplot, a waitress named Kira—he'd oh so cleverly altered the spelling—was being held captive by a villainous man. Or so she said. Kira was holding another woman captive, and the hero saved her by shooting Kira. "It didn't make sense," the hero said, by way of explanation. "If someone was holding her captive, why did she work in a town forty-five minutes away? She had another secret." Kira died, bleeding out on a concrete floor.

Claudia read the book and demanded changes. Pete responded with a list of new potential pen names.

ABOUT CARI DUBIEL

Twitter @caridubiel

Cari Dubiel juggles writing, librarian-ing, mom-ing, and bassooning in Northeast Ohio. Her novel, *How to Remember,* is in production with Inkshares. She is a past Library Liaison to Sisters in Crime and the co-host of the ABC Book Reviews Podcast.

ASPIRANT

By Becca Spence Dobias

"Sister Trái đất thơm?" Sister Yêu asked in her calm Vietnamese accent.

Julie had received her new name, which meant "Fragrant Earth," when she'd accepted the mindfulness trainings. The other sisters, mostly Vietnamese, had oohed and ahhed over the moniker, but the young woman had been slightly disappointed. Her native language was English, and "fragrant" didn't necessarily have good connotations. "Fragrant Earth" made her think of the heaping landfill down the street from her family home in Victorville, a city of about 120,000 in what felt like the middle of nowhere, Southern California. The other sisters had gotten names that meant things like "Open Heart" and "Pure Soul." Julie—no, Sister Trái đất thơm—wasn't sure why the Elder nuns thought she was some smelly dirt.

Sister Trái đất thơm looked around at the room full of young people, all eighteen to thirty years old, who had come for the monastery's annual young adult retreat, and smiled back at their smiling faces. Even to these people, who had chosen to come to a five-day mindfulness retreat, she knew she was a freak—though she was twenty-two, she was most certainly not one of them. They saw her as something cute and quaint—like a little mouse—something to be taken care of and to gain wisdom from. Like a little Yoda or something. She knew—it was the same way she had seen the monastics when she'd first arrived.

"Sister Trái đất thơm," Sister Yêu repeated patiently. "Will you create the Facebook page for our young retreatants?"

"Of course," Sister Trái đất thơm said, snapping back to her present moment awareness.

"Thank you, Sister." Sister Yêu bowed to her, then turned

back to the retreat-goers. "In this way, you will be able to remain connected to each other, and, we hope, to your practice. When you use Facebook, you will be able to take a mindful breath and say to yourself, 'My dear, breathe. You are online."" Sister Trái đất thơm smiled slightly, remembering how lame the mantra had sounded when she'd first heard it.

"Will you add me as a friend?" Aaron asked. He was tan and muscular, and his scent was oddly familiar and attractive. Though he was from San Diego, he felt very East Coast to Sister Trái đất thơm—no-nonsense, tough but kind, a dry sense of humor.

"I will," Sister Trái đất thơm said and smiled. She reached a hand up to feel her bald head, then re-centered herself in the moment, noticing her feelings. She was attracted to Aaron—she had been all week. She could imagine his arms around her. He was so genuinely interested in what she had to say. She realized she was flirting—something she hadn't done since she'd begun the ordination process six months ago by submitting her letter of intent.

The feelings of guilt, of shame, swept over her immediately. *This is how you ended up getting raped,* she heard a small familiar voice in her head say. She was proud that a louder voice—the one she had been nurturing since she'd come to the monastery—said, *It's just a thought, Julie. Thoughts aren't facts. You're thinking.*

Aaron smiled at her. "Awesome!" he said. "I'll look forward to it." He paused and laughed. "I mean, I'll do my best to be in the present moment. But I'll be happy when you find me!"

Sister Trái đất thơm laughed too. He saw her as a person, not some sage. He could tell she was a regular person who had just decided to come here and do this. Maybe he could imagine her with hair.

The retreat was all but over. They had all gone home, save for two attendees, both young men, who were extending their stay.

I wish Aaron had extended his stay, Sister Trái đất thơm noticed herself thinking.

There was a lot of work to be done cleaning up the monastery, and Sister Yêu delegated the jobs. She walked between the aisles of monks and nuns, who were sitting in neat rows with their brown and gray and orange robes and tall backs, bowing to them and assigning them various duties.

She bowed to Sister Trái đất thơm and said quietly, "There is a folder in the office with the retreatants' names and contact information, for the Facebook group. You may use your old login information if you wish, but many monastics find this distracting. I recommend creating a new account. If you do decide to keep your account, I suggest you remove contacts besides very close family and friends, and change your name to reflect your dharma name."

Sister Trái đất thơm nodded and returned Sister Yêu's bow.

The office was a small room attached to the dining hall. Inside was a plain oak desk and a small filing cabinet containing emergency contact information for each of the monastics as well as the monastery's financial documents.

On the desk was a pencil, a pen, an old digital camera, a small black laptop, a telephone, and the folder Sister Yêu had described.

Sister Trái đất thơm sat in the metal folding chair, her back straight, and opened the laptop. The wallpaper was a picture of an ensō, the Zen brushed circle, with calligraphy inside that echoed the older nun's words. "Breathe. You are online."

Sister Trái đất thơm took a breath, feeling the cool air move through her nostrils and into her lungs, then reemerge, warmed by her body.

She opened the web browser and typed "Facebook.com." It was strange to see the familiar login page.

Should I use my old account? she wondered.

She sat, breathing, staring at the login screen, unsure. Sister Trái đất thơm recoiled a bit at the thought of her friends learning her dharma name. She imagined them at parties and bars, wrinkling their noses at the unfamiliar words.

It's not as if they know Vietnamese, she thought and entered her login information, surprised at how easily the password flew from her fingers.

Why aren't you more grateful? she scolded herself and then caught the thought.

I am being unkind to myself, she said internally, then, *I'm getting good at this. I am breaking old mental habits.*

There was a beat and then she scolded herself again. *Why are you so prideful?*

Her cycle of self-deprecating and self-congratulating thoughts was interrupted by the loading of her friends list and her own profile picture in the corner. Sister Trái đất thơm gasped. It was like looking at an old friend—someone very familiar, but definitely not her. In the picture, her hair was long and brown, freshly highlighted at the salon, a gift from her mom—when they were still on speaking terms. Sister Trái đất thơm was laughing and looking slightly off-camera. She looked young and carefree—wistful. It was so different from how she usually felt, and she looked so pretty. It had been why she'd picked it.

The next thing Sister Trái đất thơm noticed was how different the site seemed from the last time she had logged on over six months ago. It was just so...loud. There was so much information; it was jarring. She wanted to turn down the volume.

She clicked on her profile settings and selected the option to change her name, being mindful to watch her emotions as she did so.

I should change my picture too, she thought, but couldn't bring herself to pick up the camera. She laughed, imagining trying to take a selfie with her shaved head and robe.

She realized there were pictures on the monastery website, so she found one there that she was in. Sister Trái đất thơm sat for a minute, staring before she uploaded the photo, wondering at how different it was than the old one. She seemed barely recognizable without hair, and yet the face she was making was much more representative of her usual internal weather—serious but content, calmly scrutinizing her surroundings. It was somehow much more *her* than the other one had ever been.

Next, Sister Trái đất thơm went through her friends list, deleting names one by one. Each time, she felt a little pang of loss as she removed the person from her life. She said goodbye to each thumbnail picture, severing her window into their engagements and babies and travels and new jobs.

After a while, it became a meditation in itself as she entered a state of flow. *May you be happy and peaceful*, she said in her mind as she clicked the "unfriend" button and then confirmed when the site asked her if she was sure. It was a real-world practice of the loving-kindness meditation they practiced weekly at the monastery.

She only got stuck on one or two names—her boyfriend from high school—the one before her abusive ex. He had always been kind to her, and they had shared so much. Did he count as a close friend? After a brief pause, Sister Trái đất thơm decided it was time to let him go as well.

And then her mother. She was family, true, and she loved her, but the sight of her picture brought Sister Trái đất thơm pain. Her mother, who had refused to come to her trial or to come visit her at the monastery, who had told her "It's not rape if you're dating him." It was time to let her go too, she knew, so she did.

Back at the home page, Sister Trái đất thơm paused. What was she doing again? It took her a moment to remember, the specter of her discord with her mother clouding her mind. The space where a bit earlier she had been bombarded with information about her previous life now still seemed to pulsate with the energy of those contacts—like ghosts, she realized, hungry ghosts.

Sister Trái đất thơm glanced at the clock. An hour and

twenty minutes had passed. The work hour was over, and she was late for their afternoon relaxation meditation session. She slipped her brown sandals off outside of the meditation hall and walked as quietly as she could to an empty spot, setting her pillow down next to another young nun, a Vietnamese sister whose name meant "Opening Flower." Sister Trái đất thơm could never seem to remember the Vietnamese, so she just avoided calling her by name. The sister smiled quietly at her and she smiled back.

Sister Trái đất thơm could not seem to get settled. Visions of the blue website danced before her eyes as she tried to focus on her breathing and the soft dusty wood floor in front of her.

The next day, Sister Trái đất thơm returned to the office to continue her work. She felt refreshed from a night of sleep, a good morning sitting session, and a calm, peaceful lunch of the usual rice and vegetables.

This time when she logged in, the page was less distracting, already clear of her previous contacts.

Sister Trái đất thơm created a group, taking her time and mindfully writing the description. She plugged in the camera and breathed calmly as she waited for the photos from the previous week to upload. She picked a photo from the last day to be the group photo. Sister Yêu had taken it after the young adults had received the mindfulness trainings, and they all had joyful tear-streaked smiles.

Sister Trái đất thơm couldn't help it—she put her finger to the screen and traced it gently across all the happy faces until she came to Aaron's. Her heart beat quickly under her gray robe as she found him, smiling from ear to ear. She loved his smile. It was so warm and genuine. She wanted him to smile at her again. She almost ached, missing him.

What am I doing? Sister Trái đất thơm scolded herself, trying to recenter. She picked up the folder and pulled out the retreat attendee contact list, then typed each by name and requested them as friends.

A few accepted her invitation almost immediately, and Sister Trái đất thơm jumped, not from the notifications, but at the reminder about how different their lives were. They carried phones in their pockets that alerted them to everything, including friend requests. She was grateful to not be tied to her device like that anymore. Most, though, did not respond right away.

Still on a retreat high, Sister Trái đất thơm thought, remembering the feeling of returning to normal daily life after her first visit to the monastery.

She paused when she came to Aaron's name, took a breath, and typed it in. She found him easily—his profile picture was his smiling face. In this one, he was sitting under a large redwood. Part of her hoped he would reply immediately, but she knew he wouldn't. She sat for a moment staring at the "requested" icon before moving on to the next name.

Three days passed before Aaron accepted Sister Trái đất thơm's friend request. Each day, her breath quickened as she waited for the page to load. She tried to be mindful of her emotions as it did.

I am feeling impatient, she noted. *I am feeling hopeful.* Somewhere in those three days, she had stopped reprimanding herself for having those feelings.

When he finally accepted, it was better than she could have hoped. Not only was there a notification informing her that Aaron Rosen was now a friend—she had a message from him.

You found me! it read. *I'm so glad*

Sister Trái đất thơm didn't even think. Immediately, she responded, *Of course I found you!*

She sat staring at the screen again, holding her breath. It was several minutes before she realized she was completely absorbed in the waiting and completely out of touch with her mindfulness practice. When she came to, she shut the laptop screen immediately, standing up from the chair and backing up, as if she'd seen a wild animal. She caught her breath, determined not to get caught up like that again.

"Sister Trái đất thơm, may I see you for a moment?" Sister Yêu asked following the next morning's sitting session.

"Of course," Sister Trái đất thơm said and bowed.

She followed the old nun up the earthen steps to the office. As she climbed, she remembered the closed laptop. Was she in trouble for sending Aaron a message? Could Sister Yeu tell she had been flirting?

Sister Yêu stopped outside the door and put a wrinkled hand on Sister Trái đất thơm's shoulder.

"How is it going with the Facebook group?" she asked.

"It's okay," the young nun said, breaking eye contact for a moment. "I've found each of the participants and invited them. I think twenty or so have joined so far."

"I am very happy to hear that," Sister Yêu said, smiling. "Perhaps you can share some practice suggestions with the group—some advice from your own experience about bringing their practice back home into their daily lives."

"Sure," said Sister Trái đất thơm. "I can do that."

"Thank you," the old nun said. "Perhaps a week of this and then you can allow the group to grow organically, to bloom like a flower. You can check in every two weeks or so and resume your usual work duties on the other days."

"Okay, Sister Yêu," said Sister Trái đất thơm, both relieved and disappointed.

She had another message from Aaron. Sister Trái đất thơm didn't open it immediately, instead waiting a moment, staring at the notification, savoring the delicious feeling of anticipation.

Sorry it took me so long to accept, it read. *Just couldn't bring myself to look at a screen for a couple days after the retreat. I'm usually on around 9 if you ever wanna chat*

Sister Trái đất thơm's heart fluttered. She felt giddy. She remembered this feeling—not just a crush, but a crush who might like you back!

What am I doing? she asked herself again.

We're usually already in the dorms at 9, she typed back, and this time, little dots appeared immediately, indicating that Aaron was responding.

Ah yeah, he said. *Well if u ever can't sleep, I could use some advice*

About what? Sister Trái đất thơm asked.

I just don't know if I can do it here anymore, Aaron wrote back after a pause.

Do what? Sister Trái đất thơm asked.

Just be in the outside world. I'm like craving the monastery again

Sister Trái đất thơm sucked in a deep breath. Was Aaron saying he wanted to come back for a longer stay? The thought made her dizzy. Before she could respond, she saw the little dots wiggling again.

At that moment the office door squeaked open and Sister Yêu peeked her head in. "How is it going, Sister Trái đất thơm?" she asked.

The young nun jumped, startled out of her hyper-focus on the screen. After months of practicing presence in each moment, the hypnotic draw of a chat screen had totally overtaken her senses, and coming back to the room felt like jumping into cold water.

"It's okay," she said simply.

"Very good," Sister Yêu said. "Can you help me in the garden for a moment, please?"

Sister Trái đất thơm nodded and closed the laptop, this time being sure to exit the browser first.

Sister Trái đất thơm lay quietly on her back, her hands on her belly, feeling them move up and down with her breath. She listened to her roommates' breathing, quiet and slow.

When the noise had transformed into long deep inhales punctuated by the occasional snort and gasp, she rolled onto her side.

What am I doing? she asked herself for the third time in the last few days. She knew that regardless of her answer, she was going to go through with it. She remembered that feeling well from her pre-Buddhism days—knowing something was a bad idea, but knowing she was going to do it anyway. She had thought those days were behind her, but apparently, they were not.

Sister Trái đất thơm sat up slowly and dangled her legs over the side of the tall bunk, then lowered herself with her arms till her feet touched the ground silently. The door squeaked as she opened it, and she looked back, holding her breath, but the other sisters were motionless.

The office was dark—so dark she could barely see where she was walking, but Sister Trái đất thơm didn't dare turn on a light. She clambered around in the darkness until she found the desk. Feeling her way around to the chair, she sat carefully on the edge. She opened the laptop, and the blue glow illuminated the room. Sister Trái đất thơm hugged her arms, trying to shield herself from the creepy feeling of the space.

Hi, she typed. The dots appeared immediately.

Hi! Aaron responded. *I thought you'd be sleeping*

I usually am, Sister Trái đất thơm said. *But you said you had something to talk about?*

She remembered late nights in her father's living room, on the weekends she stayed with him, using his dial-up Internet and chatting with boys from school.

Yeah... Aaron said. *How did u know u wanted to become a nun?*

Sister Trái đất thơm paused, thinking, and then typed honestly, *I never really knew. I still don't know*

Hmm, Aaron said.

I just didn't know what else to do, she said.

That makes sense. I think I'm right there with u. I just don't know if I can commit

They talked into the night. Finally, Sister Trái đất thơm glanced at the clock in the corner of the screen.

OMG I have to go! Everyone's going to be waking up, she said, no longer feeling she needed to keep up the formalities people expected of her as a monastic.

I love talking to u, Aaron typed, and she grinned.

I love talking to you too, she said.

If ur ever out here in the real world will u come see me? he asked.

Yes! she typed, shaky with excitement. *I really have to go!*

It took every bit of her willpower to close the laptop.

It was light already, the sun peeking over the mountain.

She couldn't go back to the dorms now.

In spite of how tired she was, Sister Trái đất thơm felt refreshed.

It was good to lose myself—to get absorbed in something without paying so much attention to my thoughts. I didn't realize how tiring it's been paying so much attention.

"You're here early." Sister Opening Flower smiled as she entered the meditation hall.

"I couldn't sleep," Sister Trái đất thơm said.

Her friend nodded and put her pillow down beside Sister Trái đất thơm. The other monastics filed in. When they had all settled, Sister Yêu rang the bell and their meditation session began.

Sister Trái đất thơm held her eyes open wide, trying not to fall asleep.

"Sister Trái đất thơm, are you alright today?" Sister Yêu asked as the younger nun left the dining hall after lunch.

Sister Trái đất thơm did her best to smile. "Yes, Sister Yêu. I'm fine, thank you."

"I am happy to hear that. Can we speak again in the office?"

"Of course."

Sister Trái đất thơm followed the small nun around the corner and into the space she had spent the previous night. Her heart lightened with anticipation as she thought about talking to Aaron again. Imagining sneaking out again made her forget how tired she felt. Mentally, she counted down the hours.

"Sister Trái đất thơm, I have noticed you seem to be less present with us these last few days. I wanted to check in," Sister Yêu said.

Her first instinct was to lie. She was reminded of "come to Jesus talks" with her mom in high school. Her mother had always wanted to be the "cool mom," but Sister Trái đất thơm, still Julie then, always denied everything—the beer, the pot, the sex.

It had made it that much harder after she was raped. She knew her mom knew she wasn't an angel, but there was still this façade, this act. When she'd been pretending to be so innocent for years, how could she tell her mom she'd been too drunk to form the words to protest, as much as she had wanted to?

This was why she'd come here, right? To break old habits. The old habits didn't work for her. She was learning new ones.

"The work on the Facebook page distracted me," she blurted out, unable to meet Sister Yêu's gaze. "I need a different work assignment." The thought was painful.

Sister Yêu smiled. "It is natural to become distracted, especially by technology that is made to distract us. I think you should continue with this duty and use your distraction as your practice. Does this sound alright with you?"

Sister Trái đất thơm nodded. Sister Yêu reached a wrinkled hand toward hers and touched it gently.

"Is there anything else you'd like to talk about?"

Sister Trái đất thơm, still not able to look her in the eye, said quietly. "It isn't just Facebook. It's Aaron, from the retreat."

"Aha," the old nun said, knowingly. "This is also natural. Many monastics have encountered romantic and sexual feelings while pursuing this path. This is also something you can use as your practice. You do not need to fight these feelings, but rather you can let them be. Sit with them without acting upon them and breathe into the sensations this creates in your body."

Sister Trái đất thơm exhaled, relieved. "I should have known I could tell you about this," she said.

"It's alright, dear one," Sister Yêu said kindly. "Old patterns of mind are difficult to break."

Sister Trái đất thơm looked up at her, finally, and bowed. "Thank you."

"You are very welcome," Sister Yêu said. "But also," she continued, now holding Sister Trái đất thơm's hand firmly. "Remember that you are still in something of a trial period as a monastic. The monastic life is honorable, but there is no dishonor in deciding it is not the path for you. We do not usually accept initiates so soon after they have suffered a trauma like yours. Your letter was so beautifully written that we felt your decision to stay here was not based solely on a desire to escape. But this is why we have a process before full ordination. The monastery should be a place to find freedom, not entrapment."

Before Sister Trái đất thơm could answer, the old nun squeezed her hand tightly and left the office, leaving her standing, arm still slightly outstretched.

She opened the laptop slowly, letting Sister Yêu's words sink in. Was she just trying to escape? Did she really feel free here? She didn't know.

She was surprised to see a new message from Aaron, sent the night before, after she had signed off.

It said simply, *I really want to see u*

"Sister Yêu!" she called out. There was no answer. She ran to the doorway and saw Sister Yêu halfway down the stone steps. "Sister Yêu," she called again, and the nun turned. "Sister Yêu, I need to go."

Sister Trái đất thơm fought back tears as she hugged the other nuns. Her small bag was packed with her essentials—a toothbrush and toothpaste, a peanut butter sandwich, and a

$100 parting allowance from the monastery. She was wearing clothes from the lost-and-found box from retreats. She had tied a blue bandana around her bald head.

Finally, it was time to say goodbye to Sister Yêu. The old nun enveloped Sister Trái đất thơm's hands with her own and leaned in, touching her forehead to Sister Trái đất thơm's. "As you know, you may consider this a two-week break and come back to the monastic life if you so choose. If you decide not to return as a nun, though, please know you are always welcome here as a lay practitioner, Julie," she said kindly.

Hearing her name from the nun's lips seemed to breathe life back into it. She felt suddenly transformed and could no longer hold back the tears, which erupted as happy sobs. Sister Yêu hugged her tightly, and they laughed as Julie wiped snot from her nose. Happy tears, like those that had glimmered on Aaron's face as he received the mindfulness trainings.

"Julie!" Aaron was standing on the platform as she stepped down from the train car. He embraced her, and she started to cry again.

"I can't believe you're really here!" Aaron said. "I need to hear all about your decision."

He took her hand, and they walked toward his old Subaru.

"It's *so* nice to see you again," Aaron gushed as they pulled out of the station. "I know we don't know each other well. It's just been such a long time since I've talked to someone the way we talk."

"I know," Julie said. "You're the first person who's gotten it —like, understood the Zen stuff but still sees me as a real person."

Aaron smiled and glanced over at her, his brown eyes warm. His muscles were visible under the tight short sleeves of his worn gray Beatles shirt. She could hardly contain herself. How could things be this good? She could be attracted to him. She might even be able to act on it.

"So what are your plans? Do you know where you're staying

or anything?"

"My brother said I can stay with him for a while. I don't really know what I'm doing. Officially I'm still on a leave of absence from school so I might try to re-enroll," she said.

"You think you'll be okay going back to campus?" Aaron asked, concerned.

"I think so. I have the tools now with my mindfulness."

"So if you decide you don't want to…if it's too much being in the place where it all happened…" Aaron paused. "You can take over my lease."

Julie was silent for a moment, confused.

"Take over your lease?"

"I'm doing it," Aaron gushed. "I'm going back to the monastery." He glanced at Julie, his eyes wide, his lips pursed to contain a grin, excitedly gauging her reaction. "So next year, like, I'll be the monastic and you'll be at the retreat. Isn't that wild?!"

Julie's heart dropped. She felt dizzy. "Wow…" Julie said, her voice so low it was almost a whisper. Aaron navigated onto the freeway.

"You can have my phone. I'm giving it up now to kind of detox or whatever." Aaron's voice faded as he reached for the device in the center console, then pressed it into her palm. Julie's fingers closed around the phone slowly, and she retreated into her own thoughts. They started to spiral —thoughts of abandonment and injustice, hopelessness, despair. And then…she caught them.

They're just thoughts, she said internally. *You're okay. You're here. Right now.* She noticed the feeling of her body in the seat and the hard phone in her hand. She ran her finger over the smooth screen. She felt the sensations of her breath entering her nostrils.

"When are you going?" she asked. "I'm so happy for you," she said, and meant it.

"I'll visit." Julie smiled. They were sitting in the car at the entrance to the monastery. The long gravel road stretched up the mountain in front of them. This time, she was driving. "I'm not ready to go up the mountain yet. But I promise I'll visit."

Aaron hugged her tightly and held on while he spoke. "It's ok. I want the hike. It's kind of symbolic, isn't it?" He laughed. "The solo trek up the mountain." He pulled away but held on to Julie's arms.

"Thank you for being my friend," he said.

"Thank you for being *my* friend," she said.

"Thank you for getting both parts of me," he said, and Julie wiped at a tear under her eye. "Aw, sweetheart." Aaron pulled her close again. He took a deep breath. "This is a thing. I don't want you to think you're imagining it. This is real. Like *us*, I mean."

Julie nodded through her tears.

"We're both searching," Aaron continued. "We'll figure it out. I'll be right here. You'll know where I am."

They held each other for a long time, then without a word, Aaron got out and started up the mountain.

Julie watched him until he rounded the corner, then reached for the smartphone in the console beside her. She hadn't turned it on in the two weeks since Aaron had given it to her—in the wonderful two weeks they had spent together—in the two weeks where she had, indeed, been able to act on her attraction. She was ready to turn it on now.

Julie reached up and felt her fuzzy head—her hair was growing back—then held the button on the side, powering the phone on.

Her finger moved toward the phone icon and then hesitated, moving instead toward the blue F. Instead of clicking it, though, Julie dragged the icon to the top of the screen.

"Are you sure you would like to uninstall Facebook?" the phone prompted. She confirmed.

The young woman selected the phone icon now and let her fingers tap the number pattern they knew by kinesthetic memory. It rang twice. "Hello?" a familiar voice answered.

"Who is this?"

Julie's voice shook. "Mom?"

ABOUT BECCA SPENCE DOBIAS

Twitter @totallynotbex

Becca Spence Dobias grew up in West Virginia and now lives in Southern California where she writes hard and moms harder. Her debut novel, *Rock of Ages*, is in production with Inkshares.

THE MARKING

By Grace Marshall

With a deep breath, Cara gathered her strength and sat up from the pool of sweat and blood she had been lying in for the last hour or so. The newborn at her breast stirred with the position change, but then fell back into the haze of nursing. She looked down at the bloody mess surrounding her on the floor and hoped that the bleeding was over.

"This was not how this was supposed to go," she said to no one.

Gazing around the abandoned basement storage room full of discarded office chairs and rotting files, she gave herself a full thirty seconds to remember the time before the Grave-grinners. A time when her daughter would have been delivered in a safe, clean hospital room with caring nurses and careful doctors at the ready, and she could have slept while her baby was washed and changed and checked and measured. A time when imminent death was not a potential side effect of birth. A time when she wouldn't have had to chew through an umbilical cord to separate her baby from the still-warm placenta lying next to her, after a twenty-hour labor on the musty floor of a commercial basement.

Cara shifted the baby so she could cradle her with one hand, then reached for her backpack. She fished around until she found her only set of spare clothes and a large but thin blanket she'd found a few days ago. She shaped the blanket into a serviceable cushion and carefully laid the baby down. Tiny eyelashes fluttered as the baby decided whether to sleep or cry. Cara leaned in close and nuzzled the tiny nose. With a yawn, her daughter gave in and settled into sleep. Cara studied the new face she'd brought into a terrible world. The baby, she realized, was her whole universe, and her own life was now dependent on the peaceful rise and fall of that little chest. She had to protect her daughter, above all else.

Cara needed to move quickly, despite her entire being demanding sleep. With shaking legs, she stood, testing her body to see what it was capable of so soon after the Herculean effort she had put forth for the delivery. She paused, letting a wave of dizziness wash over her. Once it passed, she was grateful for how steady she felt.

She saw that she was still bleeding and rifled through her bags. She had stumbled upon a relatively well-stocked CVS a couple weeks ago, and she needed her drugstore supplies now. She poured some water on a rag and washed herself as best as she could. Tucking another bottle of water inside her bra to warm it up before using it to bathe the baby, she broke into a pack of fresh underpants and carefully lined a pair with several pads. After forcing down a couple of Tylenol and dressing her aching body, she gingerly worked on getting her newborn ready. Her fingers shook from both nerves and the unfamiliarity of the task.

She checked her watch. She needed to find the city, and she couldn't miss the Marking.

As Cara wiped her baby clean, she longed for her own mother. About a month ago, as they were following signs to the sanctuary city, they had run out of water. Her mother had told her to stay hidden in an alley and had gone off to try to fill their canteens. Less than five minutes later she had heard her mother scream, then the unmistakable crunching of bone. Cara had stood by helplessly as her mother was shredded. Afterward, the monsters had come down the alley, their rough, scaly flesh close enough to touch as they lumbered away. She still had nightmares about the tearing and grinding noises.

Once the baby was as clean as possible, Cara reached for the bag she'd been protecting more dearly than her food supplies. Opening it up, she pulled out a package of diapers and a pristine onesie with little sunshines smiling out at her from its soft white fabric. She dressed the baby, then pulled out the real prize: an infant carrier. She frowned at the instructions and carefully made sense of how to put it on securely. Finally, she had it on, and she lifted the baby into it. The baby cooed and nuzzled against her chest. She pulled out her last item—a pack of pacifiers—and slipped one into her daughter's angelic little mouth. Then she packed up everything she could fit in her backpack and used the rest to cover the mess she'd left on the floor.

With another deep breath, she walked up the stairs. It took much more effort than it usually would have, but her system was beyond taxed. She had managed to barricade the door at the top in between labor pains, and she now carefully unstacked the various chairs and old printers that formed her makeshift security system. With her hard work undone, she slowly opened the door a crack and listened harder than she ever had before. She counted to ten to slow her breathing.

One, two, three. Inhale.

Four, five, six. Exhale.

Seven, eight, nine, ten. Inhale.

Cara stepped through the door and prayed her baby would sleep. The city would only be a fifteen-minute walk if she didn't encounter any problems. She gave the pacifier a little push to make sure it was snug between those tiny, perfect lips. "We're gonna make it, I promise," she whispered, for both their benefit.

She walked as quickly as she dared across the empty office. Rounding a corner, she spotted the front door of the building and the security desk. She had headed for the guard station with a bit of hope; she was rewarded when she yanked open one of the drawers and a taser rattled into view. She carefully tucked it in the side pocket of her backpack and crept toward the glass doors separating her from the outside world. She knew it was unrealistic to treat the building as safer—she had certainly seen the Gravegrinners trample their way through walls to devour the Unmarked—but the familiar mental habit of walls meaning safety hadn't yet had time to fade.

Outside the building, she saw the same bizarre landscape that had settled into place several months ago. Everything looked exactly as it had, except that there were no people to be seen anywhere. A couple of cars were rotting in the street. A few windows were broken here and there. Everything looked mostly normal, just abandoned. It created a disturbing sense of safety, in a way.

Cara checked her watch. Only forty-five minutes until the Marking, assuming the sanctuary city hadn't lost the Marker or been overrun by Gravegrinners. As her mind began to spin through every terrifying reality, she reminded herself to breathe.

One, two, three. Inhale.

Four, five, six. Exhale.

Seven, eight, nine, ten. Inhale.

With her next exhale, she stepped through the door and onto the street. She stayed close to the walls as she walked as quickly as she could, not quite daring to run while the baby was sleeping. As she settled into the now-familiar rhythm of walking while keeping her senses on high alert, she allowed her mind time to wander.

Seven months ago, she had been safe in her mother's house, arguing with her boyfriend about whether to keep the baby she now cradled against her chest. He had always wanted to be a dad, but she still didn't feel prepared to be a parent. She had turned away from him to try to put her thoughts in order when she caught sight of something outside. It was a falling star. She closed her eyes and wished silently for the right answer about whether to keep the baby. When she opened her eyes, the falling star was still there, and getting larger by the second. Her eyes grew round with fear as she became certain it was going to hit the house. Instead, the meteorite landed with a crash in the middle of the street. Her boyfriend had also seen the incoming meteorite, and they both leaned against the window to get a better look at the impossible. The meteorite had created a crater in the road, and now something was crawling out of it.

The monster that emerged was as tall as a house, with four thick legs whose joints seemed to be able to bend in any direction. It was mottled gray with rough skin. Her boyfriend had turned and run away from the window, but Cara stood rooted to the floor and watched as her next-door neighbor ran out of his house, waving a shotgun around and screaming. The beast turned and descended on him. It was surprisingly fast, and the ground shook with each step it took. Her neighbor fired off at least three direct hits, but the monster healed as quickly as it was hurt. Then it opened its nightmarish mouth. Silver teeth gleamed in the moonlight, large and long with jagged tips. As the first row of teeth parted, row after row appeared behind, as if the creature had endless ravenous mouths. Her neighbor watched, paralyzed in horror, as the skin around the monster's mouth wrinkled up around its lips, pushing its eyes up and away from its skull in order to see its meal over rows of brutal jaws.

For a brief instant, a terrible stillness encompassed the scene. The monster struck as quickly as a cobra, snatching the neighbor into all those horrible teeth. His legs kicked with desperation as his muffled, panicked screams emanated from inside the monster's maw. As the last row of teeth sunk into the man's thighs, each set of teeth rotated around him in opposite directions, pulling him apart with steely efficiency.

Suddenly there was a crash, and she was covered in debris. She turned toward the sound and saw another creature staring down at her. She screamed in terror as it leaned toward her. Just above the horrible mouth were six dark, unblinking eyes and a small slit near the top of its head. The slit seemed to be sniffing at her. She felt a gruff exhale on her face and hoped death would come quickly. But then the creature brushed past her toward the kitchen where her boyfriend had gone to hide. She heard her boyfriend scream in the same terrified way her neighbor had, followed by wet tearing noises and a sickening sound like chicken bones in a garbage disposal. She stood frozen in shock and fear until finally she heard the thump of the monster walking away. She collapsed on the floor, sobbing with terror and grief.

The next couple of days were unlike any the world had ever experienced. She and her mother huddled in her basement, watching TV and searching the internet for information about what they should do. Slowly the story came together—the monsters, dubbed "Gravegrinners" by the news, had appeared all over the globe at the exact same moment. Witnesses described them falling from the sky as small meteorites that would then grow and become fully developed within a matter of seconds. They seemed to be choosy about their victims. Scientists worked to identify what the people who had been consumed had in common. One theory after another was developed and then discarded. People reported that they had been repeatedly passed over by the Gravegrinners. Demographic and genetic information was analyzed. Finally, one cluster of survivors in the same town all recognized one another from a support group, and that was when everything started to come together. Every single person who had been passed over by the Gravegrinners had watched someone die. Scientists discovered that people who had observed such a traumatic event had an alteration in their brain chemistry, and it seemed that the Gravegrinners could smell it. The research efforts that had been conducted to confirm this theory were truly nightmarish, especially since most of those who had not witnessed death were young.

Governments started building the sanctuary cities, barricading areas that were centered around survival resources like lakes, or farms, or stockpiles of weapons and supplies. When a sanctuary city was complete, they would post signs urging all survivors to make their way there as soon as possible. The reason was twofold—they wanted to save as many people as possible, and they were hoping to starve the Gravegrinners to death. The various military forces of the world had been working on developing a way to destroy them, but had come up empty-handed. They knew that the monsters didn't eat animals, plants, or anything except for certain humans though, so the strategy was to centralize their food source and eliminate it through a process they called Markings.

The first time Cara had heard about a Marking, she had been equally repulsed and impressed. It was an elegantly logical solution to the problem, but it was also a tragedy in and of itself. And the fact that most of those being Marked were children made Cara's heart hurt. Admittedly, she would rather children were scarred by a Marking than shredded by a Gravegrinner, but some people found the process of being Marked so unsettling that they chose to take their chances instead.

Suddenly Cara heard footsteps and was pulled out of her reverie. She looked around but there wasn't a store or office close enough to duck into. She spotted a car a few paces ahead on the road and jogged over to try the handle. Unlocked. She got in the backseat, locked the doors, and tried to hunch down. It was difficult with the carrier and her backpack on, and she was moving roughly because of fear. She jostled the baby into a crying wakefulness. Cara quickly replaced the pacifier while trying to make soothing sounds. Footsteps weren't inherently dangerous, but they weren't inherently safe either. She was far too close to getting her baby to the Marking to start taking risks now. She wanted to check her watch but was too afraid the movement might be seen outside the car.

As Cara frantically tried to calm her infant, she dared a quick peek out the car window. A woman was walking down the sidewalk, muttering to herself, and carrying an axe. The momentary pause in shushing seemed to upset her baby, who gave a loud wail of dissatisfaction. The woman's head whipped around and focused on the car. Cara knew when she saw the woman's eyes that she and her daughter were in danger. The woman smiled with crazed desperation and marched rapidly toward them. As the woman drew closer, she started to laugh, and lifted the axe above her head.

"Oh shit oh shit oh shit!" Cara screamed, giving a desperate thought to the universe that she really needed the keys to be in that car—she couldn't think of any other way to get her baby to safety. She slipped off her backpack and awkwardly climbed into the front seat, clutching her baby tightly. No keys in the ignition.

Suddenly Cara heard a crash and felt the car lurch. The woman had swung the axe down onto the rear window. It glanced off, but she brought it back up for another swing. The woman laughed maniacally. "Give me that baby to kill and I'll let you go! It only takes one to be Marked!" the woman yelled through the car window. She then reared back and brought the axe down on the car again. This time, the axe shattered the glass. The woman cackled at her success, then started chanting "Kill the baby! Kill the baby! Kill the baby!" as she continued to strike the car.

Cara started to get out of the car, thinking she could run for it, but the woman saw her reach for the door handle and sprinted around to the driver's side. "Kill the baby!" she bellowed, her anger overtaking her crazed glee. The woman brought the axe up over her head, and with a tremendous smash, broke open the driver's side window. Cara screamed in terror, and then her baby screamed. Her newly minted maternal instincts took over, and she remembered the taser in her backpack and frantically reached into the backseat. She found the weapon, aimed it at the woman, and pulled the trigger as the axe plummeted toward her. Two darts flew out from the taser and landed directly on the woman's chest. The woman immediately began to flail as the electricity struck her, and she dropped the axe and fell to the ground.

Cara didn't know how long the woman would be slowed by the shock. She reached down under the seat of the car to see if there was a tire iron or flashlight she could use as a weapon. Her hand hit something jingly and metal. She grabbed the keys, found the one for the car, and stuck it in the ignition. With a turn, the car grumbled to life, and Cara hit the gas.

Suddenly the car shook. Then shook again. Then again. She recognized the hope-breaking footfall of a Gravegrinner on a visceral level. She slowed to see if she could tell the direction it was coming from. It was in the rearview mirror. The Gravegrinner lumbered toward the woman on the ground and peeled back its rows of teeth into a smile of death. Cara floored the gas and headed toward the sanctuary city as quickly as possible, trying not to listen to the terrifyingly familiar cracking of bone echoing down the street. The woman's screams soon faded and then were cut off.

Cara risked a glance at her watch. She had ten minutes to get to the city and run to wherever the Marking was happening inside. She focused on driving, even though her baby was still screaming with a note of terror in her voice that gave Cara chills.

They rounded a corner, and there it was. Tall metal walls crowned with barbed wire formed an imposing barrier before her. She guessed that the wall was about a half a mile long and about three stories high. Armed guards patrolled, and a formidable artillery was stationed at regular intervals along the walls. Above the wall, she could see the edge of the plastic dome designed to dampen the smell of the Unmarked. She skidded to a halt and jumped out of the car.

"Help me! I have a baby! I need to get her to the Marking!"

As she leaned back into the car to grab her backpack, a guard unit jogged over. They surrounded her and escorted her up to the gate, weapons pointed outward. Someone inside opened a small door in the metal wall and pulled her in. "This way!" he said. They passed through a small airlock and then both broke into an all-out run. Cara clasped her baby's head to her chest, hoping she wasn't shaking her too much. They cut around a corner and went down another three blocks to a trailer surrounded by another set of metal walls and a plastic dome. The guards around the trailer saw them running and opened the gate. She practically broke down the airlock door in her hurry and fear.

Just as they ran through, they heard the stomping of Grave-grinners coming from outside the city. Gunfire erupted from the outer perimeter. “Keep running!” the guard yelled. He reached the door of the trailer and opened it, then turned and pushed Cara and her baby through. He slammed the door shut behind them, and a moment later Cara heard the gate close, slightly muffling more gunfire and an explosion.

The group assembled in the trailer turned to look at her. She carefully unbuckled the straps of the carrier and pulled her daughter out. “Come, bring her to the front,” a kindly woman said. The woman held her hand to guide her through the large group and helped Cara down to the floor. Cara guessed that there were about forty children in the crowded trailer. They were all gathered together in a tight group facing a chair on the opposite side of the room, where an old woman sat serenely. The younger children were all in the front, so they could see. The sounds of fighting grew louder, and the trailer shook. Some children started to cry, especially the toddlers and babies. Their parents tried to calm them, but looked frightened themselves.

The old woman in the chair spoke. “How old is your baby? She looks brand new.” The old woman wore a kind smile, and for some reason, that made Cara want to weep more than anything else that had happened that day.

“She’s about two hours old,” Cara said.

“Does she have a name?”

“Not yet. What’s your name?”

“Rose.”

“Then her name is Rose.”

The old woman’s smile was radiant with joy. “Well, then, let’s begin.”

A guard stepped behind the old woman. “Please be certain you and your children are all looking, even the babies. They may not know what they are watching, and they may not even be able to see it clearly, but as long as they are looking, it should work. Do not close your eyes. Do not look away. Watch until the end. This is the only way we can Mark you as safe."

"And don't cry. Just lead long happy lives, like I have," the old woman said.

With that, the guard pulled out a sharp knife. The woman smiled down at her namesake. Parents in the room held their children's heads so they were staring at the woman, even holding their eyes open so they couldn't blink.

One, two, three. Inhale.

Four, five, six. Exhale.

Seven, eight, nine, ten. Inhale.

The guard reached forward and with one deft stroke sliced the old woman's throat open, releasing a glimmering ruby waterfall of blood from her neck. The room went from silent to deafening as all the children—and some of the parents—started to scream and cry as they all watched her bleed out. As the last light faded from her eyes, the sounds of fighting outside stopped. The Gravegrinners were retreating. The promise of an Unmarked meal had been taken away, and they had no reason to attack the city any longer.

As everyone started to file out of the trailer, Cara sat still with baby Rose on her lap, staring at the lifeless shell of the woman who had saved her child. The woman had reminded her of her grandma, who had been the one to Mark her safe from the Gravegrinners. Cara thought back to that terrible day when she'd gone to her grandma's house after school to watch TV and eat ice cream while her mom was at work, and instead had held her grandmother's hand as she died from a sudden stroke on her way back from the kitchen with the bowls. Cara knew that, unlike her grandma, Rose had chosen to die. She did it in order to save children like Cara's. But as she looked into the flat eyes of the lifeless woman, Cara was overwhelmed with grief instead of gratitude.

ABOUT GRACE MARSHALL

Grace Marshall is an author, mother, and TV enthusiast. She writes technical documentation as her primary profession but has also been known to post randomly on her site escapeoftheinnermonlogue.com.

THE GRAVE ORDEAL OF JAWBONE JOHN SOUTH

By Daniel Lee

They say he was a tall man for his day, but slight and emaciated, pale and gaunt as a haunted night watchman. His eyes, they say, were sunken and sallow, and his beard like coarse white straw. At night he was said to give off a light of his own, and some suspected this the key to his gang's seeming ability to appear from out the nothingness and descend unexpectedly upon their victims. His age at the time of death could not be verified by any records of the day. Though some newspapers stated with confidence that he was forty-two, others claimed ages as young as thirty-five or as old as fifty. They say he was a charismatic man, raucous, quick to laugh and visibly content among friends, but cruel, prone to unprovoked bursts of violence such as the eleven murders with which he has become historically associated. But it's said too that he would confound his friends and members of his own gang with moments of tenderness and gentility befitting a man of an altogether different temperament. He would stand amid the trees of his adored Kentucky. His lips would move, yet no sound was heard. That he was famously criminal is known. That on his land no homestead was ever found is also fact. That he fashioned accoutrements from the jawbones of his victims, this too is true. And it is also true that from this peculiarity came his name: Jawbone John South.

South was an unmarried man, though in his book, *South of Hell*, biographer Jim Francis suggests that he was throughout his life enamored of only one woman, Caroline Kennedy, whose lineage is known and whose marriage to Henry Echolls of Owensboro, Kentucky, so broke South's heart that they say it was Echolls' jawbone that holstered his weapon.

The man's ability to pirouette about the law remains astonishing. Most of the crimes he's said to have committed occurred within only a hundred or so miles of Christian County, yet the man was never prosecuted. Indeed, one might suspect the lack of court documents pertaining to John or his crimes, and the relative inability or unwillingness of the local authority to take such a man down, to be in part responsible for history's swallowing up of so luminous a figure. In that way perhaps the law triumphed, for what is the life of a man such as South if forgotten? So titanic a force he seems to have been that it remains a wonder we do not speak his name in the same breath as Jesse James or Billy the Kid.

So it is that the particulars of his life have evaporated, and we are today left with little more than speculation and myth. Of his many alleged exploits, however, one above all has persevered. And it is principally for this anecdote that the man is remembered at all, at least among students, like myself, of niche history and of the bizarre. The story, they say, goes like this:

Two days before the Casper Heritage Bank robbery, the South gang was still mapping out the particulars. From the front door would enter a masked John South along with Cote Johnson and John's fellow Confederate veteran Absolum Solomon. The men would be armed each with his signature piece — John with his custom Smith & Wesson, with its wolf fang trigger, from out its jawbone holster — and would be backed by the lookout, Ely Carlson. The back exit would be covered by Jeremiah Jeroboam and the Native Sam Kintuck.

On the table still remained the matter of escape. This was, in general, the point of contention among the group. As the name among them, John was understandably perceived to be the principal quarry for any who might pursue them. So long, then, as the men were in his company, they too would be pursued. Still, the men were less than willing to split up and leave John the sole caretaker of the loot, and he in turn was uninterested in leaving it in their collective care until some supposed rendezvous. His will, of course, was seldom questioned, lest their jawbones too be made to hang from some adornment, their teeth strung like shells about his neck.

So it was that at that penultimate negotiating table the men dined, stowed away in the tool shed of Ely's uncle, some forty miles from Casper. By all accounts, it stank of must and awfulness. It was there that Ely and Jeremiah slapped cards on the makeshift table, hastily assembled from two sawhorses and an old door, and slapped hands on the back of young Cote. It was they who'd found the boy, they who'd introduced the runaway to John, a meeting that ended with young Cote's induction. It was he who now sat slurping up sofkee, scooping plate after plateful into his bottomless gullet, at which sight Jeremiah proclaimed, "The boy shovels more'n a gravedigger!" And it was then, they say, that John had his epiphany.

By all reasoning, it *was* a perfect plan, the men agreed, and nearly the whole of the following day was consumed with selecting a proper plot, subduing the groundskeeper, and digging the pit. The unearthed box was upturned over the hole and emptied of its occupant. As it was, it lay more than a foot shorter than John stood, and try as he might to construct an extension, old Absolum's carpentry skills left the thing still wanting in length so that in repose within, though his arms be at his sides, John's resemblance to the crucified Christ — with knees bent sidelong — was unmistakable.

With evening upon them, John acquiesced to the state of the casket, seeing as he would not be inside but for a couple few hours. Its walls were lined with newspaper, and that night John accepted from his men a toast to his ingenuity. He would, for all intents and purposes, vanish from beneath the nose of the law while his dispersed men knew exactly where he — and the money — would be, only to return when the coast was clear to exhume their captain and split the winnings.

The day came. A red sky. A sticky humidity. A chicken for breakfast. A two-hour ride into Casper. A round of beers as the clock hand ticked minute by minute closer to the changing of the guard, midday lunch.

One thing that can be corroborated is that there was, on that day, no changing of the guard. Casper Heritage records are surprisingly detailed on this point. There was to be no midday lunch. Instead, as morning became afternoon, and as John and his men watched from the sunbeam-striped saloon across the street, the one standing watchman became two, then three, then four. And from their perch no doubt the South gang perceived their opportunity lost.

How the bank knew to increase security remains a mystery. Had someone seen them enter town and announced their approach? Or, more apocalyptic to John, was there a traitor in his midst? Whatever words were whispered at that final negotiating table, whatever arguments made, John was not swayed. And at 4:00pm on July 18th 1885, the South gang rushed the Casper Heritage Bank.

The Native Sam Kintuck was shot dead before he even made it inside, the watchman's next bullet just grazing Jeremiah, his third sent astray as he was himself gunned down. And so the gang secured the back exit.

Across the front entrance there was an exchange of gunfire, a hallowed sea of flame igniting about the air between the men and in its settling upon the earth two guards laid out parallel, final expressions of agony upon their faces. And the remaining gang stepped them over, into the bank, wherein the last watchman was slain, its staff and clientele held at gunpoint until the money was brought out and handed over.

In this time several deputies had gathered outside, and with the emergence of the criminals another round of gunplay ensued. The men managed to mount their horses and begin their escape, though a momentary glance from Cote to one of the lawmen was all the confirmation John needed of his gut sense. He shot the boy dead right there on the street before turning and taking off at a gallop toward the cemetery.

Absolum, Ely, and Jeremiah stayed by him even as the pursuing horsemen of the law grew hotter upon their heels and the shapes of the headstones before them took on the qualities of silhouettes in the deepening twilight.

John stepped into the box and stood at the precipice as though a mutineer walking the plank above an empty ocean. He transformed into a folded up likeness, an origami man inside a little wooden house. He laid on his back, twisted at the waist so to curl up his legs to fit. He clutched the sack of money in his fist, stuffed in beside him as though it were the plush effigy of an animal joining him for the night's long slumber. Now he breathed in his last full lung's worth of fresh air, and perhaps briefly contemplated the seeming endlessness of the world about him in those moments before it was taken, and his universe reduced to that within the casket.

The lid was placed over him, one nail at a time driven into the walls of the frame. And the light of the moon was hidden as well, the world gone dark with that most crippling of all nights, content not only to blind but to deafen, and to keep from us the secrets of all the senses save touch, which serve only to reveal, moment by moment, inevitably, horror, if not in fact then in the mind's eye.

The box was lowered into the hole, allowed to rest directly upon what remained of its former occupant, and with a speed unknown to any of the three men before that night, the pit was filled, the soft soil shoveled without care until it reached the lawn. And then they stowed the tools, mounted their rides, and rode hard as the lights of the lawmen's lanterns appeared like fireflies at the edge of the trees.

And those lights gave chase with a heretofore unseen commitment, following the men well past their anticipated distance and into the night so far that it became day. Their backs were sore and their minds ill at ease with the thoughts of both the nature of their pursuers — be they human or something supernatural — and their captain, still interred in dirt, inert.

They decided to part ways, one man in each direction but that from which the lawmen came. It's a matter of record that Jeremiah Jeroboam boarded the 8:20 out of Slaughters headed north, doubtless trying for the state line. Absolum turned west, though his reasons are unclear. His home was in Stamping Ground, though it was surely not his intention to make his way there, not now. Ely made for his uncle's house some forty miles away.

It seemed the huntsmen required neither sleep nor moment's pause for sake of tracking, as the men fled in cold sweats across the longest, blackest country of their lives. There were strangers, perceived as chances along the way for salvation, invariably either avoided or frightened off, as the fugitives passed in the night, bleary-eyed and ravenous. Among these was Peter Panaticker, in whose surplus store Absolum nearly hid. Panaticker would later describe the man as ancient and reminiscent as some forgotten smell of myths from long ago, as though the walking husk of a dead god, a hollow tabernacle of whisky and ash that spun on its heel at the sight of the store owner, then stood swaying in the dark until the rain began to fall and he staggered away toward an oily horse tied at the post.

The train departed Sebree without Jeremiah, who doubled back and would have caught sight of three horsemen riding sidelong the locomotive, rifles upturned lances, blades like shark fins cutting through the downpour above the surface of the black mountains in the distance: bayonets.

It's unclear precisely when Ely decided as well to turn back. What is known is that he lacked his partners' luck, and when the lawmen returned to Casper they did so with his corpse, carried over their heads like a triumphant king returned from some victory abroad but prostrate and gored upon the serrated blades of their rifles.

What, in this time, must have transpired within John's casket? One might presuppose that those first anticipated couple few hours were themselves agony, for surely upon the driving of that final nail, let alone the dropping of the box into the hole and the subsequent covering up by six feet of soil, the ultimate quality of this plan must have become clear.

Suppose the men did not return. What then? Suppose they chose instead to wait out his air and appetite, wait out what remained of his life within that box, perhaps as vengeance for the death of Cote, and divide the money three ways instead of four. He must have felt himself a fool, and his decision a terrible, terrible miscalculation.

Upon the realization of his confined quarters, they say John began clawing at the wood, scraping and screaming to his last. And then, lungs emptied and voice chords shot, he lay alone, imprisoned and immobile, as though a child's pet passed on and buried in a cigar box in the yard. Perhaps buried before its time. How many, he must have wondered, of those lain to rest in the graves about him were not themselves fully passed at their lives' perceived terminus? How many awoke in the nights following their inundation to find themselves so trapped?

There are the stories of the paranoid who would insist they be buried with a string around one finger, run through the earth and attached to a bell above their graves. Thus, should they awaken to the horror of horrors, the ringing of the bell would sound their return. From these stories, they say, comes the expression "saved by the bell."

John South had no such string and no such bell. Perhaps his alleged bioluminescence made for something of a glow within the box, and perhaps, were that the case, this permitted him some little relief. But we must presume this was likely not the case, and that the man was shrouded in blackness like nothing he'd theretofore known.

Perhaps he calmed himself with the anticipation of the counting of the money, or with a rhyme, or with a popular song from his Rebel days:

Somebody's darling, somebody's pride,

Who'll tell his mother where her boy died?

But what games the mind must play upon a man in such a predicament. Hours passed. One wonders whether he was conscious of the time, and at what point he must have known the agreed-upon moment of his salvation had come and gone.

He began to hear a drumming reverberating down from

the surface like the footsteps of the multitudes, as though an army passed above him. It was raining. A sprig of lightning resounded within his chamber deep and loud, a shrieking voice transformed into the cries of the dead in the neighboring graves, and the sound of the sifting of the packed soil as it trickled in through the holes and cracks where Absolum's extension had been hastily fashioned — these like the repercussions of his neighbors' movements nearer him. Perhaps he imagined the coffin's previous tenant lying crushed beneath him, tracing his corroded finger along the bottom wall, searching for and finding its weak spots and cracks. He felt a tremor at his back.

He pressed his chest to the coffin lid, struggled to move. Clapped his palms to the side walls and felt the worming of the scavengers snaking their way inside the box. Drew his fists to his throat in fevered prayer and perceived the air, thin and stale, at last replaced with the stench of the dead earth outside. It was at that moment more than he could take, and he wrestled his fang-trigger gun from its holster, screwed the nose into his chin and squeezed, only to realize his last bullet had been made to rest within the skull of young Cote Johnson, and that from this nightmare he would find no such immediate reprieve.

And so, in this way, three days passed. It remains unclear whether the men were on the run for all that time or whether they had in fact tried to wait him out, never suspecting that after so long he could have still been alive. And indeed, on that morning of the fourth day, when the caked pounds of rotted soil were swept away by survivors Jeremiah Jeroboam and Absolum Solomon, and at last the sarcophagus exhumed, it was not a man emerged from that box but some other, alien creature, stinking of piss and pale like some amphibian native only to the subterranean world.

They say he was never the same after that. They say he scarcely spoke again, and then only under his breath. That children venturing near his property had the habit of disappearing. They say there were at night great holocausts upon his land, which on investigation revealed themselves to be the burning scourges of some spectral event, sent down screaming and wailing from out the fiery heavens, as though stones from out the fists of the Almighty. And those who bore witness to these remains would later swear that across the charred faces were still visible the indentations of enormous clenched fingers.

Who can say what cosmic war was waged within that pit? What foul condemnation or inevitable judgment took place that so incurred the wrath of the Great Unknown? He would dance naked about the smoldering craters of the fallen stars, howling and speaking in tongues, blaspheming. He would move through town, and men would step from his path. He became a local legend, a ghost story. So much so that after his passing, there was talk that perhaps even then he was not really gone, and that in the final cruel move of that providential chess game, he had been doomed once more to visit the grave a living man. Some go so far as to add that his casket was later disinterred by a group of curious youths who described an interior covered in scratch marks.

Absolum died but a month after the Casper Heritage robbery, allegedly of sheer exhaustion and stress beyond the bounds of what his aging heart could take. Jeremiah, with his cut of the Casper loot, moved to Alabama, where he married school teacher Henrietta Thatcher and made a life. He was shot dead at the age of fifty-two while again attempting a robbery of the Casper Heritage Bank.

And as for John South, by some his body is said to rest in the same plot, in the same cemetery, some say within the same box, as on those three nights in 1885. But by those who claim subscription to the story of its disinterment, it's said he rose from that place and for decades after still walked among the living, though whether as one of them or not, they cannot say.

ABOUT DANIEL LEE

Twitter @dannyboylee

Daniel Lee is the author of the novel AFTER DEATH, which won First Place in the Nerdist Sci-Fi Contest and is forthcoming from Inkshares. He lives in Los Angeles, where he makes his living as an editor of movie trailers. See more of his work at Dan-Lee.net

WENDELL, WENDELL, & WENDELL

By Patrick Edwards

"I think I have a plan..."

Wendell looked at the two companions on either side of him, both also named Wendell, and then back down at the digital city map display on the table.

"Wendell, can you—"

"Which one?" said the Wendell to his left.

"Oh, yeah... I guess we should come up with nicknames or something."

"I like that idea," said the right-side Wendell.

"Well," said middle Wendell, "I made the machine that opened the first portal... so maybe I should be Wendell One?" He looked at Left Wendell. "And that'd make you Wendell Two?"

"Hell no, not numbers," grumbled Left Wendell. "It sounds like we're just copies of you. And besides, we both had machines that split open doorways between parallel universes... that's the only reason yours worked—it had mine to connect to."

"But yours acted as a grounding unit," countered Middle Wendell. "*Mine* opened the door. And you didn't even build yours. Your brother—*our* brother, Kevin, is the particle physicist in your world."

"*Was* the particle physicist, remember? He accidently sliced himself into a thousand pieces messing around with this parallel dimension crap."

Right Wendell reached around the middle one to rest his hand on Left Wendell's shoulder. "Sorry to hear about your loss of our brother, man."

"Yeah... it's okay." Left Wendell sniffed and let an awkward chuckle slip. "He was kind of a pretentious dick, though. Not that he should've died or anything, but still..."

"I hear you," said Middle Wendell. "My Kevin is a concert pianist. Talk about pretentious dickery..."

"My Kevin is a writer," said Right Wendell.

"Damn."

"You win."

"We still need nicknames," said Middle Wendell as he adjusted his wire-frame spectacles. "I'll be Glasses Wendell." He looked Left Wendell up and down, focusing on the well-manicured landscape of facial hair.

The owner of that facial hair rolled his eyes. "Sure, I'll be Beard Wendell."

"Okay, back to the plan," said Glasses Wendell, "So Beard Wendell and," he nodded to his right, "Handsome Wendell will enter the—"

"Wait! Why the fuck is he *Handsome* Wendell? We all look the same."

"I don't know, look at him..." Both Glasses Wendell and Beard Wendell looked at the Wendell on the right. "There's something about him, he's tan and..."

"Damn," said Beard Wendell, "you're right, I can't put my finger on—Hey! Dude, did you get a nose job?!"

"No!"

"Oh wow, you did," added Glasses Wendell. "That is not our natural nose."

"It wasn't a *nose job* nose job! I broke my nose and my septum got messed up. I needed surgery to breathe better..."

"I vote we call him Nose Job Wendell."

"No chance in hell are you calling me that... I feel like we're skipping over the obvious. Just call me Gay Wendell."

Beard Wendell and Glasses Wendell cringed.

"Uh," said Glasses, "I don't feel comfortable with that..."

"Yeah," said Beard, "that feels wrong."

"Of course we support you and think that's totally great..."

"Oh, hell yeah. Totally supportive... The dudes of your world are lucky."

"Guys, seriously? I'm gay. It's okay. This is me, a gay man, telling you it's fine to call me Gay Wendell. How can that be offensive?"

The other two looked at each other and then back at him.

"You know what?" said Beard. "I think Handsome Wendell works just fine."

The newly minted Handsome Wendell rolled his eyes. "Whatever. Let's get back to the plan."

Glasses pointed at the map. "We need to get to the machine before Evil Wendell—" He glanced left and right. "We cool with that name?"

"What about Shitty Wendell?" asked Beard.

"Oh, I like that!" said Handsome.

"Fine," said Glasses. "We need to get to the machine before Shitty Wendell finds it, because if he does, there's no telling what awfulness he'll use it for."

"And more importantly," added Handsome, "if Shitty Wendell gets the machine it'd mean we'd be stuck here in this version of Earth. I will go insane if we stay here much longer."

"Yeah," said Beard, "we need to get the hell out of here."

"Agreed." Glasses pointed at the map. "We're here and the machine is just a few blocks away in that building there. We could just make a break for it, but the cameras would see us. I think I've found a route of sky-bridges and covered walkways that will get us to the machine without being exposed to the drone cameras."

"Even if we weren't trying to hide, I'd prefer this method," said Handsome.

"Yeah," agreed Beard, "outside is a fucking nightmare."

"Oh," said Handsome, "Remember not to swear once we leave. We don't know which buildings have decency fines."

"That's right," added Glasses, "We don't have that much left in this world's currency."

"Alright, let me get it out of my system... fuck! fuck! Fucking asshole shitting on a dick..."

"Are you—" Glasses Wendell started.

"Tits!"

"Are you done now?" Glasses asked.

"Yeah... oh no. What if we need to talk about Shitty Wendell while we're out there? We can't say 'Shitty.'"

"We'll figure it out. We gotta go. The minute-to-minute rent of this privacy room is draining our funds."

Handsome put his hand out, palm down.

Beard arched an eyebrow. "Seriously?

"C'mon," pleaded Handsome.

Glasses placed his hand over Handsome's. "Just do it."

Beard sighed and put his hands over the others.

"Go team Wendell!" exclaimed Handsome.

"We are so lame."

The three Wendells stepped into a hallway lined with similar privacy conference rooms. As they approached the hall's exit, the entire door panel lit up like a TV. A woman dressed in a garish orange business suit appeared in the door screen. She spoke in a joyful tone that could never have been mistaken for genuine.

"Good afternoon, Valued Guests! We're sad to see you leave. Would you be interested in learning more about our monthly conference room subscriptions?"

A massive green button with golden letters reading "Yes" appeared in the middle of the door. Additionally, a tiny red circle that read "No" appeared in the lower left corner of the door. Glasses reached down and pressed the No button. The animated woman frowned.

"I'm so very sorry to hear that. Before the door can be unlocked, please watch this mandatory twenty-one second ad for Citadel Properties, the leading purveyor of commercial real estate. You may skip the ad with a payment of six credits."

"Pay it," said Beard.

"We need to save our money," countered Glasses.

"He's right," added Handsome.

The window to skip the ad closed and the commercial began to play. It was full of jarring music and provocative images seemingly having nothing to do with commercial real estate.

"I hate this fu— this effing world so effing much," grumbled Beard Wendell.

"Seriously, it's just the worst." added Handsome Wendell.

The ad ended, allowing the door to slide open. They left the hallway and stepped into a massive bustling atrium. Flashy vendor booths laden with plastic tchotchkes lined the walls. The ceaseless barking of the proprietors mingled with the hundred other conversations to form a cacophonous verbal stew. Neon lights shaped like trees were scattered about the floor space. The three Wendells worked their way through the crowd toward an archway built to resemble two anthropomorphic bananas holding hands.

"Okay," said Glasses, "We head through there. It's a tunnel connecting this building with the next one over. It's called the, uh, *Tube of Visceral Fruits...*"

"The wha—"

A woman wearing a glittery gold business suit hopped out in front of them.

"Look at you three dashing gentlemen!" she boomed. "Let me guess, you're all related?" She laughed at her own joke while taking a big step closer. She gestured toward a nearby booth that displayed a glowing green "Rx".

"How are your collective mental equilibriums doing today? If you're feeling like you need a boost, you should try our new *Happy Time Tablets*. They're top ranked in the *Best Life* blog's annual 'Pick Me Up Pills' market review."

She took another step closer, just barely outside the circumference of reasonable personal space.

"I'm required to warn you that severe homicidal urges are a possible side effect. But don't worry! If you start feeling all murdery, just pop a couple of our *Zen Head* gelcaps. You'll be feeling nice and calm...and *happy*, of course!"

The three Wendells stared at her dumbly. Her smile never wavered as she crossed the personal space threshold, her breath fogging up Glasses' glasses.

"Oh!" she continued, "I have to also tell you that *Zen Head* can make you drowsy. But don't worry! That just means you need a dose of *Jump Start*. You see it—"

"Do you have any free samples?" asked Handsome.

"Oh sure!" Her smile got wider, if that was even possible. She dove behind her booth. Handsome nudged the other two forward and rasped, "Go!"

A few minutes later, they were exiting the Tube of Visceral Fruits, all looking a bit paler and more world-weary than when they'd entered.

"Let's never discuss that place again," whispered Glasses.

"Did that pineapple who was stabbing the intestines out of the coconut have a giant erection?" asked Beard.

"We're not talking about it!" snapped Handsome.

They looked around the new building's lobby, finding it nearly identical to the one they'd just left. Glasses spotted their next destination across the way. It was an escalation ramp, a moving walkway that rose up at an inclined angle to the next floor. The problem was the incline was just steep enough to prevent any standing position. They were like escalators, only terrible.

"We need to get to the second floor. There's a sky bridge that can take us to the next block over."

They started to walk forward, but a jarring sound made them flinch. They turned toward the center of the room, where a man and woman were drawing a crowd. She had crusty blue dreadlocks and wore a lime green poncho. A kazoo was pressed to her mouth.

The man's hair was shaped like two cones pointing up at forty-five degree angles and he was wearing a semi-transparent orange vest with matching pants. He stood next to a device that looked like a metal box on legs with an antenna sticking straight up. Glasses had seen something like that before on his Earth, an obscure and awful-sounding instrument called a theremin. The man reached out and waved his hand over the antenna. The wholly unpleasant sound that followed confirmed that his device was indeed, a theremin.

The woman blew into her kazoo as he continued to wave his hands around the theremin antenna, creating a truly horrendous auditory experience. Even more disorienting was the fact that the Wendells appeared to be the only ones not enjoying the music. Everyone in the lobby stopped what they were doing and turned toward the performers. The Wendells crept in closer to get a better vantage. People rushed in from the various atrium exits to hear the impromptu concert. In less than thirty seconds, a solid wall of human bodies had formed between the three Wendells and their next destination. Everyone seemed to share the drug saleswoman's disregard for personal space—the crowd barely left enough room for air. The spectators started clapping along with the music, but the song's rhythm kept changing, so the clapping was never able to stay on time.

"This is the worst thing I've ever heard in my life," groaned Handsome.

"It's like The Macarena had an unholy lovechild with The Chicken Dance," said Beard.

"You have those songs in your Earth too?" asked Glasses.

"I can't take this," said Handsome. "Let's push our way through and get out of here."

"Remember not to nudge anyone," warned Glasses. "Nobody seems to care how close they are to each other as long as you don't actually touch. If you bump someone, they could file a complaint."

They all winced at a sudden high-pitched note from the theremin. There was no way to tell whether the musician made a mistake or if that was what he meant to do.

"I know I've said this before...but I really really hate this place," said Beard.

"Agreed," added Handsome.

"Yeah, yeah, c'mon." Glasses led them toward the back of the lobby, searching for a gap in the crowd.

"Seriously," Beard continued. "Remember that one Earth we went to that had literal fire raining down from the sky? I'd rather be back there. That's how much I hate this place."

After slowly shimmying their way around the throng of impromptu concert attendees, the Wendells finally found themselves in front of the escalation ramp. Glasses paid the one-credit fee and they stepped onto the inclined moving walkway. Beard immediately lost his balance. The other two caught him.

"Hold on to something," warned Glasses.

"On to what? There's no handles or railings!"

They all leaned forward, placing their hands against the walkway in an angled push-up position.

"This has got to be, like, almost a forty-five degree incline. Have these people seriously not invented steps?"

"Now that you mention it... I don't think I've seen stairs anywhere here."

"They figured out how to set everyone up with digital armbands that can act as smart phones, wallets, and personal IDs... they have actual flying cars... outside, there's probably two drones to every one person... they have the technology to constantly monitor our behavior and instantly fine us for legal infractions... but they never thought to invent stairs. Fu—I mean *Fork* this *forking* place."

They reached the top of the ramp, having to awkwardly crawl off it before standing back up.

"Okay. Through the sky bridge. The building on the other side stretches two blocks. Then we'll be right across the street from the machine."

They took two steps into the tunnel and froze. Glasses hopped back into the building behind them.

"Oh shi-ooot!" he yelped. "What the heck is that about?!"

"That is...that is disorienting," noted Handsome.

The interior of this tunnel that spanned the neighboring buildings was one big digital screen. Standing inside the tunnel gave one the sense of floating in the middle of an endless blue sky. No ground. No horizon. No sun. No sense of up or down.

"They weren't kidding when they named this thing *Sky Bridge*," noted Beard.

Glasses stayed just outside the tunnel, keeping his feet planted on a floor that actually looked like a floor.

"It's not real," said Handsome. "It's a screen. Just focus on the far end."

Glasses dabbed a bead of sweat from his brow, but otherwise didn't move.

"Close your eyes," offered Beard. "We'll lead you across."

Glasses took a deep breath, nodded, and squeezed his eyes tight. Handsome and Beard each rested a hand on his arm, and they walked across the Sky Bridge.

"Oh my god! No!" hollered Beard.

Glasses began trembling and squealed, "What?! What is it?! *What*?!"

"Oh, stop," said Handsome. "We're across."

Glasses opened his eyes. He saw actual floor. The terrible blue expanse reached back behind him. He looked up at Beard, who wore a devilish grin.

"Very funny," Glasses grumbled.

"Hey, I couldn't help myself...besides, I'm actually relieved there's something that can rattle you. You've been so robotic through this whole thing. I was starting to wonder if you were like a cyborg version of us or something."

"It's okay." Handsome patted Glasses on the shoulder. "A fear of heights is very common, at least on my Earth."

Glasses readjusted his spectacles. "It's not simply a fear of heights. I could stand at a window at the top floor of skyscraper and be fine. It's the helplessness. I couldn't stop my brain from imagining *what if I really was just out in the middle of an endless sky...well, I'd fall of course...but how would I save myself? There's no answer.* Then I go into panic mode."

"Ah, I see," said Beard, "so it's more of a control freak thing."

"Well, that part's all done now," said Handsome. "Now it's

time for you to get back in control and lead us through—" His eyes drifted out over the second-story landing and down to the cavernous open space that stretched out before them. "What is this place?"

"It's, uh, a convention center or something."

It looked like the largest indoor flea market ever conceived. There were hundreds of colorful vendor booths similar to those in the other lobbies. But there were also about two dozen large tents displaying unique, colorful logos. The center pole of each one was topped with a large light bulb.

"What kind of convention?" asked Beard.

"Great question, Guest Friend!"

A floating holographic head the size of a beach ball popped into the air in front of them. The Wendells hopped backwards in shock.

"What the fu-fork?!"

The animated head looked like a Ken doll. He smiled and said, "I'm Trevdan, Virtual Host for the All-Cap Convention Center. Our facility is currently home to the Association of Reality Show Entrepreneurs! At forty-five months and counting, the A.R.S.E. convention is the longest running professional conference in history! We are thrilled!"

They took a closer look at the throngs of people. It was a sea of plastic surgery, ostentatious clothing, and unnecessarily dramatic social interactions. Trevdan's programming must have had a directive to prevent any lull in conversation, because he boomed, "Each of the marquee tents contains a network focus group!"

The light bulb at the top of the nearest tent lit up with a bright green glow that was quickly followed with a wild cheer.

"Every time the tent light shines, a new show has been Green Lit!" The cartoon artificial intelligence chucked at his own pun. The green light on the same tent lit up a second time, which was followed by yet another cheer.

"How could they have created another show in less than a

minute?" asked Glasses.

"I smell a Spin Off!" crowed Trevdan.

"How can you spin off from a show that hasn't been made yet?" asked Handsome.

"Metrics!" exclaimed the animated display. "It's all about the Metrics!"

"What does that even—nope, never mind." said Beard.

Glasses nodded toward the moving ramp leading down to the main floor. "Let's go."

They had to sit down on the walkway while riding the ramp down to avoid toppling forward.

"I guess we shouldn't worry about saving face in this world," mused Handsome. "From what I can tell, dignity is an alien concept."

They stood back up as they reached the floor and looked toward the opposite end of the massive convention center.

"Here we go," breathed Glasses.

They managed about a dozen steps into the crowd before a besuited man with excessively waxed hair blocked their path. He smiled at them the way a lion smiles at a gazelle.

"Want to be on a TV show?! I need three wacky friends to live next door to a group of emotionally damaged singles. Having the neighbors be a set of triplets would be a great twist on the classic formula!"

"Don't acknowledge," warned Glasses.

They shuffled around the suit and the man inside it. This time they made it a full two dozen steps before the next person stepped in their path. She stroked her chin and gave them an appraising look.

"Okay, take a thought journey with me. The show is called Triple Trouble. We film you three visiting different cities around the world. You see how many laws you can break before getting arrested. We'd have to start small—petty stuff, and work up to the felonies—you know, build tension for the viewer. I'm sure we've got the legal budget for it. It couldn't cost more than what we paid to settle with that ungrateful cast from Rabid Roommates…"

"Should we just go?" whispered Beard.

"Yes," replied Glasses.

They scurried away. The producer didn't seem to notice. She was already brainstorming which advertisers they should pitch to first.

They managed to cover a full fifty feet of ground before the next obstacle popped up. There were three of them this time: a woman in the middle flanked by two men.

"Oh no! No!" said Handsome. He wagged his finger at them. "No dating competitions! No wacky races! No survival contests! No posing as professionals of some obscure niche business! We aren't interested."

The three producers looked at each other and then back at them. The woman in the middle gave a frighteningly warm smile. "But you're already under contract, Sugar."

"Say what now?"

She tapped her foot on the floor. "Should've read the fine print."

The three Wendells looked down. A green circle, ten feet in diameter, had been painted on the floor. With a closer look, they noticed a long series of paragraphs printed in a minuscule font. Glasses kneeled and brought his face down to just a few inches above the script.

He read aloud, "By standing in the *Green Circle of Yes* and speaking to a member of the executive staff, you are formally agreeing to a production contract with Eye Bangers Broadcast Network; the terms and conditions are to be determined by the engaged executive."

"What… *the fuck*," said Handsome. His armband dinged with the alert that a four-credit Decency Fine had been deducted from their account.

Beard snorted. "I can't believe it wasn't me who swore first."

"Oh, don't worry about that," said the executive. "We'll get you set up with language exemptions. Artistic Licensing stuff.

You're part of the Network now."

"Hell no, we aren't," countered Beard.

She *tsk tsk*'d. "Don't be like that. We'd hate to have to call security over and report a breach of contract. They just raised the minimum punishment to three broadcast seasons in Jailville."

"What's—*wait*," Handsome started, "You have a show where you film the people you throw in prison for contract breach called Jailville, don't you?"

The woman's smile brightened. "That show's profit margins are through the roof. It helps not having to pay your cast."

"May we have a minute to confer amongst ourselves?" asked Glasses.

The woman nodded. "You've got fifty-five seconds. I need the other five for a quick ad spot." A camera drone swooped in above them. "This scene right here is going in our pilot episode, Sugar."

The Wendells huddled up.

"Okay," said Glasses, "New plan: we run for the streetside exit over there."

"Doesn't that mean Shitty Wen—" *DING!* "Ugh, I mean *He* will probably find us?" countered Beard.

"Worth the risk," said Handsome. "A chance of getting murdered beats reality TV slave labor in my book."

"My thoughts exactly," said Glasses.

Beard shrugged. "Okay."

"I have an idea," said Handsome.

They all turned back toward the executives. The lead woman smiled. Before she could say anything, Handsome pointed into the crowd of passing people.

"I heard that woman in the purple dress is a psychic who can only read minds on Tuesdays...And she's married to two different people who have no idea the other exists!"

The three executives almost gave themselves whiplash with how fast they turned their heads.

"We'll call it Two-Timing Tuesday Telepath!" one of them

exclaimed.

"Run!" shouted Handsome.

They sprinted for the exit. Shrieks for "Security!" echoed behind them. As they approached, the doors lit up to play an advertisement.

"Screw this," said Handsome, and he pressed his thumb to the screen to pay the skip fee. They flung the doors open and the sights and sounds of the outside world assaulted their senses. The blinding light that attacked their eyes had little to do with the sun. Hundreds upon hundreds of drones zipped through the sky, each one surrounded by a bright holographic ad display. Most blared short, ten-second jingles on replay, forming a cacophony of indiscernible taglines. Even more disorienting was the roaring whirlwind of airborne vehicles.

This world had indeed adopted the flying car as a preferred means of travel, and the sci-fi fan inside each Wendell had been eager to see them in action. They were all quickly disappointed to learn the truth of the matter: a city's worth of flying cars being operated manually by the average everyday person would inevitably become a hurricane of catastrophe. There were no traffic lanes. How could there be? The cars flew about at every angle and elevation. Midair fender benders were nearly constant. Most of the time, the electrostasis field being projected twenty feet above the ground was strong enough to catch the falling vehicles. But sometimes, a serious crash would happen, and the damaged cars would careen downward with such a force that the stasis field could only manage to slow them down before they hit the ground. The pedestrians all walked with their heads pointed upward, which in turn caused plenty of human-on-human "fender benders." The land-bound cars all looked like mechanical turtles with their metal shells meant to protect against falling vehicles.

Glasses pointed. "There's the building. Two blocks up. Let's go."

"There's no Decency Law outside, right?" said Beard.

"Don't think so."

"Fuck this place!" he shouted.

"Feel better?" asked Handsome.

"Much."

They hurried along the sidewalk, skirting around the sky-eyed locals, and reached the first intersection.

"Anyone else as shocked as I am that they actually have crosswalks?" asked Beard.

"Yep," agreed Handsome. "I would've expected this to be more like real-world Lizard Leap or something."

"Liz-what?" Glasses shook his head, "Never mind, the light changed. Let's cross."

As they reached the curb of the opposite sidewalk, they froze at the sound of a jarring electronic shriek. It was the sound of a flying car's hover-brakes coming to a quick stop. Then they heard a voice from above yell, "I see them!"

The Wendells looked up and saw a man hanging out of a green car, a few inches above the stasis field. He wore a green suit and green sunglasses.

"Isn't that one of Shitty Wendell's goons?" asked Beard.

"Yep," said Handsome. The green-suited goon opened his door and let a rope ladder fall down. It sizzled and froze in the air at the stasis field.

"Shizzle bizzle!" the goon cursed. He flipped a switch in his car, sending a specialized electrical charge through the emergency escape ladder that negated the stasis field. The ladder unfurled successfully to the ground.

"Did he just say—" Beard started.

"Run!" shouted Glasses.

The three Wendells took off, shouldering people out of the way as they went. They came to the last intersection and halted as traffic whirred by. Glasses looked back. The goon had descended the ladder and was rushing after them with a gold-plated pistol in hand.

Beard pointed to the right. "We've got more incoming."

Another green flying car had parked above the stasis field,

and another green-suited thug was climbing down a rope ladder. Handsome assessed the traffic between them and their destination. "Looks like we're playing Lizard Leap."

"Oh hell," muttered Glasses.

They hopped across the first lane, narrowly avoiding a speeding quintuple-bike. They darted to the left, then forward two lanes, then back one to dodge a mega-trailer truck. Then, with one more hop to the right, they made a mad dash for the sidewalk. As they tried to catch their breath, Beard turned back to the goon on the other side and raised his middle finger.

"I hope you know what this means," he called.

The goon smirked and placed his thumb to the crosswalk pedestal. The traffic lights changed instantly, causing half a dozen accidents. But the path across the street was now wide open.

"Um... what the hell?" said Handsome.

"I think he just paid to change the lights," said Glasses.

"That's cheating," whined Beard.

Handsome noticed two more green cars flying toward them from opposite directions at ridiculous speeds. The nearby goon was nearly across the street. He raised his weapon and started to speak. "Don't move or I'll—"

Right at that moment, the two additional green cars burst into the intersection above them and collided with a deafening crash. The gun-wielding goon looked up just in time to see one of his coworker's cars land right on his head. His body disappeared beneath the heap of twisted, smoldering metal.

"Holy fucking shit on a stick!" exclaimed Beard.

"I'm going to be sick," said Glasses.

"Let's get inside." Handsome grabbed their sleeves and pulled them toward the door. "It's raining cars and trucks out here."

As they approached the entrance, the door ad started to play; however, one of the two double doors was already open, so they simply slipped right by. The building lobby was surprisingly desolate, empty except for stacks of cardboard boxes.

"What'd you say this place was, again?" asked Beard.

"It used to be the offices for some business," answered Glasses, "I think it was called..."

"Bed Friends, Inc." answered Handsome. He'd flipped open one of the boxes and pulled out a small red bottle. He read the label out loud, "*Scent of Love* by Bed Friends... hmmm, must be a cologne or something."

He sprayed a quick mist in the air and sniffed. His nose immediately rankled in disgust.

"Oh my god... it smells like sweaty sex... it's literally the scent of love."

"No wonder they closed down," said Beard.

"They didn't close," said Glasses. "They were so successful they had to move to a larger office."

Beard muttered, "Hate this place."

They rode the elevator up to the top floor and stepped out into another large open space that contained nothing but more cardboard boxes.

"Okay, where's El Machino?" asked Handsome.

"Yeah, let's not spend one more miserable minute here," said Beard.

"I had to hide it when we got split up earlier," said Glasses.

"Great, so where is it?" said Beard.

"It's uh... in a box."

"Which one?" asked Handsome.

"Welllllll..."

"Oh, c'mon!"

"You don't remember where it is?"

"No, no... I know it's one of those, in that pile over there."

"Fine. Let's hurry!"

They rummaged through boxes. Besides more cologne, they found boxes of bedroom paraphernalia much too graphic and unsettling to be discussed. Beard seriously doubted that the contents of one particular box he opened could ever actually be usable on human anatomy. After a two-minute search that felt like two hours, Glasses exclaimed, "Found it!"

He struggled for a moment, but pulled the machine free. It looked like an old-timey typewriter, with two glass cylinders rising up out of it. The cylinders each contained what looked like a miniature tesla coil suspended in viscous gel. One side's gel was blue, the other's was orange.

"Spec-tac-cu-lar!" crowed a voice that sounded very much like one of the Wendells.

The three Wendells slowly turned around. Standing near the elevator, flanked by two green-suited henchmen, was Wendell. The Wendell that belonged to this world: Shitty Wendell.

Shitty Wendell's hair looked like it was made of plastic and had been styled into a shape reminiscent of the Sydney Opera House. Tiny flecks of gold dotted his faux bronze skin. Each lens of his sunglasses displayed a miniature portrait of himself. His suit was a vomitous patchwork of glowing logos for various companies that would occasionally flash and blink.

"That's okay, I don't mind if you stare," he said with a grin. "My suit has optic sensors. It can tell when eyes are looking at me. And I get paid a one-tenth credit for every second someone spends looking at one of my sponsor logos. So, don't you dare look away from me. I'm saving up to buy a bigger private plane. My current one feels a bit cramped these days."

He laughed at that, and after a moment, his two cronies laughed in support.

"Look, Wendell," Glasses started.

"My name is not WEN-dell!" Shitty Wendell shouted. "It's Wen-DELL! The emphasis is on the second syllable. WEN-dell sounds like an accountant at an office supply company. Wen-DELL is a renowned taste-maker. A professional connoisseur of all things luxury. An emperor of style. That is who I am. That is who we all are. It's time for you three to stop selling ourselves short. I want you three to join me. We should be the Masters over every version of Earth in the multiverse.

Who else is more qualified? We took the laws of physics and ground them under the heel of our custom-made Italian leather boot."

"*We?*" said Handsome. "There's no *we*." He pointed at Glasses. "*He*'s the one who figured out how to bridge the parallel dimensions. How can you take credit for that?"

"That's what I do! I take starter ideas and turn them into world-changing phenomenons!" Shitty Wendell threw his arms up with a dramatic flourish.

"You steal ideas and take credit for them," said Glasses. "That doesn't make you a visionary."

"It makes you a dick," added Beard. "And for the record, your name's not Wen-DELL. It's Wendell… *Shitty* Wendell."

"And we'd never work with you," said Handsome, "You're an embarrassment to the Wendells of every Earth."

Shitty Wendell stared intently at Glasses. "Is this how you feel, too?"

Glasses wrapped his arms firmly around the machine. "It is."

Shitty Wendell shrugged and said to his thugs, "Kill the other two and then torture the nerd until he agrees to help."

The thugs raised their gold-plated pistols. The Wendells frantically scanned their surroundings, looking for anything that might help. Then the room started to vibrate. Everyone froze. They heard a deep pulsing sound that went, "*Wub wub wub wub*".

A dark blob of movement pulled all their eyes toward the panoramic glass wall in time to watch a black helicopter come to a standing hover, just a few feet away from the building. The side panel slid open, revealing a person clad in black tactical body armor, holding a weapon that resembled a giant boom microphone stuck on the end of an assault rifle.

"Uh… duck?" said Beard to the other two Wendells.

"Shoot him!" screamed Shitty Wendell, and he pointed his pistol at the helicopter.

The shooter in the helicopter pulled his trigger. The air

in front of the weapon seemed to wiggle and bend. The wall of glass shattered inward. An unseen force knocked the four Wendells and two green-suited thugs to the ground. Their ears popped.

As they all attempted to reorient themselves, a plank was lowered to form a bridge between building and helicopter. Three people in tactical armor rushed across, holding more conventional-looking guns this time. A familiar fourth person followed after them. She was the executive from the reality show convention, the one from the floor contract. She wore an armored vest over her suit, holding a pistol in one hand and a small stack of documents in the other.

"Kim Killsmith, you bitch!" growled Shitty Wendell.

She smirked at him. "Stand down, Mr. Ever'te. The Network has these boys under contract. We need them undamaged for pilot season... hmmm, I can't believe I didn't notice how much they look like less awful versions of you. You want to join the cast as the fourth brother no one likes?"

Handsome whispered to Beard and Glasses, "She's growing on me."

"Fuck you, Kim," Shitty Wendell growled. "You have no idea who they are! What's really at stake here?"

"Millions of credits of broadcast revenue are what's at stake here," she replied, "And that's all I need to know. Now stand down."

"Fuck you," Shitty Wendell repeated. He glanced at his thugs.

"Don't do it," warned Kim Killsmith.

Glasses Wendell tugged at the sleeves of the other two and nodded toward the nearby stacks of boxes. They began to inch their way closer.

Shitty Wendell looked up at Kim with a sneer. "Fuck. You."

With that, he and his two thugs raised their pistols. Kim and her escort did the same.

"Go!" shouted Glasses. The three Wendells dove behind the stacks of boxes as the gunshots rang out. Well, they assumed they were gunshots. The sounds were loud and abrasive and punctuated with screams of the combatants. But they noticed that rather than a nondescript "pop" the sound was more akin to a cash register's "Cha Ching."

One of the green-suited thugs fell through the stack of boxes hiding the Wendells. Blood streamed from a trio of wounds in his chest. His gun landed on the floor between Glasses and Beard.

"Grab it," whispered Handsome.

"I don't want it," said Glasses.

"Yeah, I'm not much of a gun guy," added Beard.

"Oh, for the love of... give it here," said Handsome. He snatched up the gold-plated pistol.

The sounds of shouting and cash register gunshots subsided. Handsome risked a peek around the boxes. The other thug and the three Network guards lay motionless. Kim Killsmith was sitting on the floor, leaning against the wall. She was alive, but blood trickled from wounds in her right leg and arm. Shitty Wendell stood over her. Handsome raised his pistol at Shitty Wendell's back and pulled the trigger.

Nothing happened.

Handsome's armband beeped. He looked at the display. It read "Insufficient Funds: Please deposit 863 credits to pay Trigger Fee."

"Oh, c'mon!"

Shitty Wendell snickered, "Bye, Kim."

Handsome reared back and hurled the pistol. It connected squarely with Shitty Wendell's head. He let out a pained moan and dropped to one knee.

Handsome moved to rush forward, but Beard sprinted past him, diving into the stunned Shitty Wendell. After a moment of grappling, Beard managed to wrestle away the gun before connecting with a solid punch. Shitty Wendell groaned and stopped fighting back.

Beard looked at Handsome. "So, was the gun out of bullets?"

"No! You have to pay a thousand credits to shoot someone here."

"Damn, this place is awful."

"The worst."

Shitty Wendell chuckled, "So that's it, then? You three dork-naughts just going to leave? I'm offering you all the money you could ever want! All the power you could ever want! What could be better than that?!"

Glasses walked up alongside Handsome and Beard.

"The beauty of an infinite universe."

Shitty Wendell scoffed, "Oh, shove that foo-foo whimsical nonsense up your ass! Fine! Leave! You think I won't find you? I've got pictures... video of the machine in action. It might take a few years, but I know with enough financial incentive, there's an egghead out there who can recreate your little toy. And then I'll tear a new asshole in every reality, every universe. So, by all means, leave. Go. I'm tired of looking at you pathetic excuses for myself."

Beard looked at the other two, "What do we do?"

"Kill him," croaked a pained voice.

The three Wendells looked over at Kim.

"About that," said Handsome, "I don't think any of us are capable of straight-up murder."

She dabbed at a drop of blood in the corner of her mouth and said, "I'll do it... happily."

"Yeah, I'm pretty sure none of us are cool with assisted murder either," said Beard.

Kim rolled her eyes. "Pussies."

"Lovely," said Handsome.

"So now what?" said Beard.

"There's got to be a way to, I don't know, incapacitate him, but without directly killing him."

"Well..." said Glasses, "I, uh, might have an idea."

He nonchalantly drummed his fingers on the machine.

*

"Hey, uh, is that what I think it is?" asked Beard.

"Uh huh," said Handsome, "that's a statue of a cartoon mouse... a forty-foot statue of a cartoon mouse."

"Not just *any* cartoon mouse," said Glasses, "that's..."

"Yep," said Handsome, "kind of hard to mistake those perfectly round ears."

"So, in *my* Earth, this is where the Washington Monument is," noted Beard.

"Mine too," added Glasses.

"It's the Benji Franklin monument in mine," said Handsome.

"Benji? Never mind. So what does this mean, exactly?" said Glasses.

"I think it means my suspicions that they've been plotting world domination via subliminal messages hidden inside entertainment media weren't just paranoid delusions," said Beard. "So stick that in your pipe, Dr. Gershwin!" He noticed odd looks from the other two and said, "He's my shrink."

"I wonder if they moved the Capitol down to Orlando?" mused Handsome.

"Oooo, let's go," said Beard.

They looked at Glasses expectantly.

He shrugged. "Sure. I always liked that pineapple soft serve they had."

They heard an electrical buzz and turned around in time to watch the glowing blue portal they'd just come through wink out of existence. Glasses glanced down at the machine in his hands.

"First, we should find a satchel to carry this thing in."

"*Satchel*? You nerd," teased Beard.

Glasses rolled his eyes.

"Hey," said Handsome, "You think we did the right thing? With *you-know-who*? I just hope we weren't too harsh..."

There's a large open field smack-dab in the middle of a place called, in most versions of Earth, Nebraska. Funnily enough, in this particular version of Earth, it's called

Ghadablast. But that's not important. What is important, however, is that a glowing blue portal appeared in the sky above this field.

A few seconds after the portal appeared, a man with plastic hair and a neon, multi-colored suit fell through it. He landed in the field with a thud. The blue portal disappeared. Shitty Wendell stood up and dusted himself off. He looked around at the empty horizon and started laughing.

"Is that the best you got?!" He shouted toward the sky. "You suck-nuggets! You think this is gonna slow me down?! I'll be king of this world in under a year!"

He stopped when he noticed dark clouds coalescing overhead. He squinted as hundreds of smoldering orange dots appeared in the sky. The dots expanded in size and then fell. As they plummeted toward the Earth, it dawned on Shitty Wendell what he was seeing.

It was literally raining fire.

ABOUT PATRICK EDWARDS

Twitter @ThePatEdwards

When he's not busy mushing words into silly stories, Pat spends his time battling inter-dimensional shadow monsters and having tea parties with his two daughters. His debut novel, Space Tripping, is currently available wherever books are sold. Check him out on Twitter @ThePatEdwards

CATCHING

By Kendra Namednil

"This is nine-one-one, please state the nature of your emergency."

"I believe my life is in danger. I live on Thirty-Eight Manganese..."

Numb but strangely electric as she rattled off her address, she glanced from her suitcase to the little digital numbers on the microwave as she spoke. They were always six minutes fast, but he would step through that door, every day, between six forty-seven and six fifty-two. Presently, it read six forty-five.

She glanced down at her two little loves, not begrudging them her place in the women's shelter.

"Okay, I have your location here. What is the nature of this..."

"My fiancé. It's not safe for me to stay on the phone. Can I put you on speaker?"

"Officers have been dispatched to your location. Is it safe for you..."

The phone clunked softly against the countertop, the volume so low that the operator on the other end might speak for an age without causing the least concern.

She smiled. It was the first time she'd smiled in a very long time, and the justification for it was not one she could put into words. She kissed her pet rabbits, and, picking them up from the couch, she slid them into their hutch.

SIX FORTY-SEVEN

She glanced at her suitcase, the statistics running again through her brain. *The presence of a gun increases the likelihood of homicide by five hundred percent.* She shook her head. He didn't have a license, but that had never stopped him. It wasn't illegal to own a firearm, and she couldn't prove that it had been brandished. *Twenty percent of victims are not the partner but friends, family, neighbors, people who intervene, police officers...* This last worried her a little, but it would be just like him to go after her friends if she sought a women's shelter. Just like him. And people were so naïve. *Twenty-one to sixty percent of victims lose their jobs because...* Possibly the stress. Possibly the missed work. Possibly the way she was a bit insular, the way she'd been too ashamed to talk. Possibly because he kept calling her there, even and especially when she had asked him not to. She went to her pets and stroked the tufts atop Flopsy's head.

"I love you, Carrot-Muncher."

He said things like that: called her princess, bought her things, loved her, shared chocolate-fudge-brownie ice cream on the good days. And he sometimes said things like "why did you make me do this to you," too, and "I'll give you a reason to be sorry." She shouldn't have visited that website, the "National Coalition Against Domestic Violence," the NCADV. It was getting her all worked up to know these things. *At least I'm not from Alaska.* Fifty-nine percent of women there were victims of domestic violence, and thirty percent had no access to resources.

SIX FIFTY-ONE

She heard his red car draw up, its tailpipe swishing as it ceased its charge up the gravel drive. They lived somewhat rural, so it would take a little while for the officers to arrive. They had to catch him in the act. Had to take him away. Otherwise, he'd tear up the will she had left, murder her bunnies, and find another woman. Another sugar-sweet, honey-pie princess for him to lure in and murder by inches.

His footfall charred the front steps, her mind conjuring brimstone. She lifted her suitcase, packed with a few days' feed, two changes of clothes, a toothbrush, and her will to live. Her resolve held steady only by the knowledge that the phone was still listening in the background. The door pulled open.

"The fuck are you..."

His usual greeting cut itself short as his eyes flashed lightning and his nostrils flared, his face transmuting from mild, amused, and deliberately cruel through all the shades of suitcase-induced rage. Faint red, then deep red, then almost purple for a second, then completely, utterly, pale, a tear burning to hang on the air as a herald of his final approach. He pulled off his belt. She almost breathed out a sigh of relief. There would be a struggle. He wanted to hurt her. He didn't feel threatened, and this was about discipline and reasserting control. She would bleed, the bruises running deep, and if the police didn't come, he'd beat her until she was unconscious, then drink from a bottle of rum and cry until she awoke, blaming the alcohol despite its absence during the beating. One of her pets might die, though. She'd come to with that reality once, and he looked to be in a killing mood. *Nineteen percent of domestic violence involves a weapon.* That statistic had seemed low to her. He advanced, his belt flicking out in an extension of a backhand, and she heard a prayer on the wind, a sound heavenly sweet and getting stronger. She cried out to cover it, to mask it. Unusual for what she generally did, but the rage relaxed a touch, replaced by cruelty.

"What? you sorry, bitch?"

She'd learned long ago that he preferred silence. His voice cracked, sometimes, goading him further. Well, he was less violent when she was silent, when she acquiesced and simpered mutely. Handed him a beer and left the room. And he was gentler drunk, except for when he wasn't. He struck her again, and again she cried out, deliberately moaning loudly now that an angel approached with distant trumpets blaring. The ground reached out and kissed the back of her head and she rolled to her stomach.

"You think you're gonna walk out, after all I've done for you? Break my back, and this is the thanks I get?"

A kick to her abdomen and chest should have rendered her bereft of breath. *NO!* He was starting to notice the glow of angels, and that was not acceptable. She screamed once and twisted, kicking up hard. The blow barely grazed his most-lauded prize, but it was the act of defiance that blinded him to the approaching holy light.

"The fuck you thinking, whore!"

His knee found purchase in her stomach and his fists were generous and polite, the one yielding to the other as each in turn caressed her upper cheeks, his class ring catching on the ridge to coax her cheek to paint itself in red. Her zygomatic bones would blush under the dark purple above them. The crescendo of hope manifest, and now there was no hiding her deed.

"You call the police? I'm going to murder you, hag!"

He was fumbling at the back of his pants, his nine millimeter almost liberated, when angels sounded twin retorts of freedom. Light caught on that moment as probity tore through his chest, casting a shadow even as the fine mist glittered. There had been shouting. Words. Nothing. She was free.

Six months later, a tear fell, and she, alone in the darkness of her childhood room, ashamed of having stood up yet another date, reached over to unlatch the hutch. "Flopsy, you love me, right?"

The weeks immediately after had passed her by; trance-like, she'd covered her discolored face. Everyone kept insulting him, saying he was evil for the evil that sometimes slipped out, and it made her defensive. But he'd bought her bunnies. He'd watch rom-coms even though he hated them, braiding her hair as she sat between his knees. He healed her even as he'd injured parts of her, reminding her that she was special, that he loved her even when everyone else had pulled away.

Lifting the larger of her two rabbits, she crossed to the window and gazed out at the moon and starscape. There had been good times, when he'd called her his princess and smiled and laughed and been there as her friends and family had drifted away. Tomorrow, she would nail her job interview. Tomorrow, she would go on a double-date. Tomorrow. Tonight, she brought her bunny down to the kitchen and, holding him the way he liked, she pulled out one of his favorite treats and microwaved a cup of hot cocoa. Tonight, the resolve of tomorrow felt real, and as she sipped, the terror of the past and the terror of the future blended, swirled, and faded away. She sat at the mouth of a cage, and, at long last, the door to the great wilds was open.

ABOUT KENDRA NAMEDNIL

Twitter @Kendra1337

Kendra Namednil was born in Northern California and began writing when she was 26, publishing her first full novel at 30. She has volunteered for many organizations, though her greatest joy was working with behavior-plan dogs with the San Francisco Society for the Prevention of Cruelty to Animals.

LIKE CLOCKWORK

By Jason Chestnut

Every day was a winding clock—a clockwork routine of shifting gears and moving parts. Josh's life was an unstoppable machine of necessity, forever grinding the years into monotony. Like clockwork, it clicked on from one day to the next, one gear after another.

Josh woke at four minutes to seven every morning and ate the same breakfast—peanut butter on toast, a cup of coffee, and a boiled egg. His suits and ties were all different, this being the only variety he embraced. He always wore his hair the same way, but couldn't remember the last time he had it cut.

The drive to work was uneventful. Josh idly hoped for an accident or the sounds of sirens. He dreamed of hurricanes and landslides, earthquakes and volcanic eruptions. But he lived nowhere near a volcano, and there hadn't been a hurricane warning in years. People may have complained that their lives were hectic, but that was nobody Josh knew. Josh didn't have bad days or even great days. He just had days.

Josh spent his nights and weekends at home, watching television. He had no friends, family, or even a pet. His only distraction was collecting shot glasses he had shipped from around the world. He didn't see the point in traveling when he could watch the Travel Channel, and he held a similar philosophy about food, friendship, romance, and sex. Josh believed he was living proof that reality can be boring.

Learton Industries specialized in educational software, training programs, and study aids. Josh worked with other programmers with similar daily routines. When he wondered why he hadn't moved onto something more exciting, he always came to the same conclusion: A deviation from his routine would be unbearable.

Today, Josh decided to take his break at his desk instead of wandering the halls as usual. This was not a huge deviation.

He had two coworkers who sat near him he considered friends as much as any coworker could be. Amy was a newlywed, and she and her husband were trying to start their own custom Teddy Bear business. She had brown hair with a bad perm and large round glasses, and she often wore dresses that were either too tight around her chest or too loose on her behind. Jim was a tall, lanky fellow with an outdated haircut and a penchant for Star Trek analogies.

"What's up, Josh?" Jim said. He was holding a small paper cup of coffee.

"Earthquakes."

"Oh," Jim said, looking over at Amy, who was peeking over the partition separating her desk from Josh's.

"Hello, Joshua." Amy always called him that, and he hated it. "That's a cute tie."

Josh cocked an eyebrow. "You don't think it makes my ass look too big?"

She giggled and disappeared again. Amy often teased him, and deflecting her playful advances was one of the few highlights of Josh's day.

"Was there a quake recently?" Jim asked, peering over Josh's shoulder.

Josh exhaled and blinked a few times, "Just had a weird dream about earthquakes, that's all."

Jim pondered this while Josh glanced at the clock on his desk. Almost time to go back to work. His new supervisor, Mrs. Arrick, was very strict about time entries.

Mrs. Arrick always had the same cup of coffee with cream and no sugar and the same mechanical conversations with the management team. Everybody considered her to be more than a little creepy. She spoke in a monotone and never smiled or frowned. She left the office at the same time every day, gesturing the same mechanical farewells to whoever she passed. Amy was of the opinion that Mrs. Arrick was sick or crazy. Jim said she was an alien sent to earth to study them.

Jim's argument that she may be an alien had almost convinced Josh, but he couldn't put stock into anything that Jim said. Believing Captain Kirk was a real person didn't make Jim a reliable source. Josh had formed his own opinion, and it was the simplest solution he could figure.

He believed Mrs. Arrick was a robot.

His work friends scoffed at the notion. Jim pointed out they would not invent the "positronic brain" until at least the early twenty-fourth century. Amy only giggled and told Josh how cute that notion was. In Josh's mind, it only seemed logical that there would be robots among them at a big software corporation. He only wished that they could at least make whatever model Mrs. Arrick was more realistic. She looked like a short, middle-aged woman with bright reddish-brown hair and bright blue eyes on the outside, but her mannerisms were all wrong.

"There was a disaster on Picard's *Enterprise*," Jim said suddenly. "Counselor Troi had to take command. Kinda like an earthquake in space."

Jim giggled, and Josh only shook his head. "What are you talking about?"

"TNG. Don't you remember?" Jim asked.

"TNG?" Josh blinked.

"Ah forget it. Anyway, Mrs. Arrick wants to see you in her office."

Josh snapped to attention, "What? When?"

"Oh, at four o'clock," Jim said, looking down at his collector's edition Starfleet watch.

"Damn it, Jim! That's in five minutes! You know how nuts she gets about being on time!"

Josh pushed past his coworker. Just like anyone else in the office, Josh hated talking to Mrs. Arrick one-on-one. To Josh, it was like talking to an animatronic puppet at a theme park —not a real conversation at all, but a lifelike simulation. He ran through things he could ask to deduce more about her, to build up his case for proving her robotic. He wanted to trip her up somehow and get her to reveal herself as artificial. But, he figured it would be like trying to beat a computer at chess.

He put his suit jacket on and walked the length of the hallway leading to her corner office. He stopped in front of Mrs. Arrick's door and ran a hand through his short-cropped hair.

"Come in," a voice said. Josh was still holding his fist up to knock. Mrs. Arrick regularly did things like this, and they drove him nuts every time. It was almost as if she had sensors or radar. He opened the door and stepped into her immaculate office.

"Afternoon, Mrs. Arrick," he said, trying not to sound nervous. "You wanted to see me?"

"Yes, please sit down," she said, in her mechanical voice. "Thank you for being prompt."

"Oh, no problem." Josh took a seat in one of the brown leather chairs facing Mrs. Arrick's regal, oak desk. On the left-hand wall were two gray bookshelves with rows of identical books. Josh could see an art déco-looking gray clock placed in the center of the bookshelf nearest him, plus a tall gray filing cabinet to its right. There were no files placed upon the cabinet, and each of its drawers were closed. There was a gray grandfather clock in the corner, and various plaques adorned the walls, hung with meticulous precision. The room smelled clean and disinfected, almost like a doctor's office.

"I understand you've been seeing Dr. Mason," Mrs. Arrick said, her hands laced together in front of her. "How is that going?"

"Well, it's been fine," Josh said, more than a little anxious. Dr. Mason was the company therapist. Josh had been seeing him once his dull, clockwork life started closing in on him. The anxiety was not unbearable, yet it was still becoming a problem. Dr. Mason had suggested that Josh find an outlet, perhaps a hobby or creative endeavor. However, that was none of anybody's business, even if it had been suggested by upper management in the first place. Josh fidgeted and felt a slight sheen of sweat form on his brow.

"Are you... happy?" The strange pause in her speech reminded Josh of that minuscule pause a calculator makes after you press the "equals" sign.

"Yes, I believe so," Josh said, trying to match Mrs. Arrick's robotic tone.

"You should enjoy your work," Mrs. Arrick droned on. "The one cog in the machine that ceases to function causes the entire machine to halt. Don't you agree?"

Josh squirmed in his seat. "Yes, I understand what you mean. You don't have to worry about me."

There were papers in a neat stack on Mrs. Arrick's desk, and she surveyed them. Josh tried to study her eyes, half-expecting to see glowing red lights or camera-like shutters flicker open and closed. His ears tried to pick up the sounds of gears or motors or the rhythmic, almost inaudible hum of electronics. *Oh, she's well made*, he thought to himself.

"You have an exemplary attendance record," she said, still looking at the papers, "and your productivity is excellent. We would hope you can keep up the good work."

"I'll do my best." Mrs. Arrick's constant use of the word 'we' unnerved Josh. "I don't mean to be blunt, but did I do something wrong?"

"No," she said without emotion or inflection. "Quite the opposite. We have considered enlisting your skills for a new project."

"A *new* project?" Josh twisted in his seat.

"Yes, a confidential, advanced project."

"What is it?"

"What do you know about artificial intelligence?" Mrs. Arrick stood, handing Josh a folder.

"Um, well, I mean..." Josh stammered, the folder sliding into his outstretched hand.

"We aim to revolutionize the software industry with a brand new form of A.I." Mrs. Arrick sat down again. "It will change human society and technological development forever."

"Human society?" Josh thought that was the clincher. He

glanced down at the gray, unassuming folder wrapped with large rubber bands. His mind raced through the gamut of irrational, fantastic scenarios reserved for science fiction. He very well may have been holding the twisted plans of a mad, rogue computer that had reached self-awareness and wanted to subjugate the inferior human race.

Then again, maybe it was just plans for another video game.

"We feel it would best serve your abilities to be part of this project."

"Me?" Josh said, almost adding: "But, I'm just a human being…what part could I play in your grand scheme of world domination?"

Instead, he only said, "But, I'm just a level two programmer."

"We have cause to believe you are far more capable than that."

There was a moment of tense silence as Josh pondered the situation. He waved away his fantastic notions and gripped the possibility they were giving him an actual important project. He was being recognized for his talents. He could get a raise. Best of all, he had something different to do. His monotonous existence would get a facelift.

Still, in the back of his mind, he half-hoped it was a world domination plot and not just an educational video game with a talking octopus.

"You don't have to answer right away." Mrs. Arrick broke the silence. "Please take the folder home and study the contents. If you feel you could handle this responsibility, we would welcome your help."

"I don't know what to say."

"We will offer a salary increase, better working environment, and a more accommodating schedule."

"Well…" Josh took everything in, "I will review this tonight. I'll give you an answer in the morning. I—thank you, Mrs. Arrick. Thank you very much."

"First thing tomorrow morning, then."

That night Josh sat in his living room, staring at the still-sealed folder on his coffee table. He had mentioned nothing to his coworkers. He figured Jim would have loved his theory about robots creating mind-controlling computer programs for world domination. Amy would have ignored him, instead making vague sexual innuendos about the buttons on his shirt or some other ridiculous thing. Besides, Mrs. Arrick had asked Josh to be "confidential" about his new task.

Josh swirled a glass of diet iced tea in his hand like a movie detective might swirl a glass of scotch when a sudden thought shot into his mind:

He'd left his work computer logged on.

He had to go back. His job had just become very important to him, and he would not jeopardize it with such a stupid, rookie mistake. Josh rushed out of his apartment, his diet iced tea lay unfinished under the light of a single, lonely lamp.

The office was dark and colder than usual. There was a strange, unnerving calm as Josh drifted between the cubicles. He rounded the corner of his own cubicle and saw the dull yellow light on the monitor signifying the computer was in "standby" mode. He slid the mouse, and the monitor clicked as the system sprang to life again. Josh clenched his teeth. His eyes darted back and forth across the rows of cubicles before returning his full attention to the computer screen. He typed in his password to unlock the system, and his desktop appeared. A web page was still open to the Google image search page on earthquakes. He considered it for a brief handful of seconds and then began the process of logging off.

He stood up as the log-out process completed. The monitor went blank as Josh wiped a cool sheen of perspiration from his forehead. Suddenly, he heard a strange clicking noise from across the room. His head jerked around and then he ducked into his workspace. He crouched over his desk and strained to listen. *Was it the cleaning crew?* he wondered. *Did their carts click like that when they pushed them along the office aisles?*

The clicking continued, and Josh thought it sounded almost like the winding of a clock. He stayed crouched and crept around the edge of the row of cubicles. Following the sound led him to a familiar doorway.

It was Mrs. Arrick's office door.

The rhythmic clicking continued and Josh edged his way forward. The clicking was definitely coming from inside, and a whole range of notions raced through Josh's mind.

This is it! he thought, *I will catch her adjusting her doodads or whatchamacallits! I knew it!*

The door flew open and slammed into Josh's face, throwing him backward. Pain shot up from his nose and into his eyes and cheeks. Josh blinked a few times before regaining his focus. Mrs. Arrick was standing in the open doorway, expressionless as usual, body language mute. Josh swallowed hard, his eyes scanning her hands for any signs of a ray gun.

"What are you doing here?" she said in her monotone voice, bereft of any surprise or concern.

"Um, I..." Josh stammered, rubbing his sore nose, "I forgot something. Then I heard noises..."

"What noises?" Mrs. Arrick said, folding her arms behind her back. Her hands had been empty, and Josh thought she was transforming them into machine guns while they were out of sight.

"Um, like clicking," he stammered and shifted his weight, planting his palms on the ground to push himself up. "Sounded like clicking or winding gears or something."

"I don't know what you are talking about," Mrs. Arrick's dry voice came back. He waved a hand with a slow shake of his head. It occurred to him at that moment that the monotony and predictability of his life might have just over-inflated his imagination. He was always hoping and looking for something terrible or fantastic to happen just to free him from the same clockwork banality. He recoiled as something dug into his palm, and he looked down to see what it was.

A small brass screw lay on the floor, and Josh scooped it up almost reflexively. He narrowed his gaze, confused about where it came from. He was still staring at it as he rose to his feet.

"Sorry, Mrs. Arrick," he said, studying the screw once more before shrugging and looking up at her. "I'm just tired."

She nodded, "Yes, tired. Go home and rest."

He nodded back, holding the screw up into his line of sight again. His eyes refocused from the screw to Mrs. Arrick, and he did an immediate double take. He lowered the strange little brass screw, settled his gaze on the strange little woman's face, and took a step closer to her. Josh tilted his head to one side and his eyes grew wide.

Along the side of her face was a noticeable *seam*. It was a divide along her cheek like the edge of a car door that, when closed, seems to blend in with the rest of the machine's body. Now, that door was ajar.

Josh's mouth hung open and Mrs. Arrick only stared back at him, expressionless. She was so still he couldn't help but wonder if she was "working." He wanted to move even closer, look beyond the seam at what was toiling away inside. Gears, springs, and cogs filled his imagination instead of any futuristic circuitry or neon-bright wiring. He imagined Mrs. Arrick more like a walking clock, wound up in the morning like a tinker toy.

Scientific curiosity suddenly gave way to absolute terror. Josh turned on his heels and darted away.

As he ran screaming through the office, the strength in Josh's legs gave out. Something was rooting him in place. *Oh no, it's some kind of robot freeze ray!* he thought. His screaming also ceased, not by choice, but by the same sudden paralysis. His entire body could no longer move, frozen mid-run, statuesque. The office lights came on and Josh's mind was aflame with a range of horrifying scenarios. He was certain the robot overlords were planning to dissect and torture him.

Jim appeared, holding what looked like the same cup of

coffee from this morning.

"I told you this was a bad idea," he said before taking a sip of his coffee. "Let's fix it."

"Don't call him an 'it.'" Amy's voice came from behind Josh. There was a faint uncomfortable sensation, a tugging at his right shoulder blade.

"Calm down everyone," came another familiar voice.

It was Dr. Mason, the company therapist. He was wearing a lab coat over his gray suit and tie, a tablet in his hand. He had thinning brown hair, a well-groomed beard, and small round spectacles.

"Everything looks fine, Dr. Mason." Amy's voice came again from behind Josh. Dr. Mason nodded and walked close to Josh, looking into his eyes, studying them.

"What about the older model?" Dr. Mason asked.

"She's toast." Jim sipped his coffee. "I don't know what you were trying to prove by having them interact like this."

Dr. Mason sighed. "It's called an experiment, James."

"Haha," Jim deadpanned.

"Download all the logs for analysis." Dr. Mason straightened again. "I'm thinking retirement is in order for the other one.

Jim shrugged and walked out of view. Josh's mind was reeling as he felt that same strange, uncomfortable tugging at his shoulder blade. Dr. Mason gave Josh a final once-over, tapped a few times on his tablet, and then walked out of view. Josh wanted to speak, scream, or even cry. But, nothing was happening. His mind was the only functioning part of the package. The engine was running, but the wheels weren't moving.

"Goodnight, cutie," came Amy's voice one more time.

And then there was darkness.

Josh blinked a few times and then sat up in bed, shaking and disoriented. His alarm clock was howling its rhythmic beeping. Groggy, he reached over and pressed the snooze button. He rubbed at his eyes and looked around, allowing his senses to adjust. He was back in his bedroom, in his pajamas, safe and sound. The clock said it was four past seven instead of four til.

Josh swung his legs around and out of the bed and found them working as usual. He yawned and was pleased to find his vocal cords also worked. He felt as if he had dreamt something, but it was crumbling in the way that dreams often do after waking. Walking to the bathroom, he reached around to rub at a strange sore spot on his shoulder. *Slept in an awkward position,* he thought to himself. He looked in the mirror and sighed. Another routine, clockwork day. *It's all just a winding clock of shifting gears and moving parts.*

Josh turned the faucet on and splashed cold water in his face. An odd, tinny sound of something falling against the porcelain basin startled him. He shut the water off and peered into the sink. He plucked the object out and looked it over, confused. It was a small, strange-looking brass screw. *Where did this come from?* he thought. He placed it on the edge of the sink and went about the rest of his routine. Same breakfast, same morning news, and a different suit and tie. He walked out the door, and a strange nagging feeling in the back of his head stopped him. He walked back to the bathroom and picked up the brass screw, slipping it into his pocket.

Somehow, he felt today would be a little different.

ABOUT JASON CHESTNUT

Twitter: @atomicboywonder

When not working on computers to pay the bills, Jason Chestnut is a writer, musician, avid reader, and gamer. He lives in Asheville, North Carolina with his wife Shannon, their two kids and lazy pug.

ACKNOWLEDGMENTS

I want to thank the entire Writing Bloc team, especially Michael Haase for orchestrating all of this! It's so great to be part of such an amazing group!

-Cari Dubiel

Thanks to everyone who commented and contributed, the Bloc is fantastic! Special thanks go to Michael Haase and Cari Dubiel for doing the extra hard yards, I very much appreciate that!

-Peter Ryan

First, I'd like to thank Michael Haase, Cari Dubiel and the rest of the members of Writing Bloc for the opportunity to contribute to this amazing collection. I'm so fortunate to know all of you. Second, to all of our readers: thank you for spending time with us and reading our stories. We appreciate you so very much.

-Susan K. Hamilton

Thanks to Miguel de Cervantes for inspiring my story (through the chivalrous deeds of the dim-witted Don Quixote); to Pepa (my late grandpa) for cultivating my imagination in the ways of cowboys and six-guns; to the WritingBloc Project Leads for making this anthology a fun and engaging experience; and to all the talented authors who've contributed to fantastic collection.

–Christopher Hinkle

Thank you Michael Haase, and the entire Writing Bloc team for including me in this beautiful anthology. I am honored to be a part of it, and your hard work is genuinely appreciated. And, as always, thank you Sam Destro (and the beagles George and Derric!) for sharing space with a person who makes up stories all day long. It's sometimes not easy for any of them!

-Jason Pomerance

I'd like to thank Writing Bloc for orchestrating this and all of the authors who contributed their genius to make it as real and amazing as it has become. I also want to thank every person that has supported *The Last Faoii,* and its sequel *Faoii Betrayer.* I could not have come this far without your help, and Faoii-Erika definitely would not exist without the universe you called for. Shields up.

-Tahani Nelson

Thank you to the whole Writing Bloc Team for your hard work and support! You are all inspiring, wonderful friends. Thank you to Deer Park Monastery and all of my Deer Park friends, and a special thanks to Amy Trâm Anh Trần.

-Becca Spence Dobias

I want to thank all of the contributing writers of this anthology for their hard work and dedication in bringing forth this wonderful collection of stories. It's been a rewarding and exciting experience.

-Durena Burns

My sincere gratitude goes out to Michael Haase, Cari Dubiel, Christopher Lee, and all my fellow Writing Bloc authors, who made working on this anthology a blast. It's a privilege to be counted among you. I owe a great debt as well to Ron Hansen, master novelist and my former writing professor, whose work has had an incalculable influence on my own. One day I will convince him to read science fiction, but until that day I hope he enjoys the story included here, which is in many ways a tribute, and which I humbly dedicate to him.

– Daniel Lee

First, I can't thank Michael Haase enough for inviting me to be a part of this collective. It has been a joy getting to know all these wonderful authors and being a part of this anthology. Most of all, I'd like to thank my mom for nurturing my imagination, by getting me into the Twilight Zone, Outer Limits, and taking me to see Star Wars when I was barely one. Ever since then I've been making my own weird and wonderful stories

– Jason Chestnut

Thank you, Michael Haase and Cari Dubiel, for taking on the monumental job of enlisting twenty authors and producing this fascinating collection of stories. Having seen the final result, I am both amazed and honored to be part of it. Special thanks go out to my fellow authors in this anthology for co-editing our stories and making them the best that they could be. It was a remarkable collaboration!

-Ferd Crôtte

Thank you Alex, Aly and Mom for support, guidance and

love. Humbled to be included with my fellow *Escape!* authors; each gracious and brilliant to the end. Stay tuned for PrOOF. Thanks to Cari D. If loving Michael Haase is wrong, I don't wanna be right.

-Michael James Welch

Thank you to Michael Haase, Cari Dubiel, and the entire Writing Bloc. Your work is important and beautiful, and I'm so grateful to be a part of this group. I'd also like to thank my dear friends who provided valuable feedback, and my daughter for being my inspiration to keep writing.

-Grace Marshall

Thank you to my wonderful wife, Katie, and our two daughters, Gabbie aka *Gabzilla* & Grace aka *Savage Beast*. Thank you to the Writing Bloc management team for creating such a delightful community. And lastly, I'd like to specifically thank Michael Haase. Sometimes I feel like a giant raging amphibious monster lost in a storm at sea when it comes to this writing business. You're the lighthouse that guides me to shore, so I can unleash my literary fury on humanity.

-Patrick Edwards

INDIE PUBLISHING TEAM

Thank you for reading. It means more to us than you know.

Look out for future anthologies and special releases from Writing Bloc by visiting WritingBloc.com

You may sign up for our mailing list on the website or submit work to be considered for future publications.

Made in the USA
Columbia, SC
09 April 2019